A MOTHER'S INSTINCTS TOLD HER SOMETHING WAS WRONG . . .

Chad emerged from his room at four. Karen was making sauce for lasagna. He didn't ask what she was cooking or comment on the pie cooling on the counter. He didn't ask if his sister was around or if Karen had heard the score of the football game. He asked only if she'd heard from his dad, then opened a can of beer, fixed himself a sandwich and carried them back upstairs.

Why in the hell was he so hot to talk to his father, Karen wondered. *Only* to his father? Was he protecting her from something?

Her mind ticked off all the things that could be wrong.

Another DUI.

He'd gotten Brenda pregnant. Or some other girl.

He was flunking out of school.

Been caught cheating.

Been kicked off the golf team.

Owed a gambling debt he couldn't pay.

Those things they could deal with. But what if he'd been involved in a hit-and-run accident? Or worse?

Karen closed her eyes and leaned against the kitchen counter. *Don't let it be too bad. Please.*

MOTHER LOVE

Judith Henry Wall

BANTAM BOOKS

New York Toronto London Sydney Auckland

MOTHER LOVE

A Bantam Book/ July 1995

ISBN 0-553-56789-6

Published simultaneously in the United States and Canada

Bantam Books are published by Bantam Books, a division of
Bantam Doubleday Dell Publishing Group, Inc. Its trademark,
consisting of the words "Bantam Books" and the portrayal of a
rooster, is Registered in U.S. Patent and Trademark Office and in
other countries. Marca Registrada. Bantam Books, 1540 Broadway,
New York, New York 10036.

PRINTED IN THE UNITED STATES OF AMERICA

OPM   0 9 8 7 6 5 4 3 2 1

MOTHER LOVE

1

Out of habit, Karen ignored the first two rings of the telephone. Phone calls in the night were for Roger—frantic parents of felonious teen-agers, wives fearful of estranged husbands, the ac-cused calling from jail, even the dying wanting to execute deathbed wills.

Karen rolled over to his side of the bed and picked up the phone.

It was Chad. She looked at the clock. Not yet five. And instantly, she was sitting up. Awake. Worried.

"Where's Dad?" he asked.

"Padre Island."

"Oh, yeah—the fishing trip. I forgot. That's why you guys aren't coming down tomorrow for the game. When's he coming back?"

"His plane ticket says Sunday morning, but Tropi-cal Storm Clifton is heading their way—and threaten-ing to turn itself into a hurricane. Your father's trying to leave tomorrow instead, but so are lots of other people."

"But you are expecting him tomorrow?" Chad asked.

"I hope so. Are you all right?" Karen half expected him to say he was calling from a police station. An-other DUI. Or worse.

"Yeah. Sure. I just wanted you to know I'm on my way home. I didn't want you to think you had a bur-glar when I come in."

1

"You're coming home *now?*" Karen asked. "It's awfully early."

He laughed. A thin, tired laugh. "Or awfully late, depending how you look at it. The house had a big party, and I haven't been to bed yet. I need to spend the weekend studying, and with a home football game, this place will be crawling with alums and parents in just a few hours. We're already overflowing with Kansas State guys down for the game. I'll get more done at home."

"Sounds like a good idea. You might even get a home-cooked meal or two."

"That'd be great. Love you, Mom. A lot."

"You sure you're okay?"

"Fine. Go back to sleep."

Karen hung up the phone, curled her body back into its sleep position, and closed her eyes. But her mind kept replaying the conversation. Maybe it was from too much beer or the late hour, but Chad's voice had sounded strained—with just a trace of a quaver, like when he used to come padding in the bedroom during a thunderstorm, back when she had been Mommie instead of Mom. "I can't sleep," he would say as he crawled in beside her. And she would curl her body protectively around his and feel him immediately go limp with sleep. She missed that part of motherhood. The physical part. A small, sturdy body pressed next to her own. Plump little arms around her neck. A tender young neck to kiss. She didn't get to touch either of her children enough. With Melissa, it was a pat every now and then, an occasional hug. Chad, after years of adolescent avoidance of his mother's every kiss and touch, now actually reached for her sometimes, but mostly on arrival and departure, not often enough.

She rolled onto her back, then tried her stomach. Her son had sounded worried.

She went to Chad's room and folded back the covers on his bed, plumped the pillows, turned on the bedside lamp in welcome.

The room looked so bare. Last year, before departing for his freshman year, he had taken down the dozen or more posters of his favorite sports and rock stars, declaring them to be kid stuff. Chad's stereo and television now resided in his room at the fraternity house. His sports trophies had been moved to the new trophy case in the family room. Only the collection of model airplanes and a row of adolescent mysteries on the shelves over the bare desk showed that a young boy had once lived in the room.

A dated picture of Chad's girlfriend, Brenda, sat on the bedside table, a more current one gracing his room at the fraternity house. The Brenda in this picture still had straight hair. And a rounder face. Less beautiful. Karen felt jealous sometimes. She was now the number-two woman in her son's life. But she was wise enough not to compete. Brenda had been good for Chad, balancing out some of his wildness.

Back in bed, she didn't try to sleep, just listen. When she heard him come in, she went downstairs.

He was standing inside the back door, looking around the kitchen, a backpack and small duffel both hung over one shoulder. He looked almost puzzled, as though there was something different about the room. Karen took a quick look around. But it was the same cheerful room it had always been—big round table, captain's chairs, large braided rug on the brick floor. She slipped her arms around her son who was no longer a boy. He was bigger than his father, more solid. Yet it was hard to think of him as a man, hard to call him a man.

"Did you and Brenda have a fight?" she asked.

"No," he said, hugging her back, clinging a bit, putting his cheek against her hair. "She's in Tulsa visiting her sister. I'm just feeling shitty from too much beer. Maybe I should have done without the whole fraternity bit—the partying gets out of hand sometimes. And some of the brothers are low-life jerks."

"And some of them are nice guys. I can't believe you're missing a home game," Karen said, relinquishing her hold on him.

"It's only Kansas State. I would have hung around if you and Dad were coming down. But I need to study. And sleep."

"Well, save some time for your sister. She could use a big brother every now and then."

Karen insisted that he take a couple of aspirin with a glass of milk to waylay a hangover. He looked as though the light were already hurting his eyes.

"You want something to eat?"

"No. We had pizza at the party. Two dozen of them."

He followed her up the stairs. She hugged him again outside the door to his room. "It's good to have you home, son. I miss having you around."

"Yeah. I miss you guys, too. Sometimes I wonder why I was in such a hurry to grow up and leave home. I don't have a mom around now to bandage skinned knees and proofread papers."

Back in bed, Karen thought of her children safe in their own beds just down the hall from her. Her babies. Almost grown. Their simultaneous presence under her roof made her feel both comforted and sad.

The happiest time of her life had been when the children were little, when she and Roger got by on less. Life was more purposeful then. Love simpler.

Teenage children had tested her love. Over and over. Chad had wrecked three cars and had his driver's license suspended for an endless six-month period. And he and a vanful of boys had been caught by the police smoking pot. Fortunately, it had been

the Nichols Hills police doing the apprehending.
Nichols Hills was an island of wealth surrounded by
the sprawl of northwest Oklahoma City, and the Nichols Hills police were far more gracious about the er-
rant children of their community's wealthy residents
than the Oklahoma City police.

And sullen, sixteen-year-old Melissa was starving
herself in the name of beauty and had sex with her
boyfriend at every opportunity. Karen didn't approve
of the dieting, the sex, or the boy. Without Roger's
knowledge, she had put their daughter on birth-con-
trol pills. She had not found a remedy for Melissa's
out-of-control dieting.

But their children were smart and beautiful. Melissa wouldn't be sixteen forever. And with Brenda
helping the process along, Chad's rough edges and
wild ways were already smoothing out—just as his father said they would.

After he graduated from OU, Chad planned either
to go to law school or to earn an MBA. Right now he
was leaning toward an MBA and maybe heading for
Wall Street. Melissa wanted to go east or west to college and study languages at someplace prestigious.

Roger refused to accept the possibility that either
child would actually leave the state. When the time
came, they would change their minds and stay close to
home. Roger wanted Chad to go to law school. In-
state. And eventually practice with him. Or there was
the other dream—that Chad would be an NCAA
champion golfer and turn pro at the end of his college career. And Roger would be his son's caddy, traveling around the country with him, the proud father
who first had taught his son to play.

Even now, Roger managed to watch almost every
competitive hole of golf Chad played, traveling out-of-
state for collegiate golf tournaments. Karen also enjoyed watching their son play. But mothers tended to

be more realistic. Chad was on the university golf team, but his freshman season had been only passable. Not brilliant. His position on the golf team this year was not assured.

As for Melissa, Roger had always assumed that his daughter would probably marry well and follow in her mother's footsteps as a proponent of gracious living, Junior League, and responsible volunteerism. But in Europe last summer, Melissa had stunned him. The child actually spoke French well enough to make herself understood—and made a brave attempt at German. But when she announced that she wanted to major in modern languages at college and become a translator at the United Nations, he didn't offer words of encouragement.

He did take pride in her tennis. She was as good at tennis as Chad was at golf, and Roger was there for every tournament. And wanted her to play in college.

Tennis. Golf. French. DUIs. Karen's mind was wandering so. She considered giving up on sleep altogether. But it was Saturday morning. There was no reason to get up at dawn.

She crawled out of bed anyway and opened the drapes. The sprawling backyard looked black and white in the hazy first light. Surrealistic even. Like a dreamscape.

She went to the bathroom, then returned to her bed and sat on the side by the window, staring out at the predawn sky. The weatherman had promised another warm day. Indian summer. Daytime temperatures once again in the upper eighties. Another balmy evening—like last night. Much too warm for a fire in the big stone fireplace in the fraternity-house living room.

But her son's clothes had smelled of smoke.

2

"$\mathcal{I}$ couldn't find her," the girl's worried voice whispered over the telephone. "I looked all over, Mrs. Frank. I thought maybe she'd already left. But her car was still in the parking lot behind Frumps. I didn't know what to do. It was already so late, and I was afraid my dad would already be freaking out."

"You left her at a party with a bunch of drunk college boys?" Inez asked, taking a breath, staying calm, keeping dread at bay until she knew if it was warranted.

"They weren't all drunk," the girl was explaining. Cindy was her name. Rose's best friend in Norman. A nice girl. "And other girls were there, too," Cindy said. "But Rose must have already left."

"Wouldn't she have told you if she was leaving?"

"I don't know," Cindy said, still whispering. "I looked for her all over. Really I did. And anyway, even if she was still at the party, the fraternity house is only a couple blocks from Frumps. She could have walked back to her car. I didn't know what else to do, so I went on home. Then I got worried and called your house. Sammy got up and looked, but Rose isn't there. The bed is still made, he said. I hated to call you at the hospital, but I thought that you should know."

Inez glanced at the clock on the wall. Five-thirty in the morning. And her daughter was not at home.

7

Rose was supposed to pick her up here at the hospital at seven when the shift ended. The dread, deep inside of her, began clawing its way upward. "What was the name of this fraternity house?" she asked.

"I don't remember the name. It's a big brick house on College Street. Rose waited on these three guys earlier in the evening. One of them invited her to the party and gave her the address. Told her come by after she got off. She insisted that I had to go, too. She'd be too embarrassed to go by herself. Just for a little while, she said. We left her car at Frumps and took mine."

"Was Rose drinking?"

"Some," Cindy admitted, her tone reluctant. "Maybe more than some. I told her she should cool it, but everyone has to find out about hangovers on their own. Maybe she fell asleep someplace. Or passed out."

"With a boy, you mean? Would she do that?"

"I don't know," Cindy's hushed voice said. "She still talks about that guy in Oklahoma City. Steve. But the guy who asked her to the party gave her a big tip and told her she looked like Demi Moore. Rose doesn't understand about fraternity boys. They don't go with girls like us. That boy asked us to the party so they could all have a good laugh."

"Is my car still at the restaurant?"

"I don't know. Maybe she came back for it."

"If Rose doesn't come at seven, I'll call a cab to take me to my car. Then I'll come to your house and get you. I want you to show me where this fraternity house is."

"But my parents," Cindy whispered anxiously. "My dad . . ."

"Please, go get your mother. I'll explain to her."

The fraternity house was huge. Like a hotel. Or a Southern plantation house. A red-brick building with stately white columns marching across the broad front porch, one of many large houses with Greek letters on the front that were located near the university campus.

No one had ever explained the significance of the Greek houses to Inez, but she assumed the students who in lived in them had more money than the students who lived in the more impersonal, high-rise dorms.

She pulled her aging station wagon into the adjoining lot, parking next to a shiny little red car that would only hold two people. She left Cindy waiting in the car.

There was no bell, so she used the brass door knocker. For a long time. Then she tried the door. It was unlocked, and she entered the dim recesses of the first floor. Beyond the large entry hall was a dining room filled with a dozen or so tables. She walked down the tiled hall to a large living room with chairs haphazardly scattered about, sofa cushions on the floor, ashtrays overflowing, large Styrofoam cups everywhere, a big-screen television silently playing an old black-and-white movie to an empty room. Clark Gable and Mryna Loy. The inside of the house wasn't as nice as she had expected. Its woodwork was scarred. Wooden floor tiles were missing, drapes faded, the carpet on the stairs badly worn.

"Is anyone home?" Inez called out.

She waited, then called again—louder.

And again, this time up the stairwell.

Finally, she heard a lock turn, a chain being unlatched, a door open. A bathrobe-clad woman with white, slept-on hair appeared in a doorway at the end of a smaller hallway that led from the entry hall.

"What are you doing here?" the woman asked.

"I'm looking for my daughter," Inez explained.

"She came here last night. To a party. And she never came home."

"Yes, there was a party. A very loud party," the woman said with a sigh and patted at her unruly hair. "But it mercifully ended about two."

"Who are you?" Inez asked.

"I'm Mrs. Cate, the housemother. I live here," she said, gesturing to the open door at the end of the hallway.

"I'm Inez Frank. My daughter's name is Rose. Could I look upstairs?"

"No, I'm afraid not. There's two floors of sleeping boys up there. But I'd be glad to ask around for you when the boys get up. It shouldn't be too long. There's a home football game today. They have to get the house cleaned up before their parents start arriving."

"I'll sit here and wait for them," Inez said, pointing to an upholstered bench by the front door.

"I really don't think she's here," Mrs. Cate said sympathetically. "The house has rules about girls staying over. And no girl in her right mind would want to."

"Maybe one of the boys knows where she went or who she went with," Inez explained.

Inez went outside to tell Cindy she would be a while. Cindy was hunched over in the front seat, crying. "I couldn't hang around here all night waiting for her," she said. "She knows how my dad is."

"I know," Inez said, patting her shoulder.

Inez went back inside and sat on the bench by the door. The housemother returned shortly with a cup of coffee. "I called the chapter president on his private line," Mrs. Cate said. "He's coming downstairs to talk to you."

"Do you make the boys behave?" Inez asked.

Mrs. Cate laughed. "I think that's what fraternity

housemothers used to do. Nowadays we mostly plan
the meals, order the food, and oversee the kitchen
help. And act as a hostess when parents and alumni
visit.''

A few minutes later a tall, skinny boy with red hair
came down the stairs. He was wearing wrinkled tan
shorts, a T-shirt, and high-top athletic shoes with no
laces and no socks. Old, filthy shoes. Only rich boys
and homeless people wore shoes like that.

He approached Inez with a look of concern on his
face, his hand outstretched. "Tom Fitzhugh," he said.
"I'm chapter president. How can I help you? Mother
Cate said something about your daughter not coming
home last night."

He had used water to flatten his hair. His face bore
creases from his pillow. A decent-looking face. Inez
relaxed a little. "My daughter, Rose, came to your
party with her girlfriend, and she never came home,"
she explained. "I want to know where she is."

"Yes. Two high-school girls were here. One of the
members invited them, I understand. One girl had
dark hair, the other was a blonde."

"Rose has dark hair. Apparently, she was drinking a
lot. I thought she might have fallen asleep someplace."

"Not here. But I'll be glad to ask around and see if
anyone knows where she went," he offered.

"Yes, please," Inez said. "I'll wait here."

"Everyone's still asleep," he protested.

But already, Inez had picked up her cup of coffee.

Half an hour later Tom Fitzhugh returned. He
knelt on one knee in front of her. "Almost everyone
remembers seeing her. She got kind of drunk," he
said. "No one remembers seeing her leave. But the
party was all over the house. Dancing downstairs in
the rec room. People watching television and playing
cards up here in the living room. The beer kegs were

out on the deck. Sometimes couples go upstairs. People were milling around and coming and going a lot."

"Could she still be downstairs?" Inez asked.

"I really don't think so, but we can go look."

Inez followed the skinny young man down a narrow enclosed staircase to a large basement room that smelled of beer and stale tobacco and had popcorn scattered across the floor like a snowfall. Plastic glasses and Styrofoam cups covered the tabletops, and a large green trash can in the corner was overflowing with them.

"There was a popcorn fight," Tom Fitzhugh explained with an embarrassed shrug. "It turned out to be a pretty rowdy party."

Inez looked behind the furniture, inside a basement laundry room, in a storage closet containing folding chairs. She was close to tears. "I want to look upstairs in the boys' rooms."

"No. I'm really sorry, but I can't allow that."

"Were all the boys in their beds? No one missing?"

"Some of the guys go home weekends. But right now every bed has someone sleeping in it. We've got about a dozen guys from our Kansas State chapter who came in last night for the game."

"I guess you know that my next stop is the police station," Inez said.

"Don't you think you should give your daughter a chance to come home first?" Fitzhugh said, not unkindly. "It's not the first time a girl has stayed out all night."

"It's the first time my daughter has," Inez said.

"I'm sure she's all right. Maybe she went to a friend's house. Or fell asleep in her car. I don't think she was accustomed to drinking that much."

Fitzhugh asked Inez to write down her telephone number and promised to call her if any of the members remembered anything else about her daughter.

And he asked her to let him know when Rose came home.

"Not all the boys are like you, are they?" Inez asked.

"How's that?"

"You seem like a nice person. Not all the boys who live here are nice, are they?"

"A few are kind of crude," he acknowledged. "Your daughter didn't belong here, Mrs. Frank. A couple of the guys thought it would be funny to get her drunk. I guess I should have tried to stop them. I'm sorry now that I didn't."

Inez's feet felt heavy, almost too heavy to move, as she walked back to the car. Don't think, she told herself. Just do what you need to do. You can think later.

"Did you find out anything?" Cindy asked as Inez slid into the car.

"No. I'll take you home and go to the police now."

"No. I'll go with you," Cindy said.

"Why did Rose want to go to a place like that?" Inez asked, staring at the large fraternity house.

"She wanted to see what rich boys were like. She thought they might be nicer than other guys since they were going to be lawyers and doctors and businessmen. I told her that fraternity guys could be real jerks, just like any other guys, but I don't think she believed me," Cindy said, folding and unfolding her hands in her lap. "She hasn't lived in Norman long enough to figure out about the haves and the have-nots. I wish my parents had never moved here. I hate going to that high school. Most of the kids have their own cars, and the girls wear 'outfits.' No matter how nice I think I look when I leave home, I get up there and realize that I look like shit."

Yes, Inez thought. Coming to Norman had been a mistake for her family, too. A college town. It had sounded so wholesome. A good place for children.

But the young people here did drugs and got drunk and killed themselves in car wrecks just like in south Oklahoma City. Only they had better clothes and fancier cars to die in.

Chad was up by nine.

He ate only a few bites of the waffle Karen prepared for him. And even that much seemed a chore. He chewed slowly, swallowed with difficulty, and finally apologized for not finishing. His stomach was protesting from all the beer, he explained. Served him right for going past his limit.

He thumbed through the newspaper then pushed back his chair and announced he'd better hit the books.

"Was there a fire last night?" Karen asked. "Your clothes smelled of smoke when you came in."

He hesitated—as though trying to remember. "Yeah. A fire. For hot dogs. We built it in the parking lot."

"I thought you had pizza at the party."

"We did. It was a long party."

"Were you with another girl?" Karen asked.

"Why do you ask?" he asked carefully, fingering the edge of the place mat.

"Mother's intuition, I suppose. You came home unexpectedly. You seem upset. There's no alarm clock in your room, yet you were up awfully early for a boy who got only a couple hours' sleep and is nursing a hangover. And you didn't eat your mother's featherlight, made-from-scratch pecan waffle covered with real maple syrup straight from Vermont. I thought maybe you had a guilty conscience. You're not seeing someone else, are you? Brenda would be—"

"Brenda and I are fine," Chad snapped.

"I'm sorry," Karen apologized, touching his shoulder. "None of my business. Okay?"

"Yeah," he said, his expression softening. And he took her hand and kissed it—an oddly romantic gesture from a son.

After he'd gone back upstairs, Karen cleared his dishes from the table and poured herself a cup of coffee, thinking she would have her turn with the newspaper.

But she sipped her coffee and stared out at the backyard through the open French doors—a spectacular half-acre backyard with a brick veranda, tiled swimming pool, paddleball court, gazebo, lush landscaping. A pair of cardinals were splashing at the ornate, two-tiered sculptured birdbath, which brought regular complaints from the gardener. He didn't like dealing with the bird droppings that soiled the veranda and brick walks. But the birds enjoyed splashing in the water. And Karen enjoyed watching them.

The coffee was good and strong. The way she liked it. On mornings when Roger was home, she made a weaker brew.

But she found no pleasure in strong coffee this morning, no satisfaction in the beauty of her backyard. And she was too distracted for the morning paper.

She didn't believe Chad. He hadn't said, "No, I wasn't with another girl last night." Instead, he'd thrown the question back at her. He'd been with another girl last night. While Brenda was out of town.

Karen hoped Brenda didn't find out.

She wanted better from her son. Wanted him to be a better man than his father.

Her husband didn't know that Karen knew about his infidelity. She'd kept silent because she believed that, in spite of his affair, Roger valued their marriage and their family. Or was it that she desperately needed to stay married to him?

She had often wondered how women faced the public humiliation of husbands straying. Of divorce. Of being left for another woman. Of having carefully constructed worlds shattered. Identities taken away. Becoming outcasts. When Karen saw such women at the market or at parents' meetings at the school, she hardly knew what to say to them. She found herself muttering empty funeral words. *If there's anything I can do* . . .

Roger would never humiliate her. She believed that he'd strayed only for sex—and hadn't done that for three years. Karen was sure of that. And there had only been the one woman. Rhonda Parker. Karen had done the right thing, waiting it out, pretending that she didn't know. Being seductive. Insisting they go to Hawaii for their anniversary that year. Buying sexy lingerie.

In spite of the reality of her own imperfect marriage, Karen wanted her children to have good marriages that precluded any infidelity. After Chad moved into the fraternity house at the end of August, she'd found an unfinished letter he'd been writing to Brenda. Which a mother shouldn't have read. But she did. It made her cry. *My love for you is a holy thing. I will die loving you.*

But going with a girl wasn't the same as being married. And in spite of the beautiful letter and years of dating only Brenda, Chad had not formalized his commitment to her. She wore his fraternity drop but not his fraternity pin. Not an engagement ring. They didn't have a home and family. Perhaps Chad's sin was an understandable one. Maybe he wondered what he missed by not dating around. And he had been upset about last night. She felt certain his distress was due to more than too much beer. That alone said something. A lesser person would not have cared.

Had Roger cared? Had he ever suffered pangs of guilt when he had sex with cool, elegant Rhonda?

For a time Karen had thought about evening the score, of finding a man to have an affair with—a sensitive man who said the right things and made her feel beautiful and adored. But an affair with that sort of man would not be the same as an occasional romp in a motel room, which was what she fervently hoped had been the nature of Roger's affair. And for that reason, she stopped mentally auditioning the men in her world for the part.

Only occasionally, usually when she was driving alone in a car, floating in between home and other places, did lovely soft images flit across her mind. Fingers touching across a restaurant table. Walking hand in hand through a mountain meadow. Being alone in a room full of people. Sometimes these fantasies starred the man—boy really—she had loved before Roger. But usually not. She was more comfortable keeping the man in soft focus.

She had shown the letter to Roger—the one Chad had been writing to Brenda. Roger had looked at it for a long time. "That's how I feel about you," he had said. "I haven't been very good about telling you, though. Not for a long time."

She didn't have any love letters. But Roger had stayed with her. In the three years since the business with Rhonda, he'd not strayed again. He was as committed to their marriage as she was. And that lifted her heart.

Commitment was more important even than love.

3

"*H*ey, Larson." the dispatcher's voice barked over the telephone intercom.

Gary picked up the receiver. "Yeah."

"I've got a woman here who wants to make a missing-person report. Her teenage daughter. I tried to get her to fill out the forms and come back Monday morning if the girl hasn't come home by then. But she says she's going to sit out here until someone sees her."

Gary allowed himself a sigh. Missing persons generally were a nuisance. In a basically middle-class community like Norman, teenagers and husbands generally came on home. And when they didn't—well, there was a big world out there in which to lose oneself. Only occasionally was there a crime associated with a missing person.

Detectives usually got weekends off. Gary was on call, which—if he was lucky—required only availability. But as he explained last night to his wife, he was behind at the station. He would need to go in tomorrow and catch up on paperwork. Which was true. But mostly he wanted an excuse to get out of the house, preferably before Sharon woke up. She was weepy again—ever since she'd been to her cousin's baby shower. She didn't want to drive up to Cowboys for an evening of dancing. She didn't want to go to the football game or shop for a new sofa. She didn't even want to go see her sister in Oklahoma City. Gary was never

18

quite sure what his role was supposed to be when his wife was in one of her funks. She regarded any effort on his part to cheer her up as insensitive, yet she resented being left alone. An escape under the banner of "work" was the safest out for him.

But already he felt guilty. Maybe he should have talked her into an afternoon on the lake.

He'd call her later. Offer to grill hamburgers in the backyard this evening. Rent a movie. Buy a six-pack.

The woman with the missing daughter was a nurse.

She was wearing a white sweater over a white uniform with an official-looking gold pin on her collar.

She looked Hispanic. Fortyish. Pretty round face. Slim hips. Heavy bosom. Her black hair was pulled smoothly back into a ponytail. Plain gold wedding band. Utilitarian digital watch. Little makeup. Her chin bore a determined tilt, but there was fear in her eyes.

A teenage girl with bleached hair followed the woman to Gary's cubicle. The girl hung back, leaning against a file cabinet as the woman soundlessly approached the desk in her nurse's shoes. Half rising from his chair, Gary reached out to shake hands. "Detective Gary Larson. What can I do for you?"

"I'm Inez Frank, and this is my daughter's friend Cindy Fisher." She cleared her throat in an attempt to conceal her nervousness. "My daughter's name is Rose. Rosalie actually. Rosalie Victoria Frank. She didn't come home last night. This morning, the car she drove was still parked behind the restaurant where she and Cindy work. Cindy drove them in her car to a party at a fraternity house—the Iota Beta fraternity house at 710 College. Cindy couldn't find Rose when it was time to leave. Before coming here, I went to this fraternity house. The president of the house said that Rose wasn't there, but he wouldn't let me look upstairs. He said that none of the boys who live there know where she is."

She spoke with great care, as though she had mentally rehearsed her words. She had the slightest of accents. Probably grew up in a bilingual household.

"And you don't believe the fraternity president?" Gary asked.

"I don't think that he lied. But someone might have lied to him. Someone in that fraternity house might know where my daughter is. A lot of boys live there. And they have some boys from out of town sleeping there. I don't think the president talked to every one of them."

"Mrs. Frank, it's still early. Probably your daughter had a little too much to drink and is sleeping it off someplace."

She nodded. That was what she hoped for. "But Rose has never stayed out all night before," she said. "I work nights, and she comes right home from her job so her younger brother won't be alone."

"How old is she?"

"Seventeen. Will you please help me find her?"

"Mrs. Frank, a seventeen-year-old isn't considered missing until twenty-four hours have gone by. Missing teenagers usually have either run away or are sleeping it off," Gary explained.

Inez Frank chewed on her lip, considering. "She wouldn't run away," she said.

Behind her, Cindy Fisher was nodding. "She wouldn't do that, sir. I talk about running away sometimes—my dad is a jerk and hits me and my mom sometimes. But Rose said she couldn't ever do that to her mom."

"Where do you and Rose work?"

"Frumps—on Campus Corner. We're waitresses. I got her the job. Rose is my best friend."

"But you left the party without her," Gary reminded the girl.

"But I looked all over first," Cindy insisted. "I looked for a long time. And besides, Rose's car was only a couple of blocks away. She knew I couldn't stay long. She knows how my dad can be. And besides, I felt so out of place. I wanted to find her and get out of there."

"What about Rose's father? Where's he? Could she be with him?" Gary asked Mrs. Frank.

The woman shook her head no. "My husband is a patient in Veterans Hospital in Oklahoma City. She wouldn't go up there by herself in the middle of the night."

"You know, don't you, chances are that Rose went off with some boy?" Gary asked. "And probably she'd been drinking."

"She's gone drinking with a boy before. But not when her brother is home by himself. She didn't come home. She didn't call. And I can't think of any good reason why. Only bad reasons," she added, her voice breaking. Cindy Fisher stepped forward and put her hand on the woman's shoulder.

"Is anyone at your house now to answer the phone in case Rose calls?" Gary asked.

Inez Frank nodded. "My son. I called him just a few minutes ago. Rose hasn't called."

"Maybe she hasn't come home yet because she's afraid to face you," Gary suggested. "Or embarrassed."

Inez Frank considered this. A thread of hope.

"What does your daughter look like?" Gary asked, reaching for a pen.

Mrs. Frank had a picture for him—a school picture of a pretty girl with a dimpled smile. Smooth dark hair like her mother.

"She is five feet five," Inez Frank said. "One hundred and twenty-five pounds. Her eyes are brown, and she has a broken tooth in front that she's saving money to have fixed." The woman paused, her eyes filling with tears. "She's a sweet girl. A kind person. I love her very much."

Karen was making out a grocery list when Melissa came downstairs. "Who's taking a shower in Chad's bathroom?" Melissa asked.

"Chad's taking a shower in Chad's bathroom," Karen said brightly.

"I can't believe he's actually decided to honor us with his presence. What's the occasion?" Melissa poured herself a glass of orange juice, regarded the glass, then returned half the juice to the container.

Melissa's hair was still in hot curlers, but she was already dressed in her new wraparound denim dress. A size four. Melissa had been thrilled about that. Karen had been appalled.

"He has a lot of studying to do," Karen answered, "and thought it would be quieter here. What's with you? You're awfully dressed up for Saturday morning."

"Trevor called. His parents decided not to go to the football game. We're going to use their tickets."

"I thought we were going shopping," Karen said. "What about Chad's birthday present?"

Melissa had the grace to look guilty. "I know, Mom. I'm sorry. But Trevor wants to go to the game."

"And you always do what Trevor wants?" Karen snapped, knowing she should keep her mouth shut. Of late, Melissa always found a reason not to shop. Or lunch. Play tennis. Anything that involved spending time with her mother.

"Don't you always do what Dad wants?" Melissa retorted.

"Your father happens to be my husband," Karen said. "And no, I don't always do what he wants. We discuss things. He doesn't expect me to break my promises to other people to suit his whims."

"It's not like Trevor's dragging me. I *want* to go with him. We'd just buy Chad some shirts and jeans. And the sheepskin seat covers he wants for his car. You don't need me for that."

"Maybe not for that specific errand, but I do need you, Melissa. I need you a great deal." Karen reached for her daughter's hand. Melissa allowed her to hold it for a few seconds before pulling away.

"Would you like a waffle?" Karen asked, unable to stop herself. If she hadn't asked, Melissa might have dribbled a couple of tablespoons of batter into the waffle iron and made a corner of a waffle to munch on, sans syrup and butter, of course. But the battle lines between mother and daughter had been drawn. If Karen got Melissa to eat something, it was viewed by them both as a victory for Karen.

Melissa put her juice glass in the dishwasher. "No, thanks."

"Come on, Melissa. Half a glass of juice isn't enough breakfast."

"I'll have a hot dog at the game." She began pulling out hot curlers and raced up the stairs. Karen watched her go, not knowing whether to scream at her or cry.

Six months ago they'd been friends, and Melissa had been a healthy-looking teenager with a size-eight body and short hair perfect for a tennis competitor.

Now she looked like she was suffering from a wasting disease. And she had to get up thirty minutes earlier in the morning to curl her hair. She was remaking herself, it seemed, to Trevor Washburn's specifications. And Trevor liked girls with hand-span waists and long, fluffy hair.

Trevor also had encouraged her to give up tennis. The tournaments and daily practicing took too much of her time. He wanted her to sit on the bleachers and watch after-school football practice with the other players' girlfriends. He wanted her to be at home when he called, to be out front waiting when he came by to pick her up in the morning, to type his school papers. Melissa's function in their relationship was apparently to please.

Not that Karen didn't understand. She did understand, which made it all the more painful. Melissa had developed early and grown to her present five feet, ten inches, by the end of the seventh grade. She had been the tallest girl in her class until the ninth grade when a few other girls caught up with her. And she had been pudgy. Not fat. But certainly not svelte. Not competitive in the high-school dating game.

Tennis had helped immensely. A lovely lean athlete's body emerged from adolescent adipose. Karen had been thrilled—and relieved. Suddenly shopping with her daughter for clothes became a joy rather than a challenge.

Then along came Trevor, Melissa's first real boyfriend. He was more important than tennis, than her family, than her friends, than her health.

Monday, Karen vowed, she'd call a doctor. Get some advice. Except she wasn't sure what sort of doctor to call. Melissa refused to go to Iva Burk anymore, saying she was too old for a pediatrician. Maybe eating disorders belonged to internists.

Or psychiatrists.

But Iva Burk was a grandmotherly sort who would listen sympathetically and offer reassurance. And that's what Karen wanted. Reassurance. Surely Melissa's behavior was just another phase.

4

*T*raffic was impossible in Norman on home-football-game Saturdays. Before and after games, it was faster to walk across town than drive. On days like today, when the weather was pleasant, lots of people did just that, parking miles away from the stadium and going the rest of the way on foot.

But now that the game was under way, much of the local citizenry and virtually all of the visitors to the town were tucked away in the stadium watching the Oklahoma Sooners in their annual contest with Big Eight rival, the Kansas State Wildcats, Gary had no trouble driving to the campus.

He could hear the cheers from the stadium as the radio broadcaster announced that the Sooners had just scored their third touchdown with ten seconds remaining in the first half.

Gary considered catching the last half, but decided he wasn't in the mood for crowds and cheering. He wasn't in the mood for much of anything, he realized. Some days he understood why people ran away.

Was that what the Frank girl had done? Run away? Opted for a fresh start? Some teenagers did that when the pressures of home and school were too much for them.

He'd had information about the Frank girl relayed to all officers on duty and put in calls to county law officials and those in nearby communities, including

Oklahoma City. Anything further could wait until Monday. By then, the girl would probably have come home or at least called her mother.

He wondered if Rosalie Frank would ever have any idea how much worry and pain she'd caused. Maybe that was a tack he should try with Sharon. Having kids wasn't all it was cracked up to be. They bring as much sorrow as joy. Of course, at one time, the thought of having a child had warmed his heart. Now all he wanted was an end to unhappiness.

The University of Oklahoma campus was a beautiful place with wonderful old trees, traditional collegiate Gothic architecture, spacious parkways, spectacular flower gardens that were replanted with the seasons and now were ablaze with chrysanthemums of every possible hue. Gary had gone to school here, but his college experience was quite different from that of the more affluent students who lived in the huge sorority and fraternity houses just south and west of the main campus. He had lived in one of the older, unair-conditioned dorms and paid his way with student loans and the small salary he earned as school-bus driver. Weekends, he'd drive home to Ardmore to see his mom and Sharon. He'd gone with Sharon since junior high, never even had a date with any other girl, hadn't especially wanted to. But then, Sharon used to smile and laugh. All the time. He used to think Sharon was the happiest person he'd ever known. Even during sex, she'd laugh with the sheer pleasure of pleasing and being pleased. "Isn't this jus' the most fun you've ever had!" she'd say.

The front lawn of the Iota Beta house had been turned into a game-day parking lot. Five dollars a car, the sign said.

Most of the Greek houses south of the campus had been built in the past two or three decades. But a number of fraternities and sororities still occupied pre–World War II buildings in the older residential neighborhood just west of the campus. Iota Beta was one of those older houses. From the outside, it looked pretty grand. Inside, it was shopworn. The woodwork was scarred. The wallpaper had seen better days. But the windows sparkled, and the scarred furniture gleamed with fresh polish.

He found the plump housemother in the kitchen, overseeing the preparations of after-game refreshments. A tradition at the house, she explained. The boys would bring their dates, and some of the parents would wait at the house for the traffic to thin. She was sorry to hear the Frank woman hadn't found her daughter, she told Gary as she took off her apron. "I felt sure the girl would come home later that morning," Mrs. Cate said.

She poured two cups of coffee and carried them to her private sitting room, which was furnished with what was left of her "own things," the housemother told Gary. "I gave everything else to my children. This is the last stop before assisted living, I imagine."

"Can you help me at all?" Gary asked. "I'd like to know what time the girl left the party and with whom."

"I questioned several of the boys," Mrs. Cate told him. "Everyone seems to agree that no girls were in the house after two—or two-thirty at the latest. The boys think the Frank girl left earlier than that with her girlfriend. The two had been the only high-school girls at the party, and apparently everyone noticed them. Their clothes were different, their sweaters too tight. Sorority girls have a look about them, you know. They wear hand-knit sweaters, expensive blazers, good shoes. Nothing cheap or flashy."

Mrs. Cate accompanied him on a tour of the first floor and the basement recreation room. "Is the place

always this clean?'' Gary asked, taking in the immacu-
late rec room with its freshly waxed floor.

"The pledges clean every Saturday morning, but
they do an especially good job on home-football-game
days—for the parents and alumni. The members even
clean their rooms in case their parents go upstairs.''

He looked through the upstairs on his own. The
hall needed paint, and its threadbare carpet smelled
faintly of urine and vomit. The bathrooms were clean,
but the plumbing was old and stained. Some of the
rooms would pass a military inspection, but others
had been only perfunctorily tidied—bedspreads
pulled over rumpled bedding, articles of clothing
kicked under the bed. A few of the beds were still
occupied by apparent hangover victims.

"Do girls ever spend the night?'' he asked. Mrs.
Cate was back in the kitchen, arranging cold cuts on a
tray. A skinny black woman was cutting a sheet cake
into squares.

Mrs. Cate shook her head no. "Boys take girls to
their rooms and close the door sometimes. But a girl
wouldn't want to sleep over. Boys walk down the hall
to the bathrooms in their underwear or naked. And
the only bathroom for girls is down here on the first
floor.''

"A lot of drinking at the parties?''

The woman sighed. "Yes. A lot of drinking. Beer
mostly. The university has tried to put a stop to underage drinking, but I think it's impossible to enforce.
They'd have to post a policeman at every house to
check IDs.''

"Do you go to the parties?''

"Heavens, no. I'm paid to have blue hair and stay
out of the way. The alumni house board wants me in
the house, but chaperons went out years ago. The
boys are in charge of themselves. Boys who get too
wild and tear up things usually get kicked out as

pledges—before they get initiated and are allowed to live in the house. Pledges who don't make their grades don't get initiated. And members who don't keep up their grades are kicked out of the house. They do have standards. It's not as bad as that movie.''

"*Animal House.*"

She nodded. "Not that bad. At least not in this house. I remember last year when a gang of naked fraternity boys were accused of urinating on the tepee that the Indian students had put up for Indian Heritage Week. And I've heard rumors from the other housemothers. Not very nice stories—about rooms with peek holes where they take girls to have sex. And things they do to the pledges that are too disgusting to repeat. But the IBs aren't that bad.''

"But not all that good either?" he asked.

"Some of the boys are decent enough—and serious about their studies, but I always wonder why they want to hang around the rest. It's an image, I guess. *Fraternity man.* They feel more important than the students who live in the dormitories and don't have nice cars. Fraternity men date pretty sorority girls from good families. When they graduate, they have an inside track on jobs when fraternity alumni are running the company.''

"Do you think that any of the boys would hurt a girl?"

She shrugged. "I don't know. Some of them talk about girls in the wrong way. I hear them sometimes, but maybe that's just to show off. I know there's a lot of sex, even with all the worry about AIDS. But I think it's all consenting. I've never seen evidence of anything else. But that doesn't mean a whole lot. I don't see most of what they do—except eat. They do eat a lot. Like pigs, some of them. Their mothers would weep if they could see how their sons act and talk at the dinner table.''

He gave her his card. "If you think of anything I should know, or if you hear anything—anything at all —please give me a call."

"I hope there won't be trouble," she said. "There was trouble at one of the houses, and the university kicked them off campus. Their housemother was a friend of mine. We played bridge on Tuesdays. Now, she lives in the guest room at her daughter's house and has nothing but Social Security."

Gary drove to Frumps. Like Cindy Fisher had said, it would be a short walk from the fraternity house. Not more than five or ten minutes.

Rosalie Frank probably had either left the Iota Beta house with a boy or been picked up by someone on her way to her car.

Still, he'd check with whoever was selling tickets at the bus station Friday night. And with the cab companies. Passenger trains hadn't stopped in Norman for years. He doubted if she had the money for a plane ticket, and the airport was in Oklahoma City. But he'd call the airlines, too.

As he walked back to his car he checked his notebook for the address of the Frank home. It was on the east side. Like his own.

Basically a middle-class university community, Norman had no enclave of poverty. But the less affluent lived on the east side. The Franks lived in a row of modest duplexes. Rental property. Many had camping trailers or boats parked in driveways—Gary had a boat in his driveway. East-side folks did their vacationing at state lakes. Sharon used to like that. Fishing. Cooking on the Coleman. Long walks. Snuggling in front of a campfire, downing a six-pack, listening to their favorite country station on the portable radio. Making love in a sleeping bag. Good times.

Gary had no reason to stop by the Frank house. Inez Frank would have called the police station if her daughter had come home. But he stopped anyway, pulling his car in behind a faded blue station wagon with a hospital parking decal on the window. The wagon's front tires were almost bald. The back ones were not much better.

A look of fear crossed Inez's face when she opened the front door. "Nothing to report," Gary said hastily. "I was in the neighborhood."

She was wearing jeans and a white pullover. No makeup. Her hair was in one thick braid down her back. Wonderful heavy hair so black it looked blue. A strong, sad woman with a classic face. Someone an artist would want to paint.

Her son shook hands. Sammy. A skinny twelve-year-old with crooked teeth who could have passed for ten.

Gary wondered what they had been doing before he got there. The television wasn't on. The coffee table was clear of any open books or magazines. No food smells came from the kitchen.

What did one do while sitting around waiting to hear about a missing loved one? Pray maybe. Clean closets. Remember good times.

His wife would either be hysterical or in a tranquilizer haze, Gary decided, with her mother and sister hovering over her. Sharon never made any claim to being strong under duress. That was his job.

The living room was clean, its furnishings worn. A set of prints hung on the walls—four colorful village scenes from south of the border. A floral hooked rug covered much of the drab carpet. And a row of family pictures lined a shelf over the television.

Now that he was here, Gary felt awkward. Inez did, too. He declined her offer of coffee, then wished he hadn't.

"I just wondered if you'd thought of any place Rose

might have gone. A relative's house. A friend's. Did she have a regular boyfriend?''

"No," Inez said too quickly. "No boyfriend. No relatives in town. No close friend but Cindy. We've only lived in Norman since February. I got a job at the Norman hospital that paid more than the job I had at University Hospital in Oklahoma City. And we can manage better with one car in Norman. Rose rides the school bus, and Sammy walks to his school. The lake is close by for fishing and swimming. I thought coming here seemed like a good idea. I guess it wasn't.''

She looked away, composing herself.

Then she looked straight at him. "I'm afraid of what one of those boys might have done to my daughter.''

"It's too early to even be thinking something like that," he said. "You said that Rose was supposed to come home after work so Sammy wouldn't be here alone?''

Inez nodded. "He has asthma. He shouldn't be alone all night.''

"And then she would come to get you at the hospital when your shift ended.''

Another nod.

Gary directed his next question to Sammy. "And is this the first time your sister didn't come straight home from work?''

Sammy hesitated, casting a sidelong glance at his mother. "Well, sometimes she's a little late. Some of the time I'm already asleep and don't know when she comes in.''

"And when she's a little late, do you know where she is?''

Again, the boy hesitated. "Sometimes maybe she sees this guy.''

"What guy?''

"A guy from Oklahoma City."

Gary looked back at Inez. But she was looking at her son. "Rose was seeing him again?" she demanded.

"She didn't say it was him. But sometimes she was late coming home. And she got phone calls late at night. Sometimes I'd hear her go out after a phone call."

"Why didn't you tell me?" Inez demanded.

"Rose asked me not to," he said, avoiding his mother's gaze, tears welling in his eyes.

Gary felt a stab of pity for the boy. He was probably wondering if keeping his sister's secret had condemned her to something worse than maternal wrath.

Inez turned to Gary. "This boy is in a gang. I didn't want her with him."

"What's his name and where does he go to school?"

"Steve. I don't think he goes to school anymore. He used to go to Capitol Hill High School. That's where Rose met him."

"What's his last name?"

Inez shrugged and looked to Sammy. He didn't know either. Just Steve.

"Why don't you make some phone calls and see if you can find out his last name and where he lives. I'd like to talk to him."

Inez nodded. "And what else will you do? How will you look for Rose?"

"If she doesn't call or come home by tomorrow, we'll put her name on the wire and notify all law enforcement agencies in the region. I plan to talk to the young men at the fraternity house. Other than that, I don't know where to look, where to begin. When people disappear without a trace, there's not much the police can do," he told her honestly.

* * *

Inez called her supervisor, saying only that she had a family problem. Getting more specific than that would only make it seem more real, more ominous.

The nursing supervisor sighed. "We're already short on the eleven-to-seven shift."

"I'd come if I could," Inez said.

The woman sighed again. "Just make sure you're here tomorrow evening."

Inez hung up the phone and got the bucket from the garage and filled it with soapy water. She began emptying the kitchen cabinets, one by one, scrubbing them inside and out, and putting everything back in. Sammy came to help her.

"I'm sorry," he said, carrying a nest of pans to the table.

"It's not your fault. Brothers and sisters cover for each other. I'm just disappointed in her. It's confusing to be disappointed and worried at the same time."

Her everyday dishes were odds and ends. But she still had most of the pieces of the good china that she used for holidays and birthdays. When Rose came home, she'd cook a special meal for her and use the good china. A leg of lamb. Mashed potatoes with real butter. Fresh asparagus. Her mother's garbanzo-bean salad. Corn pudding. Sopaipillas. Flowers in a vase. Candles. A meal they'd all remember for the rest of their lives.

With everything back in the cupboards, Inez went into the room she shared with her daughter and began straightening the closet. Rose had wanted her own room. Inez had looked for a three-bedroom apartment but couldn't see spending that much when money was so dear.

She was only an LPN. She used to dream about becoming an RN, but her husband had been able to work less and less, and finally, he couldn't work at all. Joe had had his own housepainting business in Houston. But as his emphysema worsened, each painting contract took longer and longer to complete. He stopped getting referrals. They sold their house. Sold his equipment and truck.

And finally moved to Oklahoma City so Joe could work in a gun store for an old Army buddy. But he became too weak even for that. Staying on his feet for longer than a few minutes exhausted him.

At first, the visits to the VA Hospital in Oklahoma City were just to have breathing treatments. Then he started having to stay for days and finally weeks at a time, being treated for the upper respiratory infections that frequently plagued him. His time at home between hospital stays grew shorter and shorter. It was always a relief when he went back, when the house once again became silent, without the agonizing sounds of his labored breathing.

He had stopped smoking when they moved to Oklahoma City. Finally. He still talked about it—how hard it had been, how he craved cigarettes, how he didn't understand why he wasn't better. He hadn't smoked in three years. But surely he knew that he was never going to get better.

Joe was a good man. Inez was grateful to him—how much he'd never know. He'd married her when the other man would not. Joe had asked her out every time he came to the diner, but she was in love with a military policeman. She had been only three days late with her period the night she finally agreed to meet Joe after work for a drink. They had lots of drinks, and she had sex with him—just in case she really was pregnant and the MP wouldn't marry her. Joe was single and the sort of man who would do the honorable thing. The MP was named Richie. He was handsome and funny and had a dimpled smile that made Inez feel all fluttery inside. She could no more have stopped herself from getting involved with Richie than she could have willed herself to stop breathing. Or so she told herself. She had worried constantly that she loved him more than he loved her, that he was just playing with her.

When Inez told him she was pregnant, Richie said that he and his wife had decided to get back together. He gave her five hundred dollars for an abortion. And kissed her forehead. "I'm going to miss you, sweet Inez. I'm sorry, but I assumed you were on the pill. Before you put out again, make sure you're on the pill."

Joe wept when she told him she was going to have his baby. Of course he would marry her. He would be honored. A *father*. Holy Mother of God, he was going to be a father. And they made love. Joe thought that she was crying with joy. Inez had wondered if she'd ever stop feeling guilty.

Rose's dimples were a permanent reminder of her real father. But Joe didn't know. For years, Inez prayed to the Holy Virgin for forgiveness. At times she thought the guilt from her horrible deed would suffocate her. But it didn't. And with time, she was able to put the guilt aside. There was too much else to think about, to worry about.

She loved her husband's gentleness, but she didn't love him. Fortunately, he wasn't a particularly sexual man. He didn't ask much of her in bed.

Her mother had kept Rose the year Inez went to LPN school. Joe made enough money then for her to do that. She still worked weekends at the diner, but that was for savings. For the down payment on a house. The day they bought their house was one of the happiest days of her life. She was eight months' pregnant with Sammy, but she and Joe and Rose joined hands and danced round and round in the empty living room of their very own home. But Joe smoked three packs of cigarettes a day. Maybe that was

her punishment. Inez was saved from disgrace by a
man whose sickness robbed his family of their home
and left them poor.

Inez's own father had been an Anglo—a service-
man stationed at Fort Bliss, Texas, who first saw Inez's
mother when he crossed the border with his buddies
for Guadalupe Day. He came across a lot after that,
courting Maria Teresa under her family's careful scrutiny.

Inez would often study the wedding photograph of
her parents in its carved frame. Maria Teresa and
Jerry. Her mother was smiling shyly at the camera, her
father looking down at his bride. Maria Teresa had
been a round, ripe seventeen-year-old virgin. Inez
wondered if her father married her mother because
that was the only way he could have sex with her.

Jerry went from an Army uniform to that of a post-
man. Maria Teresa's roundness grew with the years.
Inez knew her father had been embarrassed for the
rest of his life by a plump wife who never quite
learned English and couldn't say his name properly.
"Jerry" from her lips was "Harry."

After Jerry died in a car crash, Maria Teresa went
back to Mexico and her family. She married again, to
a widower who was the man she should have married
in the first place.

Except who was to say what one *should* have done.
The children that came with marriage, whether or not
the marriage had been wise or foolhardy, made re-
grets difficult.

Like Inez herself. If she hadn't used a lie to get Joe
Frank to marry her, she never would have had Sammy.
Precious Sammy. He brought out the tenderness in
her.

Sammy had asthma. Strange how both her husband
and her son couldn't breathe right. But thank God,
Sammy seemed to be outgrowing his disease. He

could even ride a bike now—not very far—but little by little, he was growing stronger. Inez had that much to be grateful for.

Goodness and long-suffering were so boring. What happened to passion and great love? For so long she'd had daydreams about winning the Publishers Clearing House Sweepstakes. And she had sent a dollar every week to Beverly to buy a ticket for the Texas Lottery— the same set of numbers every week, compiled from her children's birth dates. But these days she would have settled for a paid-off VISA card and a car that wasn't about to go its last mile.

Now, suddenly, she couldn't even escape into silly daydreams. Her life had been reduced to its most elemental components. Her children were all that really mattered. And one of them was gone.

thing. Like talking. Confessing. Saying how sorry he was. That he'd never cheat on Brenda again.

Except she could be jumping to conclusions. Maybe Chad was bothered about something else altogether.

She wandered down the hall into the number-two guest room, which was next on her list of projects. She had redone it in those months after her mother died when she was searching for something to distract her from grief. But she'd never liked the results. It looked like a hotel room. Sterile. Not inviting.

She seated herself on the love seat, rearranging the room in her mind, trying to visualize a different wallpaper, different pictures on the wall, perhaps a small tray table in front of the love seat with magazines and a decanter of brandy.

After that she toured the yard but could find nothing to discuss with Mr. Song on Monday. Not that he followed her suggestions. He would nod agreeably, saying "Missus have bery good idea," then he would do exactly as he wanted.

The kidney-shaped pool glistened pristinely in the sunlight. The decking was hosed clean. The gazebo had had its annual coat of white paint. In the front yard, the five hundred yellow chrysanthemum plants Mr. Song had planted around the circle drive were gorgeous. In the spring, there had been the blooms from more than a thousand tulips bulbs—all red. In the summer, the bed had featured petunias in brilliant shades of pink and purple. Sunday drivers stopped to take pictures.

Karen decided that she'd get something ready to put in the oven. Paella maybe. Or lasagna.

Then she'd read. Maybe float around the pool for a while. Take advantage of the warm weather.

Only she knew she wouldn't. She was always telling herself she was going to do that—read and float in the pool. But she seldom did so more than one or two times a summer. Reading to her was something done curled up in bed or on an airplane. The glare from the water hurt her eyes. The pool was an ornament only. Roger went in the pool about as often as she did. The kids had always preferred the larger, more social pool at the country club just down the street.

Karen had taught first grade in Norman the three years that Roger was in law school. She didn't have to. Both her and Roger's parents were more than willing to support them, to have them immediately produce grandchildren. But the newlyweds needed to be off the dole and on their own. And Karen was determined to use her degree in elementary education. She knew from her student-teaching experience that she had the makings of a good teacher. And indeed, by the time the third and last year of her teaching career rolled around, she was on her way to being masterful. Her third-grade class that year had been invited to appear on local television to perform the international dances she had taught them. Every one of her students had an entry for the local science fair. She had been named Teacher of the Year by the Monroe Elementary School PTA.

But to continue teaching school was out of the question. Roger was ready to launch his law career. Life at that point in time for a young woman like Karen meant selecting and decorating a darling starter house in northwest Oklahoma City and getting herself pregnant.

From the starter house, they moved to an expensive new house in fashionable Quail Creek, and from there to a half-million-dollar dwelling in Nichols Hills, from which there was noplace left to move up to—except to a million- or multimillion-dollar house in Nichols Hills, which Karen would never hear of no matter how rich they became. She loved this house. She wanted her children always to be able to come home to this house, where they had spent most of their growing-up years.

Even though her husband with his analytical lawyer's mind insisted that every time a coin was tossed the odds were fifty-fifty that it would come up heads, and even though Karen understood that mathematically Roger was absolutely correct, she still felt in her gut that if a tossed coin came up heads three times in a row, the fourth toss had a greater chance of being tails. And if it wasn't, the probability of the fifth toss coming up tails was even higher.

When the spaceship *Challenger* blew up, she was somehow not surprised. It was bound to happen eventually.

She grieved for the young astronauts and their families, for schoolteacher Christa McAuliffe and the motherless children she left behind. But that long string of successful space flights preceding the *Challenger* had lowered the odds. All of Roger's logic couldn't change her mind on that count. Odds and other things had a way of getting evened out.

She worried sometimes that her own life had been a series of lucky tosses. She had been born to money. Her parents were loving and conscientious. She was reasonably pretty. Reasonably intelligent. The man she married because they happened to be attracted to one another at a time in their lives when marriage was the likely next step turned out to be a good choice. Roger was a successful attorney and a devoted family man. She was fortunate to have borne two beautiful, healthy children. Her life was full of family, friends, clubs, causes. And her home.

If a fairy godmother came along giving away wishes, all Karen could possibly ask for was continued good health for her family, continued good fortune in life. She wanted for nothing. Except for Trevor Washburn to go away, which, in the normal course of events, he probably would anyway. And maybe she'd ask for a potion to rejuvenate her sex life, which had become routine. Then again, maybe not. After all, there was a certain comfort in routine. Nonroutine sex could be saved for vacations and hotel rooms, sparing the marital bed from the stress of great expectations.

Or maybe she'd just ask to be better friends with her husband. She and Roger didn't touch souls anymore.

Perhaps that, too, was safer.

But there were no fairy godmothers to hand out good fortune, and tails was bound to come up one of these days. Karen just hoped the reckoning would be something she could bear.

To date, the death of her mother was the worst thing she had ever endured. After five years, Karen still felt the void in her life. No one but a mother really wanted to hear about headaches or cramps. No one else noticed that she'd lost five pounds or was wearing a new shade of lipstick. Her mother had known she was pregnant with Melissa before Karen even knew it herself.

But facing the death of parents was inevitable for most people. Karen resented her mother's death at sixty-two when other mothers lived to a ripe old age. But those other mothers in their ripe old age were sometimes a burden, like Roger's father was starting to be. So Karen understood that life had not cruelly singled her out by killing off her mother.

She had lost a baby two years ago, a tiny baby boy born three months prematurely. He'd lived only seventeen hours. But even that may have been for the best. Another pregnancy had been Roger's idea. After his affair. One last child to heal his guilty soul. A baby would be good for them, Roger insisted. It would keep them young. The house would seem lonely without young children. Karen wondered if getting his first wife pregnant with one last baby would keep him from finding a younger second wife and having a baby with her. And sometimes, she could almost feel a sweet baby in her arms.

But she had had misgivings. Another baby would have been a cop-out of sorts. While it might be a reprieve from middle age, it would also eliminate other possibilities from her life. With her children all but grown, she could go back to school. Get a job. Start a business. Concentrate on tennis and achieve state ranking in her age category. Entertain more. Try for a national office in one of her organizations. Develop new goals. Do things to make each day and week different from the one before.

But mostly she had been afraid. A baby was an unknown. It might be deformed. Retarded. A psychopath. Upset the balance of her marriage.

When she was young, she hadn't worried deeply about such things. When she was young, she hadn't known that children brought as much worry as joy, as much pain as love.

After the baby's premature birth and death, she grieved sincerely for the child she would never know and occasionally put flowers on his grave, but she was also relieved. The decision had been taken out of her hands.

Sometimes there were other flowers on the baby's grave. Yellow roses. Roger's favorite.

They wanted a name for the tombstone and decided on Gabriel. If he had lived, he would have been named something else. Bryan or Michael or Zachery. She thought of him only as the baby who died.

Things she could bear: The house burning down. Roger losing all their money and moving them to a track house in south Oklahoma City. Losing a breast. Getting fat. Roger's father dying. Her father dying.

Roger dying. Roger becoming impotent or senile or helpless. Facing the end of her life.

What Karen could not bear was something bad happening to her children. Or even thinking about something bad happening to her children. To Melissa or Chad.

Sometimes she wanted to wring their necks. At times they were selfish and spoiled. But then Karen herself was spoiled. Roger, too. They were a family of spoiled people who could indulge themselves in most of their whims.

But although they sometimes infuriated her, her children had been her life. They were an extension of her soul, of her very being.

While Roger professed that odds on each toss were even, Karen knew that, in his gut, he believed coins could be made to come up heads most of the time. He believed that people who were smart and worked hard and played by the rules had control over their lives, that they made their own luck. They stayed out of spaceships. They drove carefully and watched out for the other guy. They knew where the fire escapes were. They worked out at a gym three times a week and drank and ate in moderation. They never made hasty decisions about investments or anything else. And they lived happily to a ripe old age and died in their sleep.

The dead baby had been harder for Roger to accept than Karen. He'd so seldom had a coin come up tails.

Roger refused to be afraid. He didn't marvel at good fortune. He took it as his due. Karen marveled at the husband she had ended up with. Why her and not the women she saw at the women's shelter where she volunteered—women who had been lustfully in love with the man they had married only to discover he was an abusive monster.

Even though Karen had grown up in a wonderful old mansion in Tulsa's Southern Hills, she still marveled at her present-day home. Such good fortune to live in such a wonderful house. It made happiness a responsibility. How could anyone be unhappy living in such a house when half the world lived in shacks?

Karen worried, however, that her house looked too much like a magazine spread and not a place where people actually lived. If her house's interior were photographed, the captions would describe a spectacular entry hall that soared upward to a stained-glass skylight, an elegant living room, its two seating areas featuring a savvy mixture of museum-quality French and English antiques. The huge formal dining room, a study in brocade and crystal. A cozy family room and country kitchen for togetherness and a showcase for American country antiques. A handsome book-lined retreat for the man of the house. A charming pink room for the resident princess. A rough-and-tumble room for the family boy. An upstairs sitting and television area. A regal suite for the master and his lady. And there were two carefully appointed guest rooms, a spacious poolside deck and charming gazebo for outdoor gatherings, lavishly landscaped grounds.

Other than Melissa's room with its clutter of mementos and posters, the house was too perfect. Karen kept repapering, recovering, and rearranging, trying to create a more inviting feel to her rooms. She piled throw pillows on sofas and beds and filled baskets with dried flowers. She had a plant service provide a continual stream of handsome, well-tended plants. She added afghans and carefully chosen eclectic clutter. Roger liked to make jokes at parties about her redecorating and rearranging. He never walked through a room in the dark. Sometimes he opened the front door and wondered if he was in the right house. Karen had made the paperhanger a rich man.

She'd hung her own wallpaper in that first apartment south of the university campus in Norman. In
many ways, those first three years of marriage had
been the best. A time of looking ahead. Anticipation.
Excitement for the future. And loving as well as love.
God, such loving.

When they had been apart, even for one night, they
came together with such intense raw hunger, a part of
her would feel shocked that two intelligent college
graduates could be so wanton, savage even, ruthlessly
going at each other. All that sweat and heavy breathing. So exciting. Thrilling. Scary. Like a mile-high
roller coaster.

She was too old for roller coasters now, and apparently too old for wantonness. But she didn't want to
be. She wanted to think that someplace, sometime,
she could could get back to it.

Melissa came home about three. She hadn't gone to
the game after all. Trevor's aunt and uncle had used
the tickets.

"I'm sorry," Karen said. "Why don't you go next
week with your dad and me?"

Melissa mumbled a maybe.

"I'm expecting you to have dinner with Chad and
me," Karen said as she took a fresh peach pie from
the oven. "At seven," she called after her daughter.

Chad emerged from his room at four. Karen was
making sauce for lasagna. He didn't ask what she was
cooking or comment on the pie cooling on the
counter. He didn't ask if his sister was around or if
Karen had heard the score of the football game. He
asked only if she'd heard from his dad, then opened a
can of beer, fixed himself a sandwich, and carried
them back upstairs.

Why in the hell was he so hot to talk to his father?

Only to his father? Was he protecting her from something?

Her mind ticked off all the things that could be wrong.

Another DUI.

He'd gotten Brenda pregnant. Or some other girl.

He was flunking out of school.

Been caught cheating.

Been kicked off the golf team.

Owed a gambling debt he couldn't pay.

Those things they could deal with. But what if he'd been involved in a hit-and-run accident? Or worse?

Karen closed her eyes and leaned against the kitchen counter. *Don't let it be too bad. Please.*

6

"*Y*our father called," Karen told Chad when he came down for breakfast Sunday morning. "He didn't beat the hurricane out of Harlingen."

Chad paused behind his customary chair at the kitchen table, his hand resting on the back. "You mean he's not coming home today?"

"I don't see how."

Chad was grubby in old sweats and even older athletic shoes dug from the back of his closet. He hadn't combed his hair. His chin was sprouting whiskers.

And he was beautiful.

Karen never failed to be affected by her son's beauty. His blond hair was thick and wavy. His skin tan and smooth. His teeth straight and white. His mouth full and sensual. His eyes dark brown. A heavy brow line and strong chin balanced out the fineness of his other features. Melissa's friends called him a hunk. In college, Karen would have called a boy like Chad "dreamy."

Melissa did not have the stunning good looks of her brother, but even during her insecure, pudgy days, she'd been a pretty child with dark shining hair, huge brown eyes rimmed with thick, dark lashes, and a generous smile that lit up her face. But of late, Karen's reaction to her daughter's appearance was more critical as she worried that Melissa's makeup was overdone, her eyebrows overplucked, her skirt too short,

50

her perfume too heavy. And now, since Trevor, she worried that her daughter looked anorexic.

But they were two very attractive children, who had been given every opportunity, blessed with parents who would do anything for them. Through drugs, sex, and DUIs, Karen kept believing that her and Roger's emotional investment in their children would pay off. Chad and Melissa would make the most of their blessings as their parents had done before them.

"So, when's Dad coming home?" Chad asked, seated now, making a show of looking at the sports page.

"He's not sure. No planes are flying, but he's trying to rent a car. It's a long day's drive, though, even when the weather is good. So, what do you want for breakfast? How about ham and eggs?" Karen asked, her voice cheery.

"No. Just toast. Then I guess I'll head on back to Norman. Is Melissa still in bed?"

"Yes, but not for long. She needs to get ready for church. Sure you can't stick around a while longer and go with us?"

"No. Not this time," he said.

Chad ate his toast and went upstairs to gather his things. "You guys coming down for the Colorado game?" he asked as he gave his mother a good-bye hug at the back door and accepted the shoe box of cookies.

"Yes, and both grandfathers. I'll do one of my famous tailgate buffets if the weather's nice. Tell Brenda to invite her folks—and her sorority little sis. Deeann, isn't it? And have Johnny bring his parents. He seems like a nice boy. But so quiet. Didn't you say his folks always come to Norman for the games?"

"Yeah. They fly into the university airpark in their private jet. His dad owns Arizona. Be sure and have Dad call when he gets in," Chad said.

* * *

Driving the Turner Turnpike from Tulsa in her snappy red Firebird, Brenda passed the time anticipating her Sunday-evening date with Chad. They had nothing planned—probably they'd go to a movie, share a pizza. But she hadn't seen him for three days, and that made tonight special.

She'd wear her new black velvet jeans with her red scoop-neck sweater. She wondered if it was too early for boots. The weather was still like summer even though the calendar said late October.

Brenda loved getting ready for dates. She allowed herself an hour or more to shower, fix her hair, apply her makeup, and dress. Even if they were just going to work out at the campus fitness center, she took care with her appearance. She liked to make Chad's eyes light up when she came down the steps of the sorority house.

Her family tended toward plumpness, so Brenda was terribly conscious of her weight. She would like to be thinner, and taller, but when she dieted too much her breasts began to shrink.

To be beautiful for Chad, Brenda spent countless hours tanning her body and suffering through aerobics. She permed, lightened, and curled her hair to fluffy blond perfection. She even managed to overcome a lifelong habit of nail biting. First she'd applied the same stuff that her mother had made her use when she was little. And as before, it burned like hell, but she still chewed away. Then she'd tried a hypnotist. But the only thing that kept her from biting her nails to the quick was to close her eyes and imagine that someday set of wedding rings on a hand with beautifully manicured nails. The wife of Chad Billingsly wasn't going to be a nail biter.

It had worked. *Visualization,* it was called. She'd

read an article about it in a magazine. *Think, therefore you are.*

She held up a hand up to admire its manicured perfection, something she did dozens of times throughout the day. Amazing how much satisfaction she got from looking at her own fingernails.

As much as she liked pleasing Chad, however, their relationship was not one-sided. He had kept his promise to go easy on the booze, which made him drive crazy and pick fights. He had also honored her request to stop doing drugs, even if it was mostly pot, which she worried would become more than just a Saturday-night thing. Chad seldom got drunk anymore, at least not when he was with her. She wouldn't let him take her home if he did. Then he couldn't have sex. And Chad loved sex with her more than he loved drugs and booze.

Brenda loved sex, too. It bound Chad to her like nothing else. But she didn't like sex when Chad wasn't himself. She didn't like it when he got rough and talked filthy. With alcohol, he came too fast. With pot, he went on and on past enjoyment. Sex was supposed to be beautiful and natural. She would have it no other way.

As a result, Chad respected her. Loved her. Wanted to marry her and have babies with her. She was playing their relationship just right. Which made her feel smug and happy.

She'd worn his fraternity drop at her throat for a year. They planned to get pinned over Christmas vacation and have their pinning serenade right before spring break. Next year, at Christmastime, they'd get engaged.

Every time a candlelight ceremony was held in the living room of the Chi Omega house, tears came to Brenda's eyes as she passed the lighted candle to the next girl in the circle. Someday the candle would stop with her. She would be the one to blow it out, signifying that she was the one with a new engagement ring. And all the squealing and tears and hugs would be in her honor.

She and Chad would get married right after graduation. June 2, on her birthday. She was already collecting pictures of wedding dresses. Her sister wanted to pass her wedding dress on to Brenda, but Brenda wanted one of her own. With a cathedral train.

The only things left to decide about her future were if she'd work and for how long. By the end of the semester, she would have completed her general education requirements. The time had come for her to declare a major. Did she want to major in something fashionable—like art history, English, or letters—or something that would get her a job?

None of her mother's friends worked. Chad's mother didn't work. But Brenda's mom claimed that women like herself and Karen Billingsly were all but dinosaurs. Extinct. Volunteerism was dying. Women nowadays had careers.

It amazed Brenda that her mother had become somewhat of a feminist in her middle years. She still went to meetings, but the clubs she belonged to now were political. She subscribed to *Ms.* magazine and wrote letters to legislators. It amazed Brenda even more that her father didn't mind his wife's new thinking. He didn't interrupt her or even look pissed when she spouted her rhetoric at dinner parties. And he didn't interfere when she told her daughters that they must major in something "real." Not art history, English, or letters. And she wanted them to go to graduate school, have careers, put off marriage until they were thirty. Susan already had disappointed her, but she had been a good sport about it and really gotten into the mother-of-the-bride role.

Brenda had always been good at math and toyed

with the idea of majoring in math education. Deeann, her sorority little sis, would be failing algebra if it weren't for Brenda's tutoring. But she really couldn't imagine Chad Billingsly married to a high-school math teacher.

Chad was noncommittal when she asked him about it. He wasn't sure he wanted his wife to work, but then he thought women like his mother were a bit boring. Dear, but boring.

"But hasn't it been nice always having her around?" Brenda had asked.

Chad had admitted that it was. "I always hated it on the days she wasn't there when I got home from school. I wanted her there to sit at the kitchen table with Missy and me and look at our school papers while we had our snack. And it was almost worth getting sick so I could stay home and have her fuss over me."

Brenda looked at the clock on the dash. Only three more hours till Chad. She already felt open and ready for him. She moved the cruise-control setting from seventy to seventy-five.

Sex was more of a problem this year. They'd both spent last year in the more impersonal freshman dorms, since freshmen weren't allowed to live in the Greek houses. Chad had a single room, and no one paid much attention to her comings and goings. But boys were not allowed upstairs at the sorority house. And Karen didn't like sneaking upstairs at the Iota Beta house. They had to ask his roommate to stay away. And sometimes guys knew that she was in there and would make lewd remarks as they went by the closed door, which spoiled her concentration. Sometimes, she and Chad went to a motel, which seemed sordid. And sometimes, they resorted to sex in the car like high-school kids.

Next year one of them would have to move into an apartment. Brenda hoped it would be Chad. She loved living in the sorority house. Loved being a sorority girl. She didn't want to give it up.

But she would if she had to. Chad was everything to her. She wanted to be his wife, have his babies, be with him every night of her life.

Brenda had asked her mother if she had ever felt that way about her father.

"I suppose. But I think I love him better now that he's not my whole life."

"How can that be?" Brenda asked.

"Love must be generous. If you suck up all a person's air, he can't breathe."

More rhetoric. Brenda would take passion any day of the week.

Throughout the day on Monday, Roger called Karen several times to report his progress. Still no flights. Other fleeing tourists had beat him to the rental cars. He'd get home when he could.

Chad called twice to find out if she'd heard anything.

The second time she was able to tell him his father would be home sometime tomorrow evening. He had a flight out early tomorrow afternoon. Routed through Phoenix. It's all he could find. Yes, she'd have him call no matter how late he got in.

7

*K*aren made a pan of brownies before changing into a gauzy caftan, freshening her makeup and retiring to the family room, where she thumbed through magazines and half watched CNN while she waited for her husband. During his last call he'd said he'd be in about ten.

It had been a good day, she decided. Busy. The busyness helped keep worries about Chad at bay.

She'd played tennis this morning with her regular Tuesday foursome then attended a luncheon meeting of the Haven House board of directors and an afternoon planning session for the annual Tri Delta Alumnae Christmas bazaar. She and Melissa had dinner in the dining room—by candlelight. Baked chicken and wild rice. Fresh green beans. Fruit salad. Melissa almost ate enough to be considered a meal before she rushed off to rehearsal. The play was the junior class's rendition of *Our Town*. At dinner Melissa had seemed surprised that her mother had heard of it and even knew the plot and that Thornton Wilder had won a Pulitzer Prize for it. She and Melissa hadn't done that well together in months.

On the ten o'clock news, a pert anchorwoman put on her serious face and announced that the Norman Police Department was asking for help in locating a missing high-school girl.

Karen studied the photograph on the television

screen. A yearbook picture of a sweet-looking girl with dark hair and eyes and a dimpled smile.

What agony for her parents, Karen thought, wondering if Melissa still carried a Mace canister on her key chain. If she always locked her car. If she avoided dark parking lots. If she never let her gas get below a quarter of a tank.

She'd ask Roger to talk to her. Warnings had more impact coming from him.

The anchorwoman was speaking via remote hookup to Norman with a female reporter standing in the front yard of a modest house—a duplex, actually —with a dark-haired woman of about forty. The missing girl's mother. A dignified woman. Not the type who would display emotion in public. But Karen could hear it in her voice. Her daughter had last been seen Friday night at a fraternity party on the OU campus, she told the reporter.

The skin on Karen's forehead tightened. *Which fraternity?*

But the camera had shifted to a jovial weatherman pacing in front of his maps and satellite images.

There were a dozen or more fraternities at OU. Most of them probably have parties the night before a home game. The girl could have gone to any of them.

Yes. Any of them. Not the Iota Beta house.

And even if she had been at the IB house, that didn't necessarily mean anything.

She considered calling Chad to ask if he'd heard about the girl. If there had been any high-school girls at the IB party.

But she was jumping to conclusions. If Chad was in some sort of trouble, it had nothing to do with a missing girl. He might, on occasion, drive too fast and drink too much, but her son would never intentionally hurt anyone. Especially a girl. Karen was sure of that.

But no one said the girl was hurt. Just missing. And

there were any number of possible reasons why a girl could be missing. She could have gotten drunk and run her car off the road. Or into a lake, like those two Oklahoma City women found in Lake Overholser twenty-five years later, still in their car. Maybe the girl had run off with a boy, or one of those religious cults had spirited her away. Maybe she was angry at her parents and was trying to pay them back by hitchhiking to California.

Karen tensed as she heard the garage door opening. *Roger*. Melissa wasn't due until eleven.

Karen hurried to the kitchen, smoothing her hair, composing her face for her husband's homecoming.

"Jesus, didn't you shave all week?" she protested as Roger swept her into his arms. "And you smell like dead fish and unwashed man. I'm sure the other passengers on the airplane were thrilled with you guys."

"Show a little respect, woman. Your man has been at sea braving wind and wave to bring his family sustenance."

"You mean you actually caught something? We'll have food this winter?"

He followed her around the kitchen while she fixed him a late-night supper, nuzzling her neck with his whiskered chin, fondling her breasts and fanny. Karen made a game of it, slapping at his hand, pushing him away, telling him he was going to give her whisker burn.

"What do you guys talk about on these fishing trips?" she asked as she cracked eggs into a bowl for an omelette. "You always come home randier than an old billy goat."

Karen sent him off to put his iced-down fish in the freezer and to take a shower. "And don't forget to shave," she called after him.

With her husband gone from the kitchen, Karen allowed her face to relax out of its homecoming smile.

She rubbed at her forehead, at the worry lines, at the headache forming behind her temples. And sighed. Roger would want to make a production out of lovemaking. Ordinarily, she would, too. Homecomings called for wine and quality foreplay. Something to look forward to. But tonight she wasn't in the right mood.

Karen poured herself a glass of her favorite merlot, downed it, and poured a second. If only she hadn't watched the news.

How ridiculous to be concerned about something that had nothing to do with her or her family, something she'd only seen on television.

If she could find out which fraternity house the girl had gone to, she could put the story out of her mind. She considered calling the television station. Or the Norman police. But that would imply more than a casual interest. Which was all it was.

Except that her son lived in a fraternity house and had been behaving strangely.

She poured a third glass of wine and took a sip. The wine helped. She was starting to feel pleasantly light-headed.

Wearing his terry-cloth robe, Roger returned damp and scrubbed. "How do I smell now?" he asked, attacking her neck.

"Delicious," she said, and allowed herself to really kiss him. She felt herself warming. Roger loved to kiss. A little more wine, and she'd be fine.

"You need to call Chad," she said, turning her attention to the fresh asparagus she was steaming. "He actually came home this weekend. Said he couldn't study at the IB house. In fact, he sounded disillusioned about fraternity life in general. Said some of the IBs are jerks. I wouldn't be surprised if he's had a run-in with one of them. He waited around to talk to you."

Hearing her own words, Karen felt better. Why, of course. Chad wasn't upset about a girl. He was upset about his fraternity brothers. Just as he had told her.

Karen thought through her new logic and could find no fault with it. She had been concerned over nothing. With an inward sigh of relief, she relaxed. She and Roger would have a lovely time.

"I want to hear all about your adventures," Karen went on. "But if you caught one of those big blue things and left it to be stuffed, we'll have to turn the basement into a club room just to have a place to hang it, and that will make it a very expensive fish."

"I was thinking more of over the mantel in the living room," he said, with a lingering caress to her fanny.

Karen poured the omelette mixture into the hot skillet as Roger dialed Chad's number at the fraternity house. "He's probably out with Brenda," he said, glancing at the wall clock.

But almost immediately he was greeting his son. And the smile on his face turned to a frown. He listened very briefly, then held up his hand. "Save it. I'm on my way."

Karen sank into a chair. "That girl . . . ?" she questioned as Roger hung up. "I saw it on the news. A high-school girl is missing. She was last seen at a fraternity house."

"No girl," Roger snapped. "They've got a legal problem with one of the boys."

"And it can't wait until morning?"

"I can't deal with it in the morning. I've got a hearing tomorrow afternoon that I should have been preparing for while I was sitting in airports," he said, hurrying away from her, untying his bathrobe as he headed for the stairs.

"Aren't you going to eat your omelette?"

"I'll warm it up later," he called over his shoulder.

"You don't warm up omelettes," she said to no
one.

Karen had been right. *A problem at the house involving a
girl*—that's what Chad had actually said. Roger wondered what Karen heard on television. But whatever it
was, he didn't want her jumping to any conclusions
until he knew what was going on.

    . . . *involving a girl.*

It wasn't so much the words themselves as the apprehension in Chad's voice that made the skin prickle
on the back of Roger's neck. Just don't let it be too
bad, he thought prayerfully as he raced south on I–35
toward Norman.

How many times over the years of his legal practice
had he worked to salvage young lives after screwups?
And kids did screw up more frequently than adults.
With adults, there was usually some sense to it—some,
if not logical, at least understandable reason. Often
with kids, however, it was just a stupid case of acting
out that cost parents sleepless nights and small for-
tunes extracting their children from the consequences
of folly.

Roger's own kids were no exceptions. Melissa had
stopped eating and was driving her mother crazy.
Chad had experimented with drugs and continued to
risk life and limb every time he got behind the wheel
of a car. The best any parent could hope for was that
the screwups would be minor. That no one's life
would be permanently altered. Roger hoped that was
what he would find in Norman. A minor, non-life-al-
tering screwup.

The meeting was to be secret. Chad had asked him
to come a Norman motel near the Lindsey Street exit
—a motel Roger always associated with a woman he
had taken there during his one and only affair—

Rhonda Parker, the wife of one of his law partners. He'd gotten away with that screwup. Karen never knew. And Roger was reasonably sure that he'd never have another affair. He had loved the excitement, but the thought of life without Karen and an intact family was too frightening. The risk wasn't worth it. Rhonda agreed. She'd been having nightmares. But he still fantasized about her. Still got a thrill when he saw her at parties. So cool and sleek. But in bed, she had been wild.

It was strange to drive into this particular parking lot and not allow himself a few erotic thoughts about Rhonda.

In Room 241, Chad and four of his fraternity brothers were waiting. Carter Fugate, wearing an OU Sooners baseball cap, acted as spokesman and presented the problem to Roger. Carter's father sat on the criminal court of appeals. A paragon of the legal profession. Why hadn't they called him, Roger wondered.

Carter had gone to Casady with Chad. A big cocky kid. Some of the parents had wanted him kicked out of school after he'd beat up an assistant football coach —actually broken the man's jaw. But the coach spoke up in Carter's behalf, or more accurately, he wrote a letter. With his jaw wired shut, he wasn't doing any talking. Just a misunderstanding, the letter had claimed. He should have handled it better. Roger always wondered if the Carter's father hadn't paid him off.

Had Roger heard about the missing girl, Carter asked, not at all cocky, his voice crackling with nervousness. The story had been on the evening news, he explained. All the local channels.

The girl had been at the Iota Beta house Friday night, Carter explained. The last place she'd been seen. They were concerned. The police had already been around asking questions. And the girl's mother. Reporters, too. They weren't sure how to handle it.

"Tell me about the girl," Roger said.

The boys exchanged glances. Except for Chad. He was looking at the floor.

"Kind of pretty. Black hair. Drank a lot," Carter said.

"How much? Was she drunk?"

"She came looking for sex," piped in Todd French, from Ardmore. A handsome redheaded kid—on the university golf team with Chad.

"And you had sex with her?" Roger asked Todd.

His question was greeted by silence. Again the exchanged glances. It was Chad who answered. "We all did."

"All of you?" Roger asked incredulously. "All of you? *Jesus!*"

"And Johnny Fontaine, too," Carter said. "His maiden voyage. But the little fag packed up and went home afterward."

"Six of you?" Roger said, trying to comprehend. "Are you telling me this girl willingly had sex with six boys?"

Carter nodded and looked to the others for confirmation. They nodded their assent—including Chad. She had been willing.

"What happened afterward?" Roger asked.

"Nothing," Carter explained. "She was passed out drunk when we left her."

"Now wait a minute," Roger said, holding up both hands in protest. "Passed out drunk is *not* consenting."

Everyone looked at the floor.

"Talk to me, damn it," Roger demanded. "Unless that girl passed out after she served as receptacle for your combined lust, we are talking about rape. *Gang* rape."

Again Roger was greeted by silence, which he interpreted as meaning the girl had *not* waited to pass out until it was over.

"So, all of you had *non*consenting sex with a probably underage high-school girl who is now missing," Roger said.

"Something like that," a big fleshy kid named Benton said. The son of a Tulsa banker. "She was dancing real hot. Asking for it in no uncertain terms. But she had been drinking straight gin and snorting some coke. She kind of came in and out of consciousness while it was going on."

"And when she was conscious, what did she do?" Roger asked.

"She protested," Chad said.

The others shot Chad angry looks. Apparently he was deviating from the agreed-on story. "Christ, Chad," Carter protested. "The little bitch got herself in that position. Don't go trying to make it sound like we were the only ones at fault."

"And what happened to her afterward?" Roger asked with a sinking heart. "Why is she now missing?"

"We don't know," Carter said with shrug. "We left her there—while we got together some money. I was going to take her to a motel to sleep it off. And put the money in her purse—over a hundred dollars. For restitution. But when I went upstairs, she'd already left."

"Upstairs where?"

"On the fourth floor, in the room where we keep the test files," Benton said.

"On the floor?"

"No, on an old sofa," Chad offered.

"Did anyone see her leave?"

They shook their heads no.

"A house full of people, and no one saw her leave? She must have been in pretty bad shape by then. Staggering. Her clothes a mess. Her hair. Surely someone would have noticed her.''

''The party had pretty much broken up by then, and most of the guys were in bed,'' offered the fifth boy, a premed major named Jackson Holmes. His dad was a neurosurgeon in Oklahoma City, his mother from an old oil family.

''So, she just got up and walked out?'' Roger injected. ''Where do you suppose she went?''

''We don't know,'' Carter insisted. ''We heard that her car was still parked over on the Campus Corner—behind the restaurant where she worked. She'd come with another girl who told the police that she couldn't find her friend and left the party by herself. But honest to God, Mr. Billingsly, we don't know where the girl went after she left the house. Maybe she really did leave with her girlfriend, and the girlfriend is lying.''

Roger ran his hand through his hair. And wished for a drink. Did they have any idea how much trouble they could be in? God, he'd never heard of such a fuckup—not from boys who had so much to lose. It wasn't like they were street scum who were going to spend most of their life incarcerated anyway. These boys had a life in front of them. *His* son had a life in front on him. And a whole family could be taken down by shit like this.

Roger wanted to scream at them. Pound them with his fists. Jesus, hadn't they learned anything from that incident at the OU football dorm? Gang rape was not a very defensible crime under any circumstances.

''Who else knows?'' he asked, forcing his voice to sound calm.

''Everyone at the party saw her,'' Carter said.

''No, not who saw her. Who else *knows* you guys had sex with her?''

''No one,'' Carter said.

''You sure?''

They nodded.

"What about Johnny? Maybe he told his parents."

"He won't say anything," Chad said. "He's scared to death of his old man and thinks his mother is a saint."

Roger stared across the room at his reflection in the dresser mirror. And was surprised at how old he looked. A man considerably older than the boys around him. They were looking at him, waiting for him to say magical words that would take the threat away.

"What do you guys think you should do?" he asked.

"I don't think that we should do anything but keep our mouths shut," Carter said, "and hope the girl is too embarrassed to say anything. Or better yet, that she doesn't remember anything. Or who knows, maybe she ran off and will never be seen again? Holmes here has been insisting that we go to the police. But Chad said we should talk to you instead. He said that you'd be on our side. And know if we should be doing anything—like establishing alibis."

Benton nodded. He was sitting on the edge of the bed, his belly hanging over the top of his jeans. "We do need alibis, don't we? We should be able to prove we were someplace else—just in case."

"Lying could open up a worse can of worms if you're caught at it. In which case, it would have been better if you turned yourselves in," Roger admitted, rubbing his temples. He needed to think. To dredge up all he knew about rape investigation. Any semen would have long since left the girl's vagina, but there would be dried semen on her clothing. Unless she'd washed everything. He supposed that if a pathologist had a good specimen, he would be able to tell that six different males were involved and could DNA-match them—pinpoint which of the sixty or seventy boys at the party had been involved. But the girl probably could point out the actual six. Or could she? How aware had she been? Maybe, like Carter had suggested, she couldn't remember a thing. And would be too embarrassed to find out why she was oozing copious amounts of cum.

If she did remember, maybe she could be bought off. Not with a hundred dollars. With a lot of money for her trouble and suffering. The families of all six boys had resources.

Then Roger realized what he was doing. He was trying to figure the odds. Could they get away with it? He had already ruled out their turning themselves in —at least at this point. They should wait and see if it would be necessary.

"What about the place where this happened? Did you clean it up?"

Benton and Carter nodded.

"The sofa?"

"The next day I left a couple of cigarettes burning on it," Carter said. "When it set off the smoke alarm, Benton and I raced upstairs, put out the fire, and hauled it off."

"Do the five of you swear to God, by everything you hold sacred, that you don't know where this girl is?" Roger demanded, "and that you had no further dealings with her after the incident you described?"

They swore. He made each of them say it, one by one. Roger believed them. They weren't bad kids. They were just young and forgot to think sometimes.

Roger agreed to play along with their waiting game. If the girl came forward, they would have to turn themselves in and let the court decide if the girl had been consenting or not.

But if she never came forward, they were to take a lifelong vow of silence.

The boys filed out of the room, leaving Roger with his son.

Chad had removed a pillow from one of the beds and was clutching it against his middle.

"Christ, Chad. Why? You're a better person than that. Help me understand?"

"I guess you have too high an opinion of me. There was a girl, free for the taking, or so I thought. And Johnny had never had sex before. We did it for him. A rite of passage, I guess. I didn't really want to when it came right down to it, but everyone was watching. I felt like I had to. We were all drunk. Carter and Benton were high. It was a shitty idea. I know that now."

"And the girl. What do you think happened to her?"

"I don't know, Dad."

"Swear to me again. You don't know what happened to that girl. Swear on your mother's life."

"God, Dad, that's creepy," Chad said, looking away.

"Swear, damn it! Look at me and swear."

Chad looked at his father, his chin trembling. "I swear."

"On your mother's life."

"On my mother's life."

The words hung in the air. Chad jumped when the air conditioner checked on. Roger put a comforting hand on his son's thigh and left it there for a time, feeling the warmth, the taunt firmness. So young. So fit and bright. Everything to live for.

"What's going to happen, Dad?"

"I don't know, son. It all depends on that girl."

"You won't tell Mom?"

"Hell, no. Imagine how upset she'd be. She's had a hard enough time with the other stunts you've pulled. This is the end of it, Chad. You hear me. No more drugs. No more driving like a bat out of hell. No gambling. No pregnant girls. You are going to slow down and fly right if you want my continued support—monetary and otherwise.''

Chad was crying now, burying his face in the pillow. Gently Roger pulled the pillow away and reached for his son, tears welling in his own eyes.

"I'm so sorry, Dad,'' Chad sobbed into his father's shoulder. "So sorry.''

Roger put his cheek against his son's head. In spite of his tough words, he would stand by this boy no matter what. It was hard to imagine loving another human being more intensely than he loved this boy.

And given similar circumstances, Roger wasn't sure if he himself would have acted differently at the same point in his life. He'd had the fantasy. Having sex while other guys watched. Proving his manhood. With a whore. With a virgin. With anything female.

8

*M*elissa came in as Karen was cleaning up after Roger's uneaten meal. She pinched off a single crumb of brownie and popped it in her mouth. "Where's Dad?" she asked, leaning against the counter. "I thought he was supposed to be home by now."

Karen explained. He'd come and gone. A client in need.

Normally, Melissa raced on by, not wanting her mother to scrutinize her rumpled clothing, her face burnished and red from lovemaking. But tonight, it would seem, there had been no tryst with Trevor after rehearsal. She was actually home on time—almost. Only twenty minutes late.

Melissa allowed her mother to pour her half a glass of milk, of which she took a couple of sips.

She actually hung around and chatted a bit. The play was coming together. She liked the whole theatrical scene, working closely with people to make something happen. So different from tennis.

"Maybe you'll be an actress," Karen said, feeling a light-headed rush of sheer pleasure from this unexpected bit of camaraderie with her daughter. Twice in one day. Enough to make her wonder if the worst was over.

Melissa shrugged. "Who knows? I just want to be *something*. Have a profession. A place other than a kitchen." The look that she gave her mother was part apology, part challenge.

"What about having a profession *and* a kitchen?" Karen said, managing the briefest of hugs before her daughter slipped away from her.

And found herself shuddering in horror at the bony feel of her daughter's body under the oversized Casady sweatshirt. Karen could have picked Melissa up and carried her, this all-but-grown daughter who was inches taller than her mother.

Karen followed Melissa into the entry hall and watched as Melissa climbed the stairs. A long-legged teenager in blue jeans and sweatshirt. Overdone hair. A normal-enough-looking girl. But the body under the clothing was not normal.

Karen clung to the newel post for support. Her daughter was starving herself.

Karen closed her eyes and sank onto the bottom step. She hadn't realized how far this thing had gone. Melissa was nothing but bones. Like Karen's mother on her deathbed.

What was happening to this family? Her daughter was *disappearing*. And there was trouble in Norman involving her son—which Karen prayed had nothing to do with a missing high-school girl who went to a fraternity party. Let it be something bearable. A pregnant girl. Another suspended driver's license. Another suspended sentence for possession. Another chance. *Please*. She needed all her resources to deal with Melissa.

Karen put on a nightgown and went to bed for a time, which was silly. She was too agitated for sleep. But she dutifully turned off the light and closed her eyes. And in her mind's eye, she could see the walls of the bedroom pull away from her, expanding outward, leaving her in the center of a huge open space. She could see herself, a dark-haired woman in a blue nightgown tossing about on a four-poster bed, drifting alone in a vast sea of hallucinogenic nothingness.

She jerked open her eyes, pulling the walls back into place.

In her robe and slippers, she went prowling around the house. Her wonderful house. She corrected the alignment of pictures, plumped pillows, pinched yellowing leaves from plants—but only out of habit. Tonight she felt like a visitor in the halls of Billingsly. An observer.

This edifice not only housed and defined the Billingsly family, it drove them, demanding support from Roger and constant care from Karen. The house set standards for Chad and Melissa, who saw themselves as having no less in their someday lives.

The house was like a fifth member of the family, and Karen had loved and served it accordingly.

As she strolled about Karen played a little game. Based on just these rooms, what conclusions would a stranger draw about the family that lived in this house?

It wasn't a grand house—not a mini-palace like some of its neighbors. This was a gracious house. A house meant to support a comfortable, genteel sort of existence.

The care with which the house was decorated and maintained indicated that the mother of the family doted on it. Large amounts of money and countless shopping trips to galleries, boutiques, antique shops had gone into accumulating this eclectic display of careful clutter. This was not the predictable work of a professional decorator.

The broad upstairs hallway served as a gallery for framed photographs that documented selected occasions in the family's life. Graduations. Birthdays. Anniversaries. Holidays. Vacations. Handsome, smiling faces. An apparently successful family. One that had every right to expect continued good fortune and more pictures for the hallway.

But the gallery of photographs formed an incomplete portrait of the family, representing happy times only. There was no picture of the father of the family meeting Rhonda Parker in a motel. No picture of the daughter in her current emaciated form. No picture of her son in orange prison garb facing an arraignment. No picture of the baby who died at seventeen hours.

Did the mother of that missing girl have a gallery of smiling faces in her Norman duplex? Surely nothing this impressive. Thousands of dollars had been invested in having these pictures enlarged and professionally matted and framed.

And downstairs, a different collection of photographs hung in the father's study. The father shaking hands with the governor. The father at a podium. The father accepting a plaque. And there were framed certificates, framed letters of congratulations. An important man. The books on the shelves were mostly law, biography, history—books that reinforced his selected truths.

The bookcases in the family room were filled with an eight-year-old set of encyclopedias, a set of leather-bound children's classics, novels mostly by women authors who generally offered no truths—only puzzlement—and left their readers wondering why they felt the need to read such books. Other shelves in a handsome case were lined with assorted trophies testifying to the athletic prowess of the family.

The mother took her role as homemaker seriously. Closets and cupboards were in order. A shopping list was written on a pad by the telephone. And a list of errands to be run.

A calendar on the wall above the phone testified to a busy life. Meetings. Tennis. Social events in the evening. Trips to Norman and to Dallas for football games. Upcoming birthday celebrations.

Karen warmed a cup of hot milk in the microwave and sat at the big round kitchen table to study the homey room with botanical prints on the wall, rugs on the floor. In the cupboard nearest the dishwasher were the everyday dishes, with the good china housed in the butler's pantry. One cupboard in the butler's pantry was used just for celebratory and entertainment paraphernalia. Punch bowl and cups. Footed serving trays. The Christmas dishes. The Thanksgiving platter. A ceramic pumpkin. Heart-shaped cake pans. A firecracker centerpiece. A musical cake stand that played "Happy Birthday."

Surely the family had been strengthened by all that celebrating, by all those lovingly cooked meals eaten around this table and the one in the elegant dining room on Sundays and special occasions.

Karen put her cup in the dishwasher and climbed back up the stairs. She sat for a while in her son's room, remembering the child who had occupied it through all his stages. Her adored son. She used to worry that she loved Chad more than Melissa. By the time Melissa came along, Chad had become an infinitely fascinating two-year-old. Melissa never seemed to catch up to him. Intellectually, Karen knew the balance would shift. Karen would always adore her son, but her daughter would someday be her confidante and best friend. That was the pattern. That was what she wanted, but she didn't feel it quite yet. Chad was the child who made her heart ache with love.

She stopped at Melissa's closed door. She longed to sit by her sleeping daughter's bed like she used to do, to smooth her hair from her forehead and watch her face peaceful in sleep. But Melissa was near adulthood. She would no longer sleep through her mother's worshipful nighttime hovering.

The chiming of the grandfather clock on the landing made Karen jump. One o'clock.

She returned to her bed, waiting in the darkness, watching the lighted face of the bedside clock until at last she heard the garage door going up—at one fifty-three.

She switched on the lamp and propped herself up against the headboard.

"Still awake?" Roger said with attempted cheerfulness.

"What the hell's going on?" she demanded of him with no preliminaries.

Roger scowled at her. And sat on the end of the bed to pull off his shoes.

"Well?" Karen said. "I'm waiting for an answer."

"Nothing's going on—at least not anything that concerns Chad," he said.

"If that missing girl was at the Iota Beta house, I'm going to find out about it anyway. So, you might as well tell me."

"It is not what you think—nothing I can't take care of," he said, carrying his shoes toward his dressing room.

Karen got out of bed and padded after him. "How do you even know what I think? He's my son, too. And I want to know what's going on with him. *Does it have something to do with that missing girl?*"

"I told you I'd take care of it." Roger was facing her, his neck turning a blotchy red. Karen was overstepping long-established boundaries. *He* took care of problems of magnitude.

When Chad was picked up by the Norman police for possession, Roger took care of it. When Melissa ran her brand-new Mustang into a parked car and left the scene without reporting the incident, Roger took

care of it. When Chad was about to have his driver's
license revoked for a second time, Roger took care of
it. When the house was burglarized, Roger took care
of it. He took care of cracks in the foundation and
family funerals. He was calm in the face of high fevers
and broken bones.

But then, that was partly why she had married
Roger instead of someone else. Roger took charge. He
was good in a crisis. He made her feel safe. She knew
that he would always be there to manage her and her
children's lives through good times and bad. And she
did love him. And their life together. Still. She realized how much when she feared he would leave her
and marry Rhonda Parker.

Why was she resistant now? Her husband was only
following long-established procedure. He was offering
her a chance to put something very disturbing out of
her mind. But for some reason, on this night, after
almost twenty-five years of marriage, she could not accept his offer.

"I want you to tell me what is going on with Chad,"
she repeated, enunciating each word very carefully.
"And you will not tell me that I'm not to worry. Not
this time."

"*Karen!* For God's sake, what's gotten into you!"

"I believe it's called fear. And as Chad's mother, I
have a right to know."

"I'm telling you all I can," he said, his voice softer
now, switching to his patient tone, making an obvious
effort to calm himself, as he slipped into his bathrobe
and carefully tied it closed. "Really I am. There's trouble at the fraternity house. Some of the boys wanted to
talk to me about it. I would be betraying their confi-
dence if I told you or anyone else. You have got to
trust me on this one, Karen. I will take care of it."

"The girl?"

"No. The trouble has to do with drugs. There. Are you satisfied. Now you know."

"Are you telling me that our son is doing drugs again? After all those promises?"

"No. But drugs are the problem at the Iota Beta house, and the situation has to handled very carefully, or some boys might go to jail, and the whole fraternity will be tainted by implication. They could get kicked off campus. Now, can we please drop this? I'm hungry and dead tired and am looking at a hell of day tomorrow."

"You still haven't told me if the girl who disappeared was at the IB house."

"Yes, *goddamn it*!" he said, slamming a closet door, whirling to face her, his neck reddening again, a vein on the right side of his throat visibly pulsating. "She was there. Now are you satisfied?"

Karen didn't follow him downstairs. But she felt guilty lying in bed while he scavenged for food.

She refused the sleeping pill he offered, but with the lights out, she reached for him. "I'm afraid, Roger."

"Don't be, baby. Everything will be all right."

She didn't feel like making love, but she needed to put things right with him.

She didn't pretend arousal but gently stroked her husband's back as he pumped his way to a climax.

After he rolled away from her and fell into a sex-induced slumber, she remained on her back, semen tickling her thighs as it slid from her vagina. Usually, she brought a hand towel to bed to sop up the wetness between her legs.

Ryan Courtney was the someone she hadn't married. Probably lots of women like her had a Ryan in their past—a sensitive, impractical young man who had touched them deeply. But women like her were not raised to marry men like Ryan—men who planned to dedicate their lives to something other than earning money and garnering power. When Karen last heard, Ryan was playing clarinet with the Cleveland Symphony Orchestra. But she seldom thought of seeing him again. He was just a memory.

She went into Roger's bathroom to search for his sleeping pills. And dried herself.

In the morning, she got up first. The story about Rosalie Frank was on page three. She was a waitress at a Norman restaurant near the campus—a college hangout named Frumps. She had last been seen at the Iota Beta house at 710 College. Police were investigating.

Karen put the coffee on, sectioned two grapefruit halves, put oatbran muffins on a plate. Roger was already up, in the shower. Karen woke Melissa and went for a walk.

When she returned, the house was empty. Both grapefruit halves had been eaten, but only one muffin was gone from the plate.

She cut out Rosalie Frank's picture and the article about her disappearance, put it in a manila folder, and tucked it away in her desk.

She was ready to leave when Mildred arrived. Karen gave her instructions for the day's housework and headed south—for Norman. She was skipping a meeting of the library committee at Casady School. They'd think she was sick. Karen never missed meetings.

The Iota Beta parking lot bore no signs that a fire had been built there. Karen even checked the adjoining sorority-house lot. No charred asphalt. No telltale ashes.

Chad had lied.

* * *

Frumps was a funky restaurant with butcher paper covering the tables and graffiti on the walls. Boys were playing pool in the back room.

Karen ordered coffee.

"Do you know the girl who's missing?" she asked the waitress, a middle-aged woman who walked as though her feet hurt.

"Yeah. Sweet kid."

"You think she ran away?" Karen asked.

"Not Rosie. She's real close to her family. Her little brother buses tables here on weekends. Sammy. They give half their paychecks to their mom to help out at home. Good kids. I'll tell you, it gives me nightmares to think what might have happened to her."

So, Rosalie Victoria Frank was a nice girl. Karen pondered the thought on her forty-minute drive back to Nichols Hills. Would she feel better if she'd found out that Rosalie was trash?

9

"*J*'d like to have my own place and fix it up all clean and nice," LaDonna said as she carefully applied paint to the spindles forming the back of one of the mismatched kitchen chairs. "In all the years that me and Russell's been married, we never lived in the same place more than six or eight months—all of them dumps. This ol' house would be a dump, too, 'cept for the paint. Painting makes a place seem like home. I tried painting a couple of times, but then decided what's the use? I was jus' doing it for someone else."

Karen knew that LaDonna's husband, Russell, after thirty years of lesser brutality, had beaten his wife unconscious on her fiftieth birthday, a beating that had taken the vision in her left eye, which was still covered with a patch.

After her morning in Norman, Karen was spending the afternoon in the Haven House kitchen, where she and LaDonna were painting the kitchen furniture with the off-and-on help of other residents. This afternoon Karen had insisted that Billie take a turn. Billie was a seventeen-year-old whose boyfriend had pulled out most of her hair during his latest rage.

LaDonna, a nonstop talker, explained daily that she was never going back to her husband, that she'd die first. Billie, her head covered with a faded navy bandanna, had nothing to say about her abuser.

"That Russell, he'd drink up both our paychecks,"

LaDonna was saying as she scrutinized the chair back that she'd just painted, "and then we'd have to skip out on the rent. Sometimes we ended up sleeping in the car. When I was growing up down by Shawnee, our family didn't have nothin' but a whitewashed shack and a few chickens, but we stayed put, and my daddy brought home his paycheck from the flour mill every Friday night. And my mama made things pretty. For a long time I didn't want to think about that—about my mama's house. But now I do. She always had houseplants—a sweet-potato vine on the window over the sink, mother-in-law tongue on the front porch, a pot of ivy on the table by the front window. Starched white curtains and starched white doilies. Floors scrubbed clean enough to eat off of. Coverlets on every bed. She didn't raise her daughter to sleep in no car. Not my mama."

Karen was grateful for LaDonna's chatter. It spared her the effort of trying to make Billie do more than shrug her shoulders or nod her head. And brushing on the thick forest-green paint was soothing.

The kitchen itself had already been painted—a pale yellow for the walls, off-white for the ancient cabinets. Also Karen's project. She had donated the paint.

Karen found it ironic that she did tasks at the shelter that she paid to have done in her own home. She'd never painted anything in her life before she started painting the shelter rooms one by one. That was ten years ago. This was the second go-round for the kitchen. Even with all that practice, she still wasn't skilled enough to paint the rooms of her own house. But then, perfection was hardly a requirement of the Haven House decor. LaDonna was right. Only fresh paint kept the decrepit, drafty old house from looking like an out-and-out dump.

George Brown, the shelter director, came over to admire their work and ask Karen if she'd check in a

woman and two children who'd just showed up at the
front door. From Wichita Falls. They'd walked from
the bus station. No luggage. They'd need clothes and
toiletries. "Come on, I'll introduce you," he said.
Karen followed his huge form down the long hallway
to the room that once had been a front parlor and
now served as an office.

The house and an accompanying trust fund had
been donated to the city thirty-plus years ago by Miss
Agnes Haven, the last surviving member of her pio-
neer family, who had turned the homestead they had
claimed during the '89 Land Run into a profitable
dairy farm that had supplied milk to generations of
Oklahoma City residents. A plaque by the front door
designated the building as the Agnes Elizabeth Haven
Home for Women and Children, but over the years it
had become known simply as Haven House. The
house was the only building left standing in a neighborhood that had been cleared for the building of the
crosstown expressway. Had the house been a few feet
farther north, it, too, would have been demolished. As
it was, it was so close to the elevated highway that the
sounds of cars and trucks whizzing by was a condition
of life at the shelter.

George was wearing a navy suit. He was on his way
to a Junior League board meeting, he explained, to
discuss the home's needs and ask for the league's continued support. Tomorrow he was addressing the aux-
iliary to the county dental society. Agnes Haven's trust
fund may have been adequate to maintain the house
in the 1960s, but income from the trust didn't even
cover the shelter's present-day utility bills. And the
house needed a new roof. New pipes. Termites were
attacking the wooden siding. The furnace was on its
last legs. The floors sagged. Even so, it was in better
shape than the other shelters in the city, even though
it had no religious affiliation—which made George's

job as fund-raiser more difficult. Yet, for ten years, he had managed to keep the doors open. No group was too small for him to address. If an individual didn't have money to give, he asked them to consider giving clothing, furniture, anything. What the house didn't actually need was stored in the basement to be sold at an annual sale.

George pleaded the shelter's case eloquently. A former linebacker for the University of Oklahoma football team, his size and uniqueness were hard to ignore. A huge black saint. A champion of women.

George had first come to the shelter a dozen years ago, after his social-worker wife had been named director. They took up residence in the first-floor director's apartment. George taught at a nearby grade school and served as the shelter's unofficial bouncer, his presence a deterrent to the angry men who sometimes showed up demanding the return of wives and children.

George's wife had left after two years for less depressing pastures. He'd stayed on as director.

During his first year as director, Karen started working at Haven House because only two other Junior League members had requested the shelter for the community volunteer service required by the league of all its provisional and active members. Other league-supported projects—the juvenile shelter, the thrift shop, the program that outfitted needy schoolchildren, the arts festival—seemed to have all the volunteers they needed. It had been as simple as that. Signing her name on the emptiest piece of paper. A one-year commitment. She'd try something else the following year. One volunteer post was as good as the next. She had no great calling to help abused women.

Very quickly, Karen regretted her decision as she became witness to all manner of despair. Most of the women came to the shelter—often with young chil-

dren—because they had noplace else to go. They were
abandoned, evicted, penniless, jobless, hungry, afraid.
These women's problems were easier for Karen to accept. And often there were solutions for their lives.
But many women were running away from brutality—
beatings, rape, incest, torture, mutilation. Karen
didn't understand the whole phenomenon of raped
and battered women and kept searching for their flaw.
Had they chosen the wrong man? Were they irritating?
Poor housekeepers? Too fat? Too demanding? Un-
faithful? Unresponsive? Why had the men in their
lives treated them so badly? She felt compassion but
no affinity.

That first year Karen counted the weeks until she
had served out her commitment. But as the time drew
to a close she kept putting off telling George Brown
that she wasn't coming back. Kept putting off men-
tioning the fact to any of the other volunteers. And
suddenly a second year had begun. Then a third.

After ten years, Karen was a fixture at the shelter.
She kept the volunteer schedule, trained new volunteers, got her wealthy friends to donate large-dollar
items—such as a new washer and dryer, a new hot-
water tank, a big-screen color television set, a tall
fence to enclose the backyard, playground equipment,
even an almost-new van when the old one wore out.

The fifth year of her service, Karen stayed away for
several months—after she learned that one of the residents had returned to a husband who'd slashed her
breasts with a butcher knife. A twenty-two-year-old
woman named Polly with fiery red hair and a college
degree. Karen could no longer deal with hopelessness.
Most of the battered women went back to abusive husbands or ended up with other abusive men. So few
broke out of the cycle. Karen still thought about Polly
every time she saw a young slender woman with red

hair. She was still sickened by the images that came to mind.

But she'd felt uncomfortable *not* putting in her two afternoons a week, not going to Haven House board meetings. She thought of George and the other staff volunteers continuing without her. She thought of her affluent, safe life and fine husband, of her children who'd never known anything but love. Maybe volunteering at the shelter was her payment for good fortune. When she went back, George said only that he'd been saving a special job just for her—a drive to restock their supply of women's and children's clothing for the residents who showed up with only the clothes on their backs. Or naked, covered only with a blanket from the trunk of a patrol car.

Karen's family and friends knew that she came here, but no one was ever interested enough to ask questions about what went on at the shelter, about what she did there. She knew Roger would prefer she not come, but they never discussed it.

Once, at Karen's request, Roger had read a feature about George Brown in the Sunday newspaper. "Is he gay?" was his only comment.

"I haven't the faintest idea," Karen said, irritated. "Would it matter if he was?"

Roger had shrugged and gone on with his own reading.

George paused at the office door. "Hey, are you okay?" he asked Karen.

She glanced across the room at the three new residents sitting on the threadbare sofa. A mother and her two small children. All towheaded. The woman's face was a mass of old and new bruises, her nose swollen and red, her left arm in a soiled cast.

"Why do you ask?" Karen wanted to know.

"The circles under your eyes. The way you forget what you're doing and stare at the wall."

His concern brought an unexpected swell of emotion in her chest. "Kid problems," she explained. "Bad ones. Suddenly my perfect life is falling apart."

"You want to talk?"

"Not yet. But I reserve the right. You go charm the rich ladies. I'll take care of those three."

Karen interviewed the woman, filled out forms, and explained to her the services and rules of the shelter and the conditions of her and her children's stay there. They had no day-care facilities, and mothers were responsible for their children at all times. Residents were required to help with the cooking and cleaning chores. Lights had to be turned out by ten-thirty. Meals were served on schedule. Sunday worship services were nondenominational and optional.

The children were Darren, age three, and Tiffany, almost two—beautiful children with perfect features and vividly blue eyes. With her battered face, it was hard to tell what their mother looked like. Christine Worthington. A dignified name for a woman whose husband beat her. But she was soft-spoken. Not whiny. She had wanted to get away. Go where her husband would never find her. The director of the women's shelter in Wichita Falls suggested that she leave the state and had told her about Haven House.

Christine had sold her wedding ring to buy bus tickets. "My father beat my mother and us kids until the day he had a heart attack and died. Tyron's father beats up on his mom. I don't want my children to grow up and be like that. Besides, if Tyron kills me, his folks will get my kids," she added matter-of-factly. "I can't let that happen."

Karen had hope for this woman. But first, Christine Worthington needed to be here with the other residents. Learn from them and their stories. Receive counseling. Understand why this had happened to her. Strengthen her resolve.

Karen helped Christine set up three cots in the same room occupied by silent Billie. They pulled a heavy white curtain across the center of the room. Then she helped Christine select a change of clothes for herself and the children from the clothing room in the basement and assorted toilet articles from a nearby cupboard.

Finally, Karen brought a stack of bed linens and towels to their tiny half room.

"Your husband ever do anything like this to you?" Christine asked. She was staring at her battered face in the dresser mirror.

Karen shook her head no.

"You're lucky," Christine said. She sat on a bare cot and gathered her two children close. The little girl was sucking two fingers. The little boy was staring up at his mother's battered face as though trying to fathom the meaning of all these strange happenings.

Lucky. Karen thought about that on the way home. A woman should feel lucky because her husband *doesn't* beat her?

Roger had been angry enough to hit her last night. He hadn't, but his fists were clenched. The urge was written across his face. She'd stood up to him. Strange to think that in all their years of marriage, she had never really done that before. She had requested. She'd even teased and cajoled. But she had never demanded. Never said that his way wasn't okay.

Had Rosalie Frank stood up to a man and gotten herself killed for it?

Karen turned on the radio. KKNG. Natalie Cole was singing with her dad. What Melissa would call "old-fogy music."

Karen needed to think about something besides Rosalie Frank and the finite nature of good fortune. She needed to start a project. Pick out wallpaper for

MOTHER LOVE   89

the number-two guest room. Have a dinner party. En-
roll in a class. Work on her tennis. Plan a trip.

She picked up the dry cleaning and stopped at the
grocery before hurrying home to prepare dinner. But
Roger's secretary had left a message on the answering
machine—he was working late and having something
sent in at the office. Melissa's message said that she
was eating at Jennifer's house. "Sure you are," Karen
said to the answering machine. How long could a person live on diet soft drinks?

She heated leftovers in the microwave and carried a
tray into the family room. The evening news carried
no mention of Rosalie Frank. Karen punched at the
remote, trying each channel, nothing capturing her
attention for long. Then she turned off the set, took a
few seconds to adjust to the silence. And thought
about the whitewashed shack that LaDonna remembered so fondly—the house her mama had made
pretty with sweet-potato vines and doilies. Karen wondered if her own children would someday remember
the house they grew up in with equal fondness.

She began taking up throw pillows.

First, she removed them from the family room.
Then the living room. Roger's study. The bedrooms.
The upstairs sitting room. She stored them in green
garbage bags that she carried to the attic. So many
throw pillows. Dozens of them. Covered in tapestry,
needlepoint, brocade, crewelwork, crushed velvet, ap-
pliqué, antique lace. Several she'd made herself, each
one representing months and months of careful nee-
dlework. For some of the pillows, she'd gone on
quests, searching for the just the right color, just the
right effect, price not an object. Many of them were
works of art costing hundreds of dollars apiece. She
had invested a small fortune in throw pillows, not because she needed them but because it was expected.

Every house of a certain value in Oklahoma City had its collection of throw pillows.

It wasn't the pillows themselves that made Karen angry. It was the fact that she had never considered *not* buying them. Which maybe was symbolic of some larger issue in her life. But right now all she could deal with was pillows.

10

"Strange how my mind keeps wanting to deal with other things," Inez said.

They were sitting with her at the kitchen table. Sammy. Her friend Beverly Martin, from Dallas. And Detective Larson, who had stopped by with doughnuts on the way to work and stayed for coffee. A good man. He cared more than just being a policeman.

Under other circumstances, Inez would be enjoying such an assemblage around her kitchen table. But it was the portent of tragedy that brought her friend Beverly and Detective Gary Larson to her side, that kept her home from work and Sammy from school.

Beverly poured the last of the coffee into Inez's cup and bustled about making a fresh pot. Inez wondered if it was all the coffee that was making her talk so much. Usually she listened more than she talked, but now the words were tumbling out.

"I feel like I should be concentrating every minute on Rose, willing her to be alive, willing her to come home," Inez said. "But I find myself worrying about Sammy's school and how long I should keep him home. Worrying about keeping Beverly away from her family. Worrying about my job and how many days of work I can afford to miss. Worrying about Joe. Today I'll have to drive up there and tell him. He called last night and asked for Rose. I didn't have the courage to tell him anything. Or my mother. I'll have to call her."

Sunday morning, Inez had called Beverly in Dallas. Beverly let her cry, hadn't tried to tell her that everything would be all right, that the police would surely find Rose. All she said was that she knew how much Rose loved her mother and how much Inez loved her Rose. And that she would be there in four hours. Her husband, Grady, broke down and cried himself when he had his turn on the phone. Beautiful Rose. Such a sweet girl. He'd pray for her. Beverly should stay as long as Inez needed her. He'd come up there, too, if Inez needed him. "You know, like for a search party. I've got two good hunting dogs."

Beverly had been her neighbor and best friend in Oklahoma City. Grady had helped with household repairs and chores that Joe could no longer do. But Grady lost his job at a meat-packing company when they closed their Oklahoma City facility, and he and Beverly used their savings to buy a neighborhood grocery in east Dallas a year ago. With her best friend no longer living next door, Inez's own decision to move was made easier. South Oklahoma City was becoming a hotbed of gangs and drugs. Inez wanted to live in a smaller town where her children would be safe.

What a joke that turned out to be.

Inez had been watching out the window when Beverly pulled into the driveway. Like two sisters, the women embraced and talked and wept together into the night, crying not just for Rose, but for life. They had worked hard, tried hard. They no longer expected soul-searing love or great riches. Those were the dreams of youth. What they now wanted was security for themselves and their children. Not to fear. But even that had been denied.

Sunday evening, Gary Larson had stopped by to pick up a list of relatives and Rose's friends. And to look through Rose's possessions. Inez had watched. So little her daughter had to call her own. Clothing mostly purchased at garage sales and secondhand stores. Cheap shoes from Payless. Wal-Mart jewelry. A few dolls and stuffed animals left over from childhood. Fashion magazines. And some books from the school library. A biography of Madame Curie. *Wuthering Heights.* A Mary Higgins Clark mystery. Beverly had returned the books this morning. She said the librarian got tears in her eyes when she realized who had checked out the books. Rose was going to be a library aid next year. Rose loved books.

Yesterday Detective Larson came wanting Rose's hairbrush for a sample of her hair—just in case they needed it for the investigation. Inez understood. If months from now, Rose's remains were found, a sample of her hair could be used for identification. Or a hair found on a man's clothing or in his car could link him to Rose. Inez held the brush for a minute, staring at the black hairs trapped among its bristles. And imagined Rose brushing her hair. A pretty, graceful girl. Someone Inez would have liked even if she wasn't her daughter. Rose had her mother's hair, but she was smarter than her mother. So bright. Always with her nose in a book from the time she was a little girl. She'd taught herself to read before she went to school. Always made straight A's. Inez had such hopes for her.

Reluctantly, she put the brush in the plastic bag that the detective had provided and handed it to him.

She knew that Gary Larson wouldn't keep coming by. At some point the police would either find her daughter or stop trying, using their time on cases that they had some hope of solving.

One minute Inez would feel supremely confident that God would bring Rose back to her. And the next minute she wondered if she would ever know what happened to her daughter. Rose's file at the police department could end up in a drawer for unsolved cases.

Hope was hard for Inez when her mind kept returning to one simple fact. *If Rose was okay, she would have called.* Even if she had run away, she would have called. Even if she was riding on the back of some boy's motorcycle on the way to God-knows-where, *she would have called.* Not to do so would be cruel. Rose was not cruel. She would not put her family through such anguish.

Inez mentally constructed hopeful possibilities. Rose was unconscious in a ditch, in which case she might still be found in time. Or she could be unconscious in a hospital bed. Inez had once been at the bedside of a man who woke up after three months in a coma. The first thing he said was "Where's my wife?" He didn't know he'd been away. Rose would wake up and ask for her mother. Inez wouldn't even care if she asked for that boy Steve.

Or maybe Rose had been kidnapped and was being held captive. Not for ransom. Kidnappers would surely choose a wealthier victim than the daughter of an LPN. But just the same, Inez had added up how much money she could scrape together. Not more than a few thousand—and that meant selling her car, her ring, the television. And if she sold her car, how would she get to work?

Gary Larson was explaining to Beverly that Rose could have been picked up by someone while she was walking back to the Campus Corner to get the car. Or someone could have been waiting for her in the restaurant parking lot. They couldn't automatically blame the fraternity members.

But Inez couldn't get that fraternity house out of her head. Iota Beta, whatever that meant. Why did they choose names that no one understood? It seemed sinister somehow. And all those boys. Boys, who would

look down on the likes of Rosalie Frank. Had one of
them taken her away and done terrible things to her?

Inez felt a wave of irritation as she watched Sammy
dip a second applesauce doughnut in his glass of milk
and take a large bite. Eating was necessary, but enjoying food seemed disrespectful to his sister. She
moved the box of doughnuts across the table, out of
his reach.

"Why don't you go back to work?" Gary asked.

"How can I leave the house?" Inez demanded.
"What if someone calls? Beverly needs to get back to
her family. Sammy needs to go to school."

"Buy an inexpensive answering machine," Gary
suggested.

Inez nodded. Yes. She could charge one at Sears.

She looked at her son. Poor Sammy. He dreaded
going back to school, not knowing how he was supposed to act. What if he forgot and laughed when
someone told a joke?

"You don't think Rose is ever coming back, do
you?" Sammy asked Gary.

"I don't know what to think. But if she doesn't,
your mother's going to need you more than ever."

Sammy looked to his mother, his eyes begging her
to promise his sister was coming home.

But Inez had no promises. Just prayers until she
knew for sure that prayers were futile. She prayed for
Rose's voice on the phone saying she was okay, for
Rose coming through the front door, for the feel
of Rose in her arms. She and Rose didn't hug much
anymore. But then, they saw precious little of each
other. And Sammy. She and Rose slept in the same
bed but at different times. Even if Rose came back,
Inez could think of no way to change the way they
lived. She had to work. Rose had to work. Even
Sammy, who was frail. Sometimes, on Sunday afternoon, they went fishing at the lake or played cards at

the kitchen table. Sunday evening the three of them
went together to see Joe. But the rest of the week they
passed in the hallway. And her children were her life.

Gary had asked yesterday if Rose might be pregnant.

Inez shook her head no. Yes, she was sure. Rose had
used almost a box of sanitary napkins only the week
before.

But the question had bothered her. What would
her daughter have done if she'd gotten pregnant?
Inez had allowed Rose to assume that her father was
the first and only man her mother had ever had sex
with, that Joe Frank was Rose's real father. Inez had
fostered those misconceptions to set a good example
for her daughter. And she'd never told her daughter
that she would stand by her no matter what, that she
would love her no matter what.

If Rose did come back, Inez vowed to tell her the
truth. Her mother wasn't a saint.

Would she also tell her that she could date Steve?
That she didn't have to sneak out in the middle of the
night to see him?

There. She was doing it again. Thinking around the
problem. Not concentrating on Rose coming home.
At mass this morning, she had stayed on, praying for
strength until her knees hurt, saying countless rosa-
ries. She'd take Sammy with her tomorrow morning.
Unless he went to school.

"That man likes you," Beverly said after Gary left
and Sammy was out of earshot.

"He's a married man," Inez reminded her. "And
I'm a married woman."

"You'll be a widow one day soon, and Detective
Larson is not a happily married man. He never says a
word about his wife. Men who are happily married
mention their wives even if it's just to say that she likes

cream-filled doughnuts, too, or she wishes that he'd get a job with regular hours—stuff like that."

"You have an overactive imagination."

"He'll be back tomorrow."

"Bev, he's *investigating* my daughter's disappearance, not courting me. And I don't want one of your looks if he does come back tomorrow. I can't think about Gary Larson. I need to think about Rose."

Late that afternoon, leaving Beverly to sit by the telephone, Inez and Sammy drove to the VA Hospital, in the sprawling university medical center in Oklahoma City. Inez never could decide if exposing her children to life as it existed in this hospital was a good or bad thing. The hospital, for many of its patients, was the end of the line. The ones who weren't bedridden lined the halls in their wheelchairs, old withered men, more than a few with missing limbs or ghastly with surgical mutilations. Some gathered in clusters talking together in hushed voices, old warriors facing the last battle, reliving previous ones. Others stared vacantly at nothing or moaned away the hours.

The chronic lungers were on six. As soon as the elevator door opened, the prevailing sound was the gasping of dying men. Up and down the halls. Every breath an effort.

The effort of breathing had enlarged the muscles in Joe's chest, making it grotesquely oversized on his otherwise wasted body. His ashen skin hung on his body in loose folds. His eyes were sunken back in their sockets, his cheeks sank into his face. Only in profile could Inez recognize that this dying form was indeed her Joe.

But he lived on with his tubes and oxygen tank. And Rose was gone.

Inez stared at the photograph on Joe's bedside table. Their family. Rose had been fourteen then. So pretty and sweet. A good daughter.

She kissed Joe's cheek and stood back so Sammy could do the same.

"Where's Rose?" Joe asked, taking a breath between words.

"Rose has disappeared," Inez said, taking his dry bony hand. "She never came home last Friday night. I think someone kidnapped her. Some man. I don't think she's ever coming back to us, Joe."

Joe seemed to listen, but his expression didn't change. The sound of his breathing filled the room. Out and in, a gurgling sound as he inhaled.

"Do you understand?" she asked, touching his face, making him look in her eyes. "Rose is gone, and I don't think we'll ever see her again. I think something terrible has happened to her. I try to pray. I want to believe in a miracle or some explanation that doesn't have her dead body dumped by a country road. But Rose is a good girl. If she were alive, she wouldn't be putting us through this grief. Even if she'd run off with some man, she'd at least call and tell us not to worry."

Inez was crying now, tears rolling down her face.

Joe's head was nodding up and down, the tube in his nose bouncing with him. "Yes. Rose. She's a good girl," he gasped. "Where is she?"

Sammy looked helplessly at his mother and went out into the hall.

She was going back to work tomorrow, Inez told Sammy on the drive back to Norman. And he would go back to school on Monday.

There was a finality about her decision. They were no longer putting their lives on hold while they waited for news about Rose. "We have to get on with things," Inez tried to explain. "Whether she comes back or not, I have to earn a living, and you have to go to school. Some things don't change."

"Can I still hope?" Sammy asked.

"With every breath."

In the night, Inez heard Sammy crying in his bed and went to him, slipping her arms around his thin body, kissing his forehead, smoothing his hair. "Did Rose know I loved her?" he asked. "I never told her. And sometimes I got mad at her and said awful things to her. Once I tore up her homework."

Inez reminded him that Rose sometimes said awful things to him, that brothers and sisters were like that. But of course, Rose knew that he loved her. And she loved him back. To calm him, Inez began to tell Rose stories. Remember the time Rose bought him a pair of hamsters for his birthday? Remember the marathon Monopoly games he and Rose used to play? Or the giant cookie she baked for him when he won the spelling contest?

"I remember one Christmas before your father lost his job," Inez said. "Before Nona went back to Mexico. She taught you and Rose the words to 'Silent Night' in Spanish, and the two of you sang it for us, standing in front of the tree, holding hands. I have a picture in the album. Do you still remember the words?"

Inez sang it with him. "*Noche de paz. Noche de amour* . . ." Night of peace. Night of love. Memories of another time. Forever gone.

"I'd like to kill the guy who took her away," Sammy said.

"I know, son. I know."

"Will anyone ask me about her at school tomorrow?"

"The teachers probably will. They'll ask if there is any news. And say they hope that Rose is found. The kids won't know what to say."

"They'll whisper about me."

"Yes. Probably. Your sister's disappeared. It's been on television and in the newspapers. That makes you seem strange."

"Do you really think that we'll move to Dallas?"

"Dallas or someplace else. But not now. I don't want to move your father. And I need to stay here with this telephone number until my hearts stops jumping every time the phone rings—just in case."

"I was thinking that maybe I could go to Dallas on Sunday with Beverly—maybe go to school down there with Greg and Brad," Sammy said. "I could work for Grady at the store after school."

"Are you that afraid of going back to school in the morning?"

"Yes," he said, softly, not looking at his mother.

"Ah, Sammy boy. What would your daddy and I do without you? I think you must be brave and stay here. I think it is your duty. Monday will be the worst day at school. After that, you won't feel so strange."

11

*W*ithout a body or other proof that a crime had been committed, Gary couldn't ask for a search warrant, but Wednesday morning, at the suggestion of the university president and the university's legal counsel, the residents of the Iota Beta fraternity house voluntarily vacated their house for the day to allow the police to look around. Gary asked the fraternity's president, a kid named Tom Fitzhugh, to be available for any questions that might arise.

The house had a full basement and four floors—more than fifty rooms altogether. Gary and three other NPD officers were being assisted by two university police officers and an agent from the state bureau of investigation. They looked in every closet, every drawer, every wastebasket, inspected every bed. They found nothing suspicious—no female clothing, no long dark hairs on any pillow to match the ones from Rose's hairbrush. The few rooms where the beds appeared to have freshly laundered sheets received extra scrutiny, with care taken to look under and around the beds and in the pockets of every garment hanging in the closet or strewn about the room.

A small fourth-floor room had suffered a recent fire. The paint was bubbled on a couple of file cabinets that contained an impressive number of previously taken examinations that were used by members and pledges as study guides. The walls and floor of the

room were smudged with soot. Fitzhugh explained
that a sofa had caught fire—from a cigarette probably
—and apparently smoldered for a long time before a
smoke detector went off. No, the fire department had
not been called. Some of the boys had put the fire out
themselves. What was left of the sofa had been hauled
away—by city trash collectors, he assumed.

"Any of the guys ever bring a girl up here for sex?"
Gary asked Fitzhugh.

"Yes, sir, it happens sometimes. During parties."

As Gary was going down the narrow stairway his
pager went off. A call from his wife.

"What's up?" he asked when Sharon answered the
phone.

"My temperature's up a degree." Her voice was
hopeful, even excited.

Gary felt a wave of irritation. "We agreed we
weren't going to do that anymore."

"*You* agreed. I pray for a baby every day. Please,
Gary, come home. I'm *ovulating.*"

Gary closed his eyes and clenched his jaw.

For twelve years Sharon had wanted only one thing.
A baby. The three times that she'd conceived had re-
sulted in miscarriages. So many times, Gary had
rushed home during the day to perform obligatory
sex because his wife's temperature chart said she was
ovulating. While he dressed to hurry back to work she
would lie with two pillows elevating her rear, her feet
propped over her head against the wall. With her eyes
closed. Silently praying.

Sex had ceased to be romantic. And now Gary
didn't want another pregnancy. He couldn't go
through the depression that followed. His and hers.
Not again.

"I can't," he said. "I'm in the middle of a case."

"You'd come if I fell and broke my arm. And this is
more important."

Gary suppressed a groan. "I cannot come home," he repeated. "And even if I could, I don't want to, Sharon. I want us to start making love again. At night. When we feel like it, not when some damned chart says we have to."

She was crying now. Repeating the same tired litany. She wanted a baby more than anything. Their marriage was incomplete without children. Their lives. She felt as though she had failed. As though she was only half a woman. He'd leave her someday for a woman who could have babies. All she wanted was another chance. Maybe this time . . .

Gary wanted to yell at her. To tell her to get out of the house. Find something in her life to care about besides having a baby. She'd lost her secretarial job at the university because of her chronic absences—and made no attempt to find another even though it meant putting their plans to buy a house on hold. She didn't want to plant a garden this year. Wasn't interested in joining a health club or going back to school. She spent her days watching television and taking her temperature, making little attempt at housekeeping.

But after the anger passed, Gary felt sad. So very sad. Poor Sharon. Poor him. Unhappiness made him weary.

In high school and junior college, Sharon had been a champion barrel racer. God, what a sight it had been to see her maneuvering her big Appaloosa through the course, then bending low over his neck, racing for the time line, horse and rider one magnificent being. How he longed for that gutsy young woman in dusty jeans and boots, her cowboy hat at a cocky angle. The pitiful, whining person who now lived in her body was not the girl he'd raced on horseback up and down country lanes, not the girl with whom he'd skinny-dipped in moonlit lakes and two-stepped the night away in cowboy bars. "Tulsa Time."

"You're the Reason God Made Oklahoma." "Some Days Are Diamonds." Thinking about it made Gary ache.

He still caught glimpses of that other Sharon at rare moments when she would forget her tragedy and sing along with a favorite tune on the radio or watch the horses race at the Oklahoma City track.

He'd offered to move to an acreage, buy her a horse. Maybe someday, she'd said, when they needed more space for their family, when it was time to teach their children to ride.

After he'd finished for the day, Gary put off going home a bit longer by stopping at Inez Frank's house to tell her about the search at the fraternity house. "I'm sorry. I wish I could tell you that we found something helpful."

"What do you do now?" she wanted to know. She looked so tired, so sad. No longer hopeful.

He shook his head. "Talk to people. Hope something turns up."

"Such as?"

"Maybe someone will remember something. I'll question the kids who were at the party. Talk to Rose's boyfriend. The people she works with. Kids at her school. Whoever I can think of."

After coffee, Inez walked out to the car with him. He dared to put a hand on her shoulder. "More than anything, I'd like to find your daughter for you," he said, terribly aware of her, of her dark eyes and smooth velvety skin, of her slim bare throat in the V of her sweater.

"I know," she said, nodding. "You're a comfort to me."

"I think about you sometimes. A lot, actually. You've got all this pain and fear inside, but you don't act pitiful. I like seeing you and Sammy together, how you don't fuss over him, but it's plain to see that the two of you really love each other. And your mouth is so beautiful. Your hands. Someday, after this is all over . . ."

She put her hand over his. "I see sadness in your eyes," she said, interrupting him. "And where there's sadness, there's still feeling."

Gary wanted to protest. To say he was ready for something else in his life other than a wife who spent her days numbed with self-pity.

Instead he allowed his fingertips to brush the ends of Inez's hair, then nodded and opened the door of his car. She was still standing by the curb when he turned the corner.

From the Frank house, Gary drove to Capitol Hill in south Oklahoma City, an area so named by its residents in the early days of statehood in hopes that the proposed state capitol building would be located there. Nothing so grand as a capitol building or anything else even remotely important had ever been built there, and over the years Capitol Hill and its environs had become an area of empty storefronts and run-down houses with weeds in the yard.

The counselor at Capitol Hill High School was helpful, calling in a few of Rosalie Frank's former classmates. Four girls. Boys, she told him, would be a waste of time. Giving information to policemen was against the code.

From the girls, Gary learned the last name of Rose's boyfriend was Navarez. Steve Navarez. He worked down the hill, in a motorcycle garage frequented by their own boyfriends.

"I wondered how long it would take until the cops came around," said Navarez—a John Travolta–looking kid with carefully slicked-back hair and a couple days' worth growth of beard. They walked around back of the building to talk.

"How'd you hear?" Gary asked.

"I called her house Saturday night," Navarez said, staring at a small mountain of discarded motorcycle parts. "Sammy told me. And yes, I can prove where I was last Friday night. That is the next question, isn't it?"

"You got it. Where were you?"

"Hanging out. I got lots of witnesses."

"Anyone I'd believe?"

Navarez shrugged.

"You didn't see her Friday night? Not at all?"

"Naw. I hadn't seen her all week. She said she wouldn't go out with me again unless I got back in school."

"I'll bet that really made you mad."

"Yeah. Madder than hell. I felt like going down there and belting her. But I didn't. She's right. A nice girl like her shouldn't go out with a dead end who didn't even finish high school. I went up to the school Friday afternoon to see about getting back in. I was going to tell her Saturday night. Surprise her."

Gary made a mental note to check at the high school. Had Navarez really inquired about getting back in school?

"Rose like to get high?" Gary asked.

"Who doesn't?"

"You know anything that will help me find her?"

"I've racked my brain, man, trying to think. But no. Someone down there got to her. Some college boy in his foreign car. Guys up here know she's hands off. And when I find out who—"

Gary held up his hand. "We don't know that anyone *got* to her. Maybe she went off of her own free will."

"Naw. She didn't do that. Not Rose. She wouldn't

do that to her mom." He started to say something else, but instead turned his back on Gary, his shoulders shaking.

Gary waited a minute before touching Steve Navarez's arm. "I'm putting my card in your back pocket. If you hear anything I should know, call me. And go back to school. For Rose."

His back still to Gary, Navarez nodded.

On the way home, Gary stopped at the grocery for two T-bone steaks, a six-pack of Corona, and a sack of charcoal. Such a pretty evening. The sky was ablaze with a pink-and-orange sunset. Maybe he and Sharon could go for a walk while the charcoal was heating.

She was sitting by the window in the bedroom, staring out at nothing. Gary knelt in front of her and buried his face in her lap. She hesitated, then put her fingers in his hair.

In the evening Roger liked to spend time with the newspapers that he'd only scanned that morning. He'd open a beer and spread the newspapers out on the kitchen bar while Karen prepared dinner. The *Daily Oklahoman*, the *Tulsa World*, the *Wall Street Journal*, the *Dallas Morning News*. On Sundays he'd add *The New York Times*. Sometimes he'd call an item to Karen's attention. Karen always looked nice in the evenings, her thick dark hair brushed and shining, her makeup fresh in honor of his homecoming. Which was nice. A pretty wife to come home to. Sometimes she'd talk about this or that as she bustled about. A comfortable routine.

Roger was, therefore, surprised when Karen stopped her bustling and stood across the bar from him demanding that he stop reading those "damned newspapers" and listen to her for a change.

She was in the middle of dishing up dinner—for

just the two of them. Again. Of late, Melissa usually avoided the dinner hour, a situation Roger was going to have to do somehing about. "Why are they 'damned newspapers'?" he asked.

Karen paused, thinking. "I guess I damned the newspapers because that seemed more diplomatic than damning you. Reading a newspaper when someone is trying to carry on a conversation with you is rude—even if it is *just* your wife. I have been conversing, you know."

"Yes. Something about a wiener roast at the fraternity house," he said.

Karen made a pained face. "I've always thought you should read the newspapers *after* dinner, while I'm tidying up. When you first come in, the sociable thing would be for you to talk to me, not ignore me."

Roger took off his reading glasses and looked at his wife. "So, if you've always felt that way, why have you waited all these years to call it to my attention?"

Karen twisted the hot pad she was holding. "Good question," she acknowledged. "I guess because I usually don't have anything very important to say. Except, that's my life. Everyday things. But tonight I do have something important to say. So for you to be reading the newspaper is especially irritating."

Roger carefully folded the paper he'd been reading, not sure whether he felt angry or hurt. His wife's behavior tonight was certainly disconcerting. And puzzling. "So, just what is this important thing that I need to listen to?" he said, immediately wishing he could rephrase the question. He had sounded condescending. And she'd picked up on it. He could tell by the way her chin rose a few millimeters. For half a second he thought she was going to clam up. Not say anything. Make him play a guessing game to discover the source of the problem.

But she spoke, tonelessly repeating the words he had apparently not listened to carefully enough to suit her. "What I said was that Chad's clothes smelled like smoke when he came in last Friday night—actually early Saturday morning. When I asked him about it, he said they'd built a fire in the parking lot to roast hot dogs. But there was no sign of a fire."

"How do you know that?" Roger asked, suddenly wary.

"I drove down there yesterday and looked."

"At the IB parking lot?"

Karen nodded.

"Christ, Karen! You act like you actually want to connect Chad to that girl's disappearance. What's with you?"

"I think it's time you told me everything that happened when you met with those boys Tuesday night. That girl Rosalie Frank didn't just walk in and out of the IB house. What went on while she was there? Why did they need to talk to you?"

Roger regarded his wife. Her back was ramrod straight, her expression and the sound of her voice deadly serious. He couldn't remember her ever being quite like this before.

Wordlessly, he pushed back the bar stool and went into the study to make the call. Chad was at dinner. He asked the pledge on phone duty to go get him. He'd already had one conversation with his son today, when Chad called to say the police had finished searching the house.

"Why did you tell your mother there was a fire in the parking lot Friday night—for roasting hot dogs?" he asked when Chad's voice came on the line.

"Because she said my clothes smelled of smoke."

"And why did they smell that way?"

"We built a fire at one of the picnic areas out by the

lake—to burn the clothes we'd been wearing. We
didn't want the police to find one of her pubic hairs
in our clothes. Or some of her blood. Carter's majoring in law enforcement. He said that they nail guys
now with DNA testing. You know, in case she did realize what had happened to her and decided to press
charges.''

"Why would there be blood on your clothing?"

"She was on her period."

Roger hung up with no comment. He sat at his
desk staring across the room at the empty fireplace.
Burned their clothes. Jesus. They had sex with an unconscious girl and burned their clothes to avoid a DNA
matchup. To avoid getting "nailed."

But then, Chad was the child of a society that con-
doned fuzz busters, cheating on taxes, laundering
money, and illicit gambling. Illegal behavior was per-
ceived as criminal only if the perpetrator got caught at
it. People were motivated less by ethics than fear of
punishment. And often Roger's job as an attorney was
to prevent, or at least minimize, any punishment that
the legal system might impose upon clients who were
guilty as accused.

Yet the conversation he'd just had with his son
made him feel acutely uncomfortable. Chad and his
fraternity brothers seemed to have little sense that
they had engaged in a criminal act. No sense of having
done wrong. Their only concern was getting away with
it.

And Roger wanted them to get away with it, too. He
didn't want young lives ruined. But he would have
preferred some sense of remorse on their part, some
indication that they had learned from their mistake,
some degree of concern for the missing girl.

He did take comfort, however, in their fear that the
girl might cause trouble. Which meant that they believed her to be alive and functioning. Which meant

that they truly had not had anything to do with her disappearance. Roger realized that in spite of their solemn oaths otherwise, he hadn't entirely believed them before.

He took a deep breath and went back to face his wife.

"The fire was out at the lake," he told her.

Karen was sitting at the table, their dinner waiting in serving dishes. Pork chops. Wild rice. Steamed squash. Hot rolls. "Then why did he tell me the fire was in the parking lot?" she wanted to know.

"He wasn't thinking straight. They had planned to build a fire there but realized the fire department would freak," he said, the lie coming easily. "So they drove out to a picnic area at Thunderbird on a whim. Just a few of the guys without dates."

"What about Rosalie Frank?"

"They were concerned because she had been at the house. A lot of people saw her there. They knew the police would ask questions if the girl didn't show up. They just wanted to know how to handle it. And, as a matter of fact, the police searched the house this afternoon—and apparently found nothing amiss. Now, can we please let the subject drop?"

"Chad had sex with that girl, didn't he?"

Roger was stunned. How could she know that? He knew that he was staring at her. Knew his mouth was open.

And she was staring back. Coldly. Not backing down.

"Why do you say that?" he said, keeping his voice a careful neutral.

"Because if he'd had nothing to do with her, you would have said so by now. Or if he'd just danced with her or only *seen* her at the party, you would have told me so. But you haven't said anything about our son and Rosalie Frank. You did mention that he was not doing drugs, but other than that, you are carefully avoiding saying anything else about that evening.''

"Isn't that rather a quantum leap to assume that my saying nothing means the worst?''

"Not really,'' she said, her hands in her lap, her gaze still meeting his, unwavering. "After all these years, I know how you think. You think that you are supposed to protect me. And Chad was in a panic to talk to you, like every other time he's been in trouble. And if he wasn't in trouble over drugs, if he hadn't been arrested for another DUI, if he hadn't been in another wreck, then what he needed to talk to you about was that girl. So that's how I know that our son had sex with a girl who is now a missing person, and I'm worried to death that you and he are covering up something more. Like an accident. Did she fall out of an upstairs window like that girl at the Pi Sigma house several years back? Did she drown in the Duck Pond. Or in Lake Thunderbird while they were roasting hot dogs? Where is she, Roger?''

"I swear to God that I don't know, and Chad doesn't either. Honestly, Karen. The girl was hot to trot and got involved with several of them. A real orgy. And they never saw her after that. I'm sorry that I didn't explain before. But it sounded so sordid, and I did want to protect you. But I can see that not knowing has been worse for you. I'm not proud of Chad or his fraternity brothers, but I believe they haven't a clue as to what happened to this girl after they zipped up their breeches.''

"So, did they go have their little hot-dog roast before or after they had sex with Rosalie Frank?'' she asked, her voice like ice.

"God, Karen, you're positively hostile,'' he said. "Our son could be in serious trouble. Show a little concern.''

"Yes, I'm concerned. And I'm scared. Confused. But I'm also disgusted. Our son's behavior is disgusting, and you seem more upset with me than you are with him."

Neither one of them ate very much. Karen didn't object when Roger switched on the television set. CNN spared them from further hostility. As soon as diplomatically possible, Roger escaped to his study.

He was getting more like her father all the time, Karen thought as she stacked the dishes in the sink. Her father often chose the seclusion of his study after dinner. But then, the reason Roger wanted a study was so he could be more like her father, whom he admired above all men.

She carried her coffee to the bar and flipped through the newspapers, clipping a brief story about the missing Norman high-school girl from the *Daily Oklahoman*. For her file. There was nothing in the Tulsa paper. She wished that she had a copy of the Norman paper.

She went to the open door of the study. "I called Dr. Burk today about Melissa," she informed Roger. "She wants the three of us to come in. Monday afternoon. I had Sally mark it on your appointment calendar. She said you were free."

Roger nodded. "Yes. Good idea. It's time we nip this eating thing in the bud."

"I think we're past the budding stage. I hugged her the other night and almost fainted. She's nothing but bones. Like someone with a wasting disease. What's happening to us, Roger? We have everything. But our daughter is trying to starve herself to death, and our son participated in gang sex with a high-school girl."

"We've had troubles before," he reminded her.

She digested his words for a few seconds. And nodded. Yes, they had survived other troubles.

"Come sit with me and have a brandy," Roger said.

"Maybe we should watch a movie and take our minds off some of this."

"No. I've left the dishes for Mildred. I'm going for a walk, maybe stop by the club." She did not ask him to come with her for fear that he would say yes.

12

*A*n oversized moon shone brilliantly over-head. Even at nine o'clock, the air was still pleasantly warm. Another mild winter was forecast. The roses probably would still be in bloom at Thanksgiving. Like last winter, when the only time she wore her mink was on a trip to Colorado. Not normal at all. Global warming probably. Next they'd be planting palm trees on the prairie.

Karen walked the two long blocks to the country club, a can of Mace in her pocket more out of habit than any real fear. One didn't expect violence in Nichols Hills.

She strolled down the long drive to the entrance of the sprawling Oklahoma City Golf and Country Club, where she took refuge with other late-evening patrons in the club's sedate, paneled bar. Early evening was the cocktail hour—men on their way home from work, couples having a drink before dinner. Late evening was for members who didn't want to be at home.

Karen sat at the bar with two women acquaintances —widows, of whom the club had a disproportionate number. These two were lean and leathery brown from daily rounds of golf. As women in their sixties, Millicent Farr explained to Karen, she and Valerie Pettigrew were too old to attract new husbands but still horny enough to want them.

"At least, I'm still horny," Millicent added. "Val here is, too, but she won't admit it. She says that men

115

no longer interest her, but I'll just bet that she has a vibrator tucked away in the drawer of her bedside table just like the rest of us unattached gals.''

"Sweetie, all I have in my bedside table is a handgun and the channel changer," Valerie drawled. "After two husbands and a couple of live-ins, I'm sick to death of men with their farts and belches and egos. And ESPN. Christ, I got so sick of ESPN! I save my fantasy time for my stock portfolio and what to have for dinner—and I don't need a vibrator for that.''

"What about that nice father of yours?" Millicent asked Karen. "Does he have a lady friend yet?"

"Several, I believe," Karen said dryly.

"And not a one of then over fifty, I'll bet," Millicent said with more than a trace of bitterness. "It's a couples' world and don't you let anyone tell you otherwise," she went on, with a knowing nod. "No matter how you feel about men themselves, you sure don't have much of a social life without one—not to mention a sex life. All there is without a man is golf, gossip, gin, and goin' places. In the past five years Val and I have visited on every continent 'cept Antarctica. And if I thought there were any men down there who'd give a woman over sixty more than the time of day, I'd charter a flight.''

Karen drank three whiskey sours, listening to stories of widowly travels, which certainly sounded more adventurous than the careful journeys she had taken with her husband and children. Valerie and Millicent had ridden camels in the Sahara, visited Tibetan monasteries, gambled at Monte Carlo, worked on an archaeological dig in Israel, seen the Queen and the Pope. Was it really impossible for them to enjoy all of that without a man at their side? Maybe they wouldn't have gone to any of those places if their husbands were still alive. Karen's recollections of Vic Pettigrew and Harry Farr were of portly men whose travel inter-

ests were limited to following the University of Oklahoma football and basketball teams around the
country.

Roger liked to travel. But he was a cautious man,
wanting planned itineraries and beaten paths. And
she was a cautious woman.

She didn't want Roger to die and leave her a
widow. But she did want them to change. When had
she realized that? Their life together needed to be less
preordained, more open and spontaneous. They
needed to explore and discover the world and each
other. They needed to laugh and sing. Maybe the
house was part of the trouble. People who lived in a
dignified house behaved accordingly. Perhaps they
should sell the house and buy a carefree condo with a
postage-stamp yard. And a second house on a beach
or a mountain—just a small rustic place with a view
and no throw pillows, where they could take long
walks and cook simple meals and make love without a
telephone next to the bed.

But she loved her house, she reminded herself. She
wanted her children to bring their children there.

She accepted a fourth drink from the bartender,
which wasn't a good idea. The alcohol was fueling her
melancholy.

She didn't like feeling this way. Only a week ago
she'd been a count-your-blessings sort of person. Only
a week ago she'd thought she was one of the most
fortunate people in the world.

And she was fortunate, *god-damn-it!* This business
with Chad would pass. And Dr. Burk would tell them
what to do about Melissa.

At midnight the bartender politely informed the
three ladies that it was closing time. Karen declined
offers of a ride from her two companions and headed
home on foot.

She remembered other nights, walking down this

sloping street with Roger, feeling tipsy and amorous, thinking how lucky they were to have a house practically on the doorstep of the country club so they could drink and mingle to their hearts' content and not have to worry about driving home. One night she tried to get him to skip with her, promising all sorts of kinky delights if only he would try.

She couldn't draw a line across their lives and say that after that day, the fun stopped, there was no more skipping and experimenting. Certainly by the time Roger took up with Rhonda it had happened. It might even have been partly why Roger became involved with Rhonda in the first place. And now, in Rhonda's wake, they had an even more careful marriage. A Holiday Inn marriage with no surprises to hurt or baffle. No high old times either. Karen had all but convinced herself that was the way mature married people were supposed to live.

After all, there were reputations and children to consider. Maturity was serious business.

Probably it was parenthood that started their reverse metamorphosis. They used to be butterflies. Now they lived within a careful cocoon. Parents didn't skip. And if mothers laughed or lusted or looked away, leukemia or kidnappers or molesters might strike their children.

How long since she had laughed—really laughed— without the benefit of booze? How long since she had been silly? Or gay? That word, in its original sense, described what was missing from her serious, vigilant, mature life. She wondered if Roger missed the way they used to be.

Karen began to skip. As though she were still young and gay, she skipped drunkenly through the neighborhood of the rich, their serious edifices staring at her over vast groomed-to-perfection lawns.

Not exactly a gay neighborhood in either sense.

She was sweating. Bourbon and mixed nuts sloshed around in her stomach.

Flies in the buttermilk, shoo fly shoo,
Skip to my Lou, my darling.
Skip, skip, skip to my Lou....

Her son had had sex with a girl he didn't know. Gang sex. Animal sex. Fornication.

Her daughter was flirting with anorexia.

Karen had loved her children more than life itself, would have died for them, killed for them, but now her love was diluted with disappointment. And she was afraid. Melissa could die. And Karen didn't believe Chad's story of a post-sexual-encounter, middle-of-the-night wiener roast all the way out at Lake Thunderbird that took place while Rosalie Frank did a vanishing act with no help from any resident of the Iota Beta house.

So, what did she believe? What ugly thoughts were pecking away at the outer edges of her consciousness?

But then, she didn't need to worry her pretty little head about such things, did she now? Her husband would take care of it.

She used to be so grateful that she had married such a forceful, gallant man. Her white knight.

She was skipping more smoothly now. Sailing along. Arms floating gracefully at her sides. Like a dancer. Like Anna Pavlova or Maria Tallchief.

Karen imagined white chiffon billowing out behind her. *Skip to my Lou, my darling.*

She should be praying for Rosalie Frank.

That's probably what Rosalie Frank's mother was doing this very minute. Inez. The newspaper said that Rosalie's father was named Joseph. He was a patient in VA Hospital. According to the metro telephone directory, the Joseph Franks lived at 1764 Dover Lane in

Norman. Inez Frank was there now, in her lonely Dover Lane bed praying into the darkness. *Please God, don't let those boys have* . . .

Karen skipped harder, winded now, pushing herself, her stomach protesting.

Religion had ceased to be something she felt in her gut and was instead something she practiced on Sunday morning at solemn services at the stately All Souls Episcopal Church. Tomorrow morning she would go there to pray, alone in the silent sanctuary, kneeling in front of the altar, a supplicant.

She would pray that Rosalie Frank was still alive. Or if she was already dead, she would pray that Chad had nothing to do with her death.

But of course he didn't. A mother, of all people, should have faith in her own son. A mother should know in her soul that the boy she had borne and raised and adored was incapable of a crime against another human being.

One night last summer Chad had come in late. Karen heard him trip and fall on the stairs. She'd rushed out of her room to find him sprawled on the steps, crying, smelling of vomit and whiskey.

He'd run over a cat. The cat had been hopelessly crushed but alive. And screaming in pain. Really screaming, Chad said. Like a person. He didn't know a cat could make a sound like that. He'd backed the car over the cat, crushing its skull, putting it out of its misery.

Karen wouldn't have been able to do that. She would have driven off into the night, leaving the screaming animal on the side of the road, hoping it would die soon. Begging God to let it die soon. But she wouldn't have had the courage to end the animal's suffering herself.

Her son was a person of courage and character and compassion.

Except he had been drunk that night. Lucky that it had been a cat he'd hit, and not a person.

She was drenched in sweat now. Nauseated. Sobbing. Shuffling along, no longer skipping, no longer a graceful dancer in chiffon.

She stumbled to the curb and threw up on Clem and Serena Falconer's perfectly manicured front lawn. In the morning, some Mexican or Korean gardener would have to clean up her vomit along with any nightly deposits of dog poop.

She walked up the drive to the back door and fumbled endlessly with her keys until the door swung open into the dark interior. She switched on the laundry-room light long enough to check the security system—Roger hadn't activated it—then walked through her dark house to the backyard. Without hesitation she plunged into the sparkling-clean, seldom-used swimming pool.

The cold took her breath away. But did not render her instantly sober. She peeled away her clothes, slinging each garment up on the deck, and began to paddle about. Naked. Everyone should skinny-dip at least once in her own swimming pool. Just think of all the poor people in China who had no pool. Didn't she have some sort of moral obligation to partake of its waters?

For a time the water felt nice. Different, at least. Buoyant. Liberating. Except that she was going to throw up again.

This time she made it to the bathroom off the laundry room.

She returned to the pool for her soggy mass of clothes and piled them on the washer then wrapped herself in a towel before setting the security system and creeping up the stairs.

She considered sleeping in one of the guest rooms. But even drunk, she didn't have the nerve. The only occasions in the past when she and Roger slept apart were when one of them had a bad cold. Even during the Rhonda Parker days, she had continued to share a bed with Roger. Not to do so would have been admitting that she knew about his affair, and that would have forced an examination of their marriage that she hadn't been ready to face.

She still wasn't ready.

Roger was already in bed, the lights out. Karen offered a silent thank-you and tiptoed unsteadily across the expanse of bedroom to her bathroom.

Once in her nightgown, she carefully slipped into bed and curled into a comfortable position on the very edge of the king-size bed, as far away from her husband as possible. Her hair was wet. Her skin smelled of chlorine. And she was cold. Very cold. She willed her chilled body to stop shivering. And go to sleep.

The headache she was going to suffer in the morning would be worth it if the whiskey sours helped her fall asleep tonight.

13

*T*he headache woke her in the night. She took three aspirin and drank two glasses of water. Probably she should go downstairs and eat a banana, for the potassium. Roger insisted that potassium and lots of water were the best treatment for a hangover. But she wasn't even sure she could keep the water and aspirin down, so the banana would have to wait.

She tried to remember the last time she'd been hungover. It was several months ago. The Grissoms' yard party. They'd stayed to play poker. Before that, the Valentine dance at the club. Before that, New Year's. Sometimes she got away with overindulging. Sometimes she didn't.

She wondered if Millicent had used her vibrator when she got home. And whether she'd fantasized about a specific or generic man while it did its job.

Karen's skin still smelled like chlorine. *From skinny-dipping.* Jesus, she'd really been soused.

If she held her head still, she would go back to sleep. She could feel it coming.

Very still. So it would forget to hurt.

The next time she woke, she had to put her hand over her mouth to keep from groaning. In a fog of pain, she very carefully made her way downstairs to eat a banana. And drink more water. She found herself awake again and went to the bathroom and drank another glass of water. She didn't dare try more aspirin.

The next time she woke, it was after eight. Roger and Melissa had already gone. She'd slept right through the alarm.

Her head still hurt. Of course. Hangovers lasted until midafternoon. No matter how you treated them. It must be written somewhere. In the morning, you swore never to drink again. By evening, you were ready for a cocktail.

Karen took three more aspirin, threw out the insipid brew that Roger had made, and fixed herself a pot of very strong coffee. And ate another banana. She felt somewhat better. Not enough. But by midmorning, she was dressed and on her way to Norman.

So many times had she made this drive over the years, to football and basketball games, to sorority functions, to dinners for university donors in the ballroom of the student union. Even when she was in school at OU, she drove back and forth to Oklahoma City almost weekly to visit the homes of sorority sisters or to shop at Rothchild's, Kerr's, or John A. Brown's— all gone now, buildings and all, in the wake of urban renewal. For special nights out, she and Roger would come to the city for dinner at the Shirvin or the Cellar, both of which had been closed for years. Most of the beautiful old buildings had been demolished to make way for mirrored towers—many of which never got built after the oil bust. Also gone were most of the oil wells that used to be so much a part of the landscape. Domestic producers couldn't compete with the price of imported crude.

Just north of Norman was the so-called Mount Williams, built as a backdrop for artillery practice during the Second World War. At the time the university's north campus had been, oddly enough, a naval installation. Much of the dirt had been hauled away over the years, but the man-made mountain had once dominated the flat countryside. Karen and a group of sorority sisters, after consuming numerous cans of beer, had climbed it one evening and stood arm in arm on top of the world, the wind blowing their hair, watching the sun go down as they sang "The Impossible Dream." Karen remembered having tears in her eyes as she sang.

Karen took the first Norman exit, which would take her to the east side of town. She had to stop and ask directions at a service station before she found her way to Dover Lane, a street of run-down duplexes. The one where the Franks lived was buff brick, trimmed in flaking brown paint. A front window was missing a screen.

She parked at the end of the block. Studying the Franks' side of the duplex, she noted the weeds growing in cracks in the driveway, the overgrown bushes, the drawn window shades. For hours, she sat there as she waited to catch a glimpse of Inez Frank and her son, Sammy. It was important that she do that. She couldn't even begin to understand why.

Finally, she gave up and drove away. She bought coffee and a package of peanut-butter crackers at a 7-Eleven, then headed west on Lindsey Street. Her headache was better but not gone.

She drove past the university's south oval, the petunia display of summer replaced with a sea of chrysanthemums in every color. She turned north on College and parked across the street from the Iota Beta house in the shade of a large elm. There she watched the boys come and go, shoot a basketball at the parking-lot goal, toss a Frisbee around the front yard. Normal-looking boys. More privileged than most. Mainstream kids, for the most part. Not computer wizards or members of the chess club, but boys who liked to party and were smart enough to make their grades and stay in school with a minimum of studying. Being "one of the guys" was more admired than scholarship. Karen won-

dered if fraternities still practiced the Beta wedge.
When she was at OU, on exam days in the large lecture halls, the smartest member of a fraternity would
sit toward the front of the room with other members
fanned out behind him, one diagonally behind the
other, to facilitate looking over shoulders.

But it was hazing that had brought the fraternity
system under close scrutiny nationwide. And in spite
of all the university's efforts to eliminate hazing on
the OU campus, it still existed. The university had
kicked one prominent fraternity off campus. Chad admitted that the Iota Betas practiced hazing. But they
were careful. Nothing dangerous. No one had ever
gotten hurt. But they had to make sure a guy wasn't a
wimp, he explained. The only exception had been
Johnny Fontaine, his roommate. Chad said that
Johnny's hazing had been perfunctory. He was a special case. His dad was a big-time alum. Mr. Fontaine
had already picked up the tab for the new deck built
across the back of the house and had offered to pay
for remodeling the first floor. But Johnny had inexpli-
cably dropped out of school. Gone home to Arizona
with his parents in their private jet after the Kansas
State football game.

Even in the nineties, for many members of the
Greek system, college was as much a time of life as a
place to get an education—as it had been for Karen
herself in the late sixties. She had earned a degree in
elementary education but had majored in courtship
and sorority. Sorority had become the focus of her life
as she immersed herself in sisterhood, singing the
songs, playing the role, loving every minute.

Karen realized that today's sorority woman looked
at the future with somewhat different eyes and expected to hold a salaried job for more than the few
years after graduation that had been usual for Karen's
generation. But a sorority woman of the nineties still

wanted to party, to meet the right young man, to marry well. She still dreamed about a pinning serenade and a church wedding. She ignored statistics telling her that she had only a fifty-fifty chance of staying married to her college sweetheart and thought of her future more in terms of his prospects than her own. She expected her career aspirations and salary to be secondary to his. Maybe young women at Vassar and Berkeley operated on a different wavelength than those who occupied sorority houses at OU, Nebraska, Texas, Old Miss, LSU. Or maybe those more progressive young women were kidding themselves. Karen couldn't imagine a woman who didn't want a home and family. And she couldn't imagine a marriage where taking care of home and family weren't primarily the province of the wife. But then, what did she know? Maybe those young men playing Frisbee in the yard of the Iota Beta house would someday share the shopping, housework, and diaper changing so that their wives could also climb corporate ladders.

Karen watched the fraternity house for a long time, studying each boy, the way he moved, the way he dressed. Most were wearing jeans or baggy shorts, like any other student. But they had a look—a walk—that set them apart.

Next, she drove south, across Lindsey Street, to park across the street from the Tri Delta house, where she'd lived as a student and now served as chapter adviser, where Karen wanted Melissa to live when she attended OU. Karen would someday have the privilege of pinning her own mother's sorority pin over her daughter's heart when Melissa was initiated into the sisterhood, becoming a third-generation Tri Delt.

Even now, as a woman of forty-seven, Karen found that her sorority membership was one of the identifying tags of her life—something newly introduced people asked her about at parties, after they'd found out who she was married to and where she'd gone to college.

The Tri Delt house, one of the largest on Fraternity Row, was an impressive red-brick Colonial, its grounds well kept, the young women going in and out well dressed, their long hair carefully sprayed into tousled perfection.

Sororities encouraged young women to be well-groomed, mind their manners, make the best grades they could, be sisterly to one another—and be sweet to everyone else. Sweetness was greatly prized. None of that had changed over the years. Sorority was a genteel way of life for those privileged enough to be invited inside.

Fraternities encouraged hazing; sororities sweetness. Yet this dichotomous system served as a mating ground for fraternity men and sorority women. Seldom did a Greek date an independent. For the most part, they kept to their own kind.

Each member of the Iota Beta house voluntarily came forward to be questioned by the police. Most of the boys who'd been at the party had seen Rosalie Frank. Only the ones who had been watching a rented porn video in the living room had missed seeing her dance —"dirty dancing," several of the boys had called it. Others described it as "suggestive." One fleshy young man called it "fuck-me dancing."

Gary even drove to Manhattan, Kansas, to the Iota Beta House at Kansas State University, and questioned the members who'd made the trip to Norman for the OU–KSU football game. The Iota Beta chapter in Manhattan was new on campus and much smaller that the one at OU.

None of KSU or OU Iota Betas who'd been at the party that night recalled seeing the Frank girl or her friend leave the house. And no one remembered seeing her pair off with any one boy. About half of the Norman IBs had dates and claimed to have left before the serious drinking began. Others were quite frank about drinking until they crawled into bed and passed out for the night. Gary found no reason to be suspicious of any one member. A few were real smart-asses, but mostly they were respectful and seemed to offer conscientious answers to his questions.

Next, Gary talked to girls who were present at the party—well dressed, mannerly sorority girls who called him "sir" when he questioned them, most in the gracious living rooms of their respective sorority houses. Two freshman pledges he saw in the lounge of their dormitory. Another freshman was from Norman and lived at home.

All of girls said they were certain that none of the IBs could have been involved in Rosalie Frank's disappearance. But several of them mentioned the girl's tight clothing, her drunken state.

Freshmen roommates Deeann Norton-Jones and Melanie Van Holt remembered seeing the two high-school girls. They hadn't known they were high-school girls, just that they were dressed differently than the other girls there, and one girl had bleached blond hair. Melanie, a tall slender girl from Tyler, Texas, did the talking. They had gone to the IB house with her twin brother, who was an IB pledge, she explained. But they left after one beer.

"Why?" Gary asked.

"Some of the boys must have been drinkin' all afternoon," Melanie said in her soft drawl. "They jus' weren't actin' very nice at all, and three of them started singin' really nasty songs. I could tell they were working up to a moonin'—or worse."

"And this was unusual?" Gary asked.

"Yeah. A little. But I might not have thought so

much about it—except we had Deeann with us. Her
father's a diplomat, and she went to a girls' school in
Europe. I'd seen drunk guys before, but suddenly they
just seemed so juvenile and crude. I didn't want Deeann to be sorry that she'd come here to school. So we
left and walked over to the Campus Corner. It was a
pretty night. Lots of kids were millin' around. A couple of guys were strummin' guitars on the street corner. No one was drunk. It was real nice.''

"The dark-haired girl—the one who's missing—
how was she acting?'' Gary asked Deeann, a fragile-
looking girl with white-blond hair and pale blue eyes.

"She was just standing there with her girlfriend.
They each had a cup of beer and weren't really doing
anything except looking around. I do hope you find
her,'' Deeann said, her hands clutched together in
her lap. "Her parents must be beside themselves with
worry.''

Gary thanked the girls, giving them each one of his
cards in case they thought of anything else to tell him.

The last girl he talked to was also a freshman. Lou
Ann Mitchell lived at home but explained that she
would move into the Theta house next fall, after she'd
made her grades and been initiated.

"Some of the people who were at the party seem to
think that Rosalie Frank came to the fraternity house
looking for sex. Did she seem to be acting that way to
you?'' Gary asked.

"'Well, she and her friend were the only cheap-
lookin' girls there,'' Lou Ann responded. "They kind
of stood out, 'specially since it wasn't an official party,
and the usual bevy of cotton whores wasn't in attendance.''

"Cotton whores?'' Gary said, not certain that he'd
heard correctly.

"Yes. Those are girls who collect the T-shirts that
frat guys give as party favors. Some of those girls dress

kind of trashy. But actually, I don't think Rosalie meant to look as bad as she did. She was in my geometry class at Norman High last spring. She came in at mid-year—from Oklahoma City, I think. She was quiet in class, but she was real smart in geometry, and sometimes the teacher had Rose put her solutions on the board. I always felt sorry for her, though. She didn't have nice clothes. I think she was embarrassed to be up there in front of the class."

"Did you speak to her at the party?"

"No. I just waved," Lou Ann admitted, looking down at her lap.

"How come?"

"I was double-dating with a pledge sister and her boyfriend. I didn't want to introduce her to them."

"Why?"

"Her clothes mostly. Rose didn't fit in. She knew it right away. I could tell. At first, she stood next to the girl she'd come with and looked around. But then someone gave her a drink, and she seemed to relax and started dancing some. We left not too long after that—when some of the members started singing dirty songs. I wish my boyfriend had pledged one of the other houses, but maybe they've all got their share of animals."

"So, some of the Iota Betas are animals. But you're certain that none of them could have had anything to do with Rose's disappearance?"

Lou Ann hesitated, a frown creasing her smooth forehead under its froth of frosted curls. "I guess I don't *want* any of them to have been involved. I wish that I'd talked to Rose. I keep thinking that if I had talked to her, then maybe she wouldn't have felt so uncomfortable and wouldn't have drunk so much."

"Do you think her drinking got her into trouble?"

"Yes, probably so. I think she was walking back to the Campus Corner, and some man picked her up

and raped her, then killed her and hid her body—
maybe it was one of those weird men from the state
mental hospital that walk all over town talking to
themselves. That one man wears an overcoat and
gloves when its a hundred degrees. Or maybe it was a
man from the hospital halfway house. It's just two
blocks away from the IB house. They all look so weird,
sitting out in the yard all day long. My parents say it's
disgraceful to let mental patients live by a college campus. Maybe you should look for Rose's body in the
basement of that place. Some of the IBs belch on pur-
pose and say crude things when they drink too much.
But they wouldn't hurt a girl.''

14

The next afternoon Karen drove to the downtown office of the *Norman Transcript* to purchase copies of last week's newspapers. Then she drove to sprawling Norman Regional Hospital in the northeast corner of town. She tucked two of the newspapers in her purse and found her way to Three West, where Inez Frank was working the three-to-eleven shift. Karen recognized the dark-haired nurse as the woman she had seen on television.

At first, Karen felt conspicuous lurking about the halls trying to catch glimpses of Nurse Frank as she entered notations on patients' charts and answered patients' calls. But there were a number of other visitors walking the halls, sitting in the lounge area. Some looking anxious. Others bored. One group in the corner of the lounge area was being led in prayer by a Bible-carrying minister wearing heavy sideburns, a navy-blue suit, and cowboy boots, asking the Lord with an upturned face and tightly closed eyes to heal Sister Thelma and restore her to her family.

She found a short article on page three of the previous day's *Transcript*, stating that Rosalie Frank was still missing. Police were investigating. Karen carefully tore the article from the page and put it in her purse.

Inez Frank had shiny dark hair and smooth olive skin, a bosom too large for her slim body. She was quite lovely in a quiet way—but tired looking. She kept trying to square her shoulders, but they would fall back into a weary sag.

Finally, with a pounding heart, Karen approached her. "Excuse me. Is Wilson Jones a patient on this floor?"

Nurse Frank frowned and checked a chart. "No. Our only patient named Jones is a woman. You might check downstairs at the information desk. In the lobby."

Her voice was low and soft. Polite. Had this woman raised a daughter who went to a fraternity house "hot to trot" and never came home?

Karen longed to do something for Inez Frank. Cook for her. Clean her house. Replace the missing screen on her window. Give her money. Buy her a new car. Take the woman in her arms and tell her how sorry she was about her daughter. About her Rosalie. Even wild girls had mothers who loved them and wanted the best for them and worried every day about something terrible happening.

The last pink tinge of sunset clung to the horizon as Karen started home. Her family would be wondering where she was, why she hadn't cooked their dinner. She hadn't even called to say she'd be late. Yet, she felt remarkably unconcerned. *Let someone worry about her for a change.* After almost twenty-five years with a perfect record, she was entitled to be AWOL for an evening. She even stopped for coffee at the Moore McDonald's.

When she turned onto her street, the streetlights already were on. Lots of streetlights. Dover Lane where the Frank family lived wouldn't have so many.

How remarkably large some of these houses were. Some big enough to be fraternity houses—or hotels. Most of them had more floor space in their living room than the Franks had in their entire dwelling.

The windows in Melissa's room were dark. The

light was on in Roger's study and in Chad's room. Tomorrow was Chad's twentieth birthday. The grandfathers were coming to dinner. And Brenda. Chad didn't want anyone else invited. Not Brenda's parents. Not any of his high-school or college friends.

The kitchen was untouched. Roger must have taken the children out to dinner. Or at least Chad. Melissa had probably thought of an excuse not to go with them.

Roger was at his desk in the study. Karen paused at the open doorway. "I'm home," she said.

He stood. "Come in and close the door. We need to talk."

Karen hesitated, then did as he asked, taking a seat on the sofa. Sitting up straight. Not leaning back. Not planning to stay long.

"Can I get you a drink?" he asked.

"No."

He gave her a surprised look at this break in the ritual. Drinks added civility to marital discussions. "Don't you feel well?" he asked.

"I'm giving up booze for now. Maybe permanently. Maybe just limiting myself to wine. I haven't decided."

He laughed. A wave of irritation swept through Karen.

"Now, what in the hell brought that on?" he asked.

"I'm tired of hangovers. And how can we expect our children not to abuse alcohol when we drink almost every damned night?"

"Come on, Karen. A sociable drink or two in the evening doesn't set a bad example for anyone," he said while pointedly pouring himself a finger of scotch from the Waterford decanter she had given him for Christmas last year. He'd given her a Rolex. She stared down at it. Who had decided that such watches were the "in" status symbol? They weren't even pretty.

Glass in hand, Roger began to pace. He did that

before serious conversations, seeming to weigh his
words. It was his way of showing that what he was
about to say was a matter of great concern.

When had he started doing that? Karen wasn't sure.
As a young husband, he'd never paced. Maybe it came
with being an attorney. Pacing back and forth in front
of the jury. Pausing for effect.

"What's going on with the house? Why are you
changing everything?" he demanded.

"I always change the house. You like to make jokes
about it at parties."

"Yes, but before you were always moving things
around," he said, stopping in front of her. She didn't
want to look up at him and didn't want to stare at his
crotch, so she sagged out of her ramrod posture and
slumped against the back of the sofa. She realized that
she still had a headache. She closed her eyes. Which
helped. Getting out of this room would help more.

"And you're always buying new things for the
house," she heard him say, his voice going back in
front of her as he resumed his pacing. "But now
you're taking things away. Taking down pictures. Taking away pillows and vases and candle holders. The
new silk flower arrangement from the dining room for
which you just spent hundreds of dollars has vanished
from view. What's going on, Karen?"

He had stopped again. In front of her.

Karen got up and perched on the corner of his
desk, her arms folded across her chest. "I thought the
house looked cluttered. I'm trying out a different
look."

"Did you forget that Chad was coming home tonight?"

"Of course not. Tomorrow's his birthday."

"But you weren't here. There was no dinner. No
message on the answering machine. No note."

"I know."

"Where did you go?"

"To Norman."

"Again? Jesus, Karen! Why?" He stopped pacing.

"I wanted to look around," she explained. "To think. This afternoon I went to the hospital to see what that girl's mother looks like. She's a nurse. A dignified woman. I went to see their house yesterday. Now I need to know what the little brother looks like. Sammy is his name."

Roger looked stunned. He shook his head back and forth. "But why?" he asked.

"I can't explain why. I can't even explain why I'm telling you, except maybe I want you to know how disturbing all this has been for me."

"Did you talk to her—to that girl's mother?"

"Yes. I wanted to hear her voice. But she doesn't know who I am."

"My God, Karen. That's so irresponsible. What if someone saw you?" He began pacing again, his forehead knitted into a scowl. "With every boy in Iota Beta a potential suspect, this family needs to distance itself from that girl's family, from the whole situation. You haven't talked to anyone about it, have you?"

"You mean, have I told anyone that our son had sex with Rosalie Frank before she vanished off the face of the earth? No, I haven't."

Roger said nothing for a minute. Debating. She could see it on his face. How much more should he tell her? Then, his decision made, he sighed. "Karen, this could be a very serious matter. That girl was falling-down drunk. What happened to her might be construed as rape. You absolutely must not say anything to anyone. Not to Melissa. Not to our fathers. Not anyone."

She stared at him. "Chad *raped* that girl?"

"Technically, yes. It's a real mess, Karen. I'm violating the trust of those boys telling you this. And please don't tell Chad that you know. But you have to realize that Chad's future and that of some other very fine boys is on the line.''

"Very fine boys? Who could be charged with rape? Good God, Roger! I can't believe I'm hearing this.''

"She was semiconscious," he explained, his tone more businesslike. They were facing each other now, Roger standing behind the sofa. "And boys will be boys," he added with a shrug. "They lined up for her. And never saw her again.''

"*Boys will be boys?* How can you stand there and say that—like you actually believe such behavior is to be expected? That they were just behaving the way any other boys would behave when the body of a helpless girl is there for the taking? Would you have done something like that? Have you done something like that?''

"No, not really," he said wearily. "The only woman I've ever forced is you—on the nights when you tell me with all the body language at your command that you'd prefer not to have sex but never utter a word of protest.''

She put a hand on the desk to steady herself. How deep this all went. All the way to bedrock. "And you do it anyway," she whispered.

Roger nodded. "Yes. There you are, naked under one of your thin little nighties, and on other nights you're hot as a pistol. So, I figure, what the hell. Sometimes I prefer it that way. Just sex. Functional, if you will. No words to complicate the process. And I don't face any sort of prison term for taking advantage of your passivity. Yet those boys could be in big trouble if what they did ever becomes known, and that girl was sauced out of her head and probably has no memory of what happened.''

"Especially if she's dead," Karen said, feeling ill, hating him, wanting to throw something at him, hit him, claw at his face, spit at him—this husband of hers who suddenly seemed like a stranger. Like the enemy. "Do you really believe that Rosalie Frank just conveniently vanished?"

She glared at him, waiting for his answer. "Well, do you?"

"Something unfortunate could have happened to her after she stumbled out of the IB house in the middle of the night. Some other person could have picked her up. If she turns up dead, we don't want anything brought out that would connect her to Chad and those boys. We don't want the police to figure out that six boys at the IB house had sex with her. We don't want those boys convicted of some crime on circumstantial evidence. So, surely you can see that you have to stop behaving so irresponsibly. *You have to stay away from Norman.*"

He came around the sofa and grabbed her arms, pulling her face close to his, his fingers squeezing into the flesh of her upper arms. "Do you understand me, Karen? *Stay away from Norman.*"

"You didn't answer my question, counselor. I'm not asking what *might* have happened to Rosalie Frank. I'm asking if you believe those boys really don't know. If you believe they had no part in her disappearance."

"God, Karen. I don't even know you." She could smell the bourbon on his breath. His fingers were pressing too hard. Hurting. Deliberately inflicting pain. Leaving bruises.

She said nothing and waited until he finally relaxed his grip, and she could pull away.

She hurried from the room, through her altered house. In her bathroom, she sat on the toilet seat and sobbed. Her careful world was in shambles. Perhaps beyond rebuilding. Never to be the same again.

And she was afraid. So afraid. *Her son had raped a girl.*

She slipped from the toilet seat and curled into a ball on the floor. It was too much. Too much. Not Chad. Not her boy.

She stayed there for a time, on the cold hard tile, grief and fear eating away at her stomach and brain.

Finally, she pulled herself to her knees and then her feet. When she removed her clothes, she could see the beginnings of bruises on her upper arms. Bruises from her husband. Like the women at the shelter. And her son had raped a girl.

Roger found her like that, staring at herself in the mirror. He stared with her. "God, Karen, I'm so sorry. So very sorry."

She held him while he cried. He was just as scared as she was, it seemed.

15

Saturday morning, Karen did the necessary shopping for Chad's birthday dinner. She hadn't made a grocery list and was forced to think as she pushed the cart up and down the aisles. A celebratory meal. Standing rib. Nonroutine vegetables and salad. Cake. Ice cream. Candles. Dinner rolls from La Baguette. A nice chablis. Champagne for after-dinner toasts. She couldn't remember what she had at home so she just bought.

How inconceivable that she should be grocery shopping for her son's birthday dinner the morning after discovering that he had raped a girl. Karen felt drugged. Not quite in touch. She saw a woman she knew from Junior League. Knew rather well. And couldn't remember her name.

But somehow she got through it, got everything out of the car. And started going through the motions. Karen, the cook.

Brenda arrived midafternoon, looking like a news-paper ad for Harold's in a navy blazer, tan silk shirt, southwestern-look wraparound skirt, silver Indian jew-elry, woven cordovan loafers, and a navy-and-tan gros-grain bow in her blond hair. She took off the blazer, tied on an apron, and insisted on helping, peeling potatoes, washing salad greens, full of chatter about school, about her parents, about her newly married sister. "Their apartment is darling. My folks paid for the furniture. His folks bought the appliances—even a

141

food processor and a bread maker. But it sure is weird to see my sister being a wife.''

"Why? How is she different?'' Karen asked as she peeked in the oven to check the meat thermometer.

"For one thing, she's so tired. And no fun. She works all day and has to shop for groceries and clean house at night. Brad helps some. He takes out the trash and stops at the cleaners. Stuff like that. And Susan worries a lot about what Brad will think—like Mom used to be about Dad before she became a Gloria Steinem convert. Will Brad like the casserole? Will he be mad because she forgot to buy shaving soap? Should she tell him that she charged some winter clothes to Mom's account at Foley's? Should she cut her hair without asking him—but what if he says that he doesn't want her to and she doesn't have time to mess with it anymore and still get to work by eight o'clock? It's really weird.''

Karen knew she should comment. Say that Susan was still a bride. Things would change. Marriage didn't have to be like that. But she wasn't sure just how marriage should be. Not anymore.

Normally, Karen took a great deal of pleasure in being with Brenda and feeling that she was a friend to the girl her son probably would marry. It was easier to be with Brenda than it was with Melissa. Karen wondered if Brenda was distant with her own mother—and if Melissa was charming and friendly with Trevor's mother. Perhaps it was some sort of cultural pattern that they were acting out. A transference of allegiance from one family to another. Young women in love impatient to leave their mother's domain. As Karen herself had been. Ready to live only for love.

A sudden memory flashed across Karen's mind of a group of motorcyclists thundering past her on the highway. Years ago. Going incredibly fast, like the wind. A hundred miles an hour. Passing Karen's car like it wasn't moving. Leather-clad hairy men, each with a woman on the seat behind him. Karen glanced at one couple as they flew by, and for just half an instant in time, found herself looking into the face of rapture.

A slender young girl, no helmet, long hair whipping around her face, her arms around her man, eyes closed, her cheek resting against his broad leather back, her life in his hands. *Totally* in his hands. The ultimate surrender. One miscalculation on his part, and she could die the next instant.

Karen had had a hard time shaking the disturbing image of that girl's face. A face from a religious painting. But how could she abdicate all responsibility for her own life? *How could she?*

Yet had Karen herself been so different? Blindly riding into the wind. Trusting completely.

How much easier it had been. The agony had begun when she stopped trusting and started questioning. Yet she was proud of Brenda for questioning, for being disturbed by a sister who had gone from courtship to a tightrope.

"I'm worried about Chad," Brenda confided as she put candles in his birthday cake. Karen had made Chad's favorite. Chocolate with caramel icing. Her mother's cake recipe—written in her own hand. It called for mayonnaise and cocoa. The cake Karen herself had always wanted on her birthday.

"Oh? Why is that?" Karen asked, focusing her attention on this small, bright, vivacious girl who loved her son.

"Well, maybe I shouldn't be telling you this," Brenda said in a tone that indicated she would anyway. "Chad said that he hasn't talked it over with you and Mr. Billingsly. But he wants us to transfer to Oklahoma State next semester. I don't want to go to OSU. I could affiliate with the Chi Omega chapter at Stillwater, but it wouldn't be the same. I want to stay at OU with my sorority sisters *and* with Chad. He'll get over it, don't you think—wanting to transfer? Maybe he's just worried about his grades. He never should have taken Japanese and calculus the same semester. And he's had a falling-out of some sort over at the fraternity house. Johnny Fontaine dropped out of school, and Chad won't even talk about it. He says that we're not going to the guest dinner tomorrow evening. He doesn't want to go to the toga party, and I've already got my costume. You won't tell him that I told you about OSU, will you? But don't you agree with me that it's a bad idea? OSU's a cow college. We'd be *Aggies*."

"If he transfers, would you go with him?"

Brenda hesitated, then nodded, a frown creasing her forehead, her green eyes full of confusion and concern. "If I thought I'd lose him, I guess I'd have to. But that would be so unfair. It would break my heart to leave OU. All my friends are here. My sorority sisters."

Melissa seemed subdued. She had changed out of her jeans without being told. She slipped into her chair wearing a plaid skirt and navy sweater, her hair in a ponytail rather than curled. Karen was somewhat surprised and relieved that Melissa hadn't insisted on including Trevor in her brother's birthday celebration.

The grandfathers came to the table in coats and ties, Roger in a golf shirt and slacks. Chad wore khaki pants and a madras shirt, his blond hair carefully combed. Karen was wearing slacks, a silk blouse, gold choker, her dark hair brushed to one side and held in place with an ivory comb. Roger said she looked lovely. Her father said she looked anemic. Before calling everyone to the table, she had gone upstairs to look at herself in the mirror. She did look pale. Not

lovely. She'd added more blush, freshened her lipstick. And put on the earrings that she'd forgotten
earlier.

With his usual flair, Roger carved the roast. Melissa
pushed her food around the plate, eating only three
tiny bites of meat and one of potatoes. Brenda was
Karen's self-appointed helper and kept filling everyone's water and wine glasses, running back and forth
to the kitchen to keep the breadbasket supplied with
hot rolls. Chad was quiet, avoiding his mother's gaze,
not in a celebratory mood.

If only his birthday had been last Friday night,
Karen thought irrationally, Chad would have been at
this table and not at a party at the Iota Beta house.
And she would only have Melissa's problems to deal
with. As it was, Karen wasn't sure which of her children was in deeper trouble.

Karen took a sip of wine, then pushed the glass
away. She didn't need any more, didn't really want it.

Walt, Roger's father, was asking the three young
people about school, about the books they were reading. He was pleased that Chad was taking Japanese
and recommended that Chad read Kenko's essays for
insight into traditional Japanese attitudes toward life.
He saw no reason why Brenda shouldn't continue with
her math studies and take advantage of her talent.
"But don't neglect literature and the natural sciences," he said. "They'll make you richer than
money."

Her father and Roger discussed state politics—
more irregularities in the last gubernatorial race were
surfacing. You'd think that candidates would be more
careful. Vernon wanted to know if Roger had thought
any more about running for the state legislature.

Karen wondered, too. He'd been talking to people.
Now he'd have to wait and see what happened with
Chad.

Her father looked impressive as always. Vernon Fullerton's mane of silver hair was carefully styled. His expensive suit had a European cut that showed off a still-youthful body, the result of tennis and daily visits to the gym. And he exuded an aura of power. He always had. Karen had been aware from the time she was a small child that people were in awe of her father. Even her mother. Karen less so. She was the princess. Her father still called her that sometimes.

Looking back, Karen realized that she had been attracted to Roger because, even as a college student, she saw in him a man who would someday be as powerful and impressive as her father.

Yet she had grown to love her gentle, soft-spoken father-in-law almost as much as her own father. At times more. When Chad and Melissa were growing up, Walter Billingsly had always had time to take them to the zoo or to read to them by the hour. He helped them plant gardens and make bird feeders. He'd taught them about nature until they got too old to care.

Roger had clerked in Vernon Fullerton's law office during law-school summers. Roger admired Vernon above all men. His own father was an embarrassment.

Whenever the grandfathers came from Tulsa, it was taken for granted that Vernon would bring Walt, who had always depended on his wife's navigational skills. Now, as an aging widower, he got lost if he went farther than a few miles from his home. And he seemed a bit more rumpled every time Karen saw him, his tweedy wardrobe aging along with him.

Until his retirement, Walt had been a botany professor at the University of Tulsa. For thirty-seven years. He knew the phylum and genus of every plant—modern day and prehistoric. But he didn't know his way across the city in which he had lived for most of his adult life. He couldn't balance a checkbook or figure

out how to use a credit card to make a long-distance
telephone call. His wife had done everything—including the raising of their son and using her own money
to pay for and maintain a fine house in Tulsa's affluent Southern Hills that a college professor never
could have afforded. Roger had learned strength and
organization from his mother. From his father, he
learned the difference between deciduous and
nondeciduous plants. And learned that, beyond earning his bachelor's and law degrees, he wanted nothing
to do with academia, where—in his harsh estimation
—ineffectual people used scholarly pursuits to escape
from the real world.

Karen understood that, at least in part, Roger
blamed his father's weakness on his mother's strength.
If she had been less strong, maybe Walt would have
been less passive. Roger had loved his mother. Admired her. And grieved sincerely when she died. But
he would never have wanted to marry a woman like
her. Never. Karen realized that her husband had been
attracted to her in a marrying kind of way because she
was sweet and accommodating. Like her own mother.
Not like his mother.

After dinner, Melissa went out with a group of girlfriends. Which pleased Karen. A Saturday night with
someone other than Trevor. Maybe she'd slip up and
eat a french fry.

Chad and Brenda played a couple of rubbers of
bridge with Walt and Vernon before Brenda headed
back to Norman, obviously disappointed that Chad
had not arranged for them to have some time to
themselves. Karen could hear them in the hall. "Just
for a little while," Brenda was saying. Pleading. "Just a
little drive."

"Tomorrow evening. I promised my dad I'd hang
around tonight."

After the grandfathers had sipped their brandy and

gone upstairs, Roger announced that he and Chad
were going for a jog, maybe stop by the health club to
work out.

Karen sat in the family room for a time, staring at
the television screen, taking an occasional stitch in her
latest needlepoint project—a Christmas stocking for
the Tri Delt alumnae bazaar.

Last night she hadn't been able to sleep. Neither
had Roger. He had wanted to love away the bruises on
her arms—and the memory of how they got there.
She actually had refused him—with words rather than
body language. Of course, she softened her rejection
by saying she was too upset, too worried. He had retreated to his side of the bed, and they lay there side
by side, staring at the dark ceiling, surrounded by silence. Finally, Karen could stand it no longer and
slipped wordlessly from the bed to finish out the night
in the number-two guest room, where she could at
least toss and turn without worrying about disturbing
Roger.

This morning he had not commented on her defec-
tion from their bed.

Tonight, both guest rooms were occupied by the
grandfathers. She considered making herself a bed on
the sofa. But that would openly announce marital discord to the children and grandfathers.

She put away the needlepoint, unable to concentrate even on mindless background stitches, and went
to take a bath. She was in bed when she heard Roger
and Chad come in, heard the door to the study close.

She was in a house with five other people and had
never felt so alone. Karen rolled over and gathered
her husband's pillow in her arms. Buried her face in
it. Inhaled his scent. She loved him and needed him.
More than anything, she wanted their family and their
marriage to endure. But a volcano was erupting,
changing the landscape of her soul, either covering it

completely or baring it to the elements—she wasn't sure which.

She imagined them downstairs in the study—her son and husband. The jogging, the lifting of weights, would have been a preliminary. Roger conducted family business from his study. The seat of power.

She should be there, hearing what was being said firsthand. She was the mother. But Chad had stopped turning to her in a crisis years ago. Not since skinned knees and visits to the principal's office.

16

*A*lmost an hour later Karen heard Chad come up the stairs, the door to his bedroom open and close. She slipped into her robe and slippers.

Roger was still in the study, hunched forward in his leather chair, his face buried in his hands.

For an instant Karen would have preferred to stop living rather than face what she could no longer deny. Her knees gave way, and she sank onto the sofa where Chad would have been sitting minutes before, finally confessing completely his sins to a father who could no longer accept half-truths.

The ceiling fan was turning at the slowest speed, making a tiny rubbing sound with each rotation. The mantel clock ticked with unaccustomed loudness. Slowly. Dragging time out.

Karen hugged her arms tightly to her body, holding herself together. "Rosalie Frank is dead," she said over the ticking. Not a question. A statement of fact. *Dead.*

Still hunched over, Roger looked up at her, his face naked, in pain. Older. His hair mussed. No longer a man in charge of a perfectly ordered life. Karen felt a stab of pity.

"Tell me," she demanded, her voice catching, her heart drumming away in her chest, perspiration collecting under her arms, between her breasts, on the inside of her thighs.

With visible effort, Roger collected himself, sitting up straight, clearing his throat and taking a breath before he began speaking. Woodenly. A recitation of the facts. "Chad's not quite sure how it happened. They left her passed-out, on her back, but her head was hanging over the edge of the sofa when one of the boys went upstairs to get her out of the house. Probably she aspirated her vomit. Or it could be alcohol poisoning. An allergic reaction to the drugs. A stroke. A heart attack. No way to know. But whatever, she was dead. They tried CPR," he added lamely.

"My God, Roger. You mean she died there in the *fraternity house?*"

An image of Inez Frank in her white uniform and lovely sad face flashed into Karen's mind. Inez hoping against hope. And her daughter was never coming home. *Never.*

"Yes," Roger said, no challenge in his voice. "She died in the Iota Beta house. In a room on the fourth floor. They panicked, and two of the boys took her body out to Lake Thunderbird."

"They threw her in a lake? Like a sack of garbage?"

Roger nodded. "Off the dam. I was appalled at first. But they hadn't murdered her, hadn't meant to harm her at all. But they could be held responsible for her death and had to figure their way out of a situation that could ruin their lives. Thunderbird's a good-sized lake. Quite deep by the dam. They weighted the body with bricks. If they're lucky, it will never be found. It probably wouldn't be the first time. I imagine there are other corpses down there."

"And it's all right with you that they did that? You sound as though you're condoning their actions."

Roger hung his head a bit, avoiding her gaze. "I don't know. Maybe I am. If they'd called the police right away, the case would have been more defensible.

Manslaughter. Some jail time. But now? They will either get away with it altogether or have gotten themselves in a situation that's a lot worse. If they'd called the police right away and turned themselves in, think of the damage to their reputations. To those of their families. Forever after, they would be associated with the incident. Like Ted Kennedy with Chappaquiddick. So, who knows, maybe their way will turn out to be for the best—provided that everyone keeps his mouth shut for a lifetime. No one can prove that the girl was raped at the IB house. No one can prove that she never left there alive. But if the case had gone to trial, some hotshot prosecutor would try to make a name for himself by ruining the lives—with full media coverage—of six boys from prominent families."

With his hands clutching the arms of the chair, Roger looked her full in the face. More in control now. His expression growing hard. Ugly even. "You had to know, didn't you? Had to push until you found out what happened. Well, I hope you're satisfied. Personally, I would have preferred to live the rest of my life never knowing. Chad wanted to protect us from all this. And now I wonder if anything will ever be the same again."

"You make it sound as though it's my fault."

He closed his eyes for a time, shifting gears. "No, Karen, nothing is your fault. But you've got to let it drop now, like it never happened."

But it did happen. And Karen knew it was, at least in part, her fault. Their fault. Chad was their son. They had raised him.

She stared down at her hands. Chipped polish. She'd missed her manicure this week. Thursday. She'd been in Norman.

"I don't understand how Chad could have done something like that—behave like an animal," she said, still looking at her hands.

Roger leaned back against the high back of his chair. "They were young and horny. They didn't think."

"And you can accept that this happened? You can excuse Chad for being involved?"

"I have no choice. You don't either. He's our son. We repair the damage and go on."

"But the damage is a dead girl. You can't repair that. And what about her family? Her mother who doesn't know if she's dead or alive?"

"I'm talking about the damage to our son and to this family. I'm sorry about the girl. Sorry for her family. But the family that I care most about is this one. And we will survive, goddamn it!" he said, clenching his jaw, slamming fist against hand. "*We will survive.* Our son's name will not be dragged through the mud. His future will not be destroyed. Do you think that Brenda's parents—or any other girl's parents—would want their daughter to marry a man convicted of rape and murder? Do you think he'd get accepted to law school? Do you think anyone would hire him? We have to manage this thing. We have to keep our boy out of it."

"And you can just act normally toward him? Good old Dad ready to lend a helping hand?"

"Yes, I can because he needs for me to. And you will continue to be good old Mom with cookies in the jar. He needs that, too—more than ever now. He needs our love and support. In the morning I want you to fix waffles. Act normal."

"Does he know that I know?"

"Yes, I told him that you'd all but guessed the truth. That I would tell you the rest."

Karen rose from the chair and tied her robe more closely about her body. She'd lost weight, she realized. She paused by her husband's chair, hoping he would reach out to her, touch her hand. But his eyes were closed, his hands limp on the arms of the chair.

She climbed the stairs, walked down the long hall, past the family pictures, past the bedroom she shared with her husband of twenty-five years, past the closed door to her daughter's room, and stood finally in front of the door to her son's room—a mother about to confront a son who had committed an act so despicable it would make her loathe any other male.

Chad was sitting on his bed, leaning against the headboard, an unopened textbook on his lap. Normally, she would sit down beside him on the bed. Touch his arm. His hair. Anything for physical contact.

But this meeting of mother and son was not a normal one.

Karen leaned against the dresser, arms folded, and stared at him. This beautiful son. Had she loved too much? Was all this somehow her fault for loving her son more than anyone else? For worshipfully admiring his beauty? For needing to touch him? For wishing she could touch him more? Had she raised him to think that he would never be held accountable for misdeeds? That he had special privileges in this world?

Chad threw out the first volley. "Dad says you don't understand."

"And what is it that I don't understand?"

"That the girl came looking for it. She wanted to find a guy to have sex with."

"Perhaps. *A* guy. Not six guys. And I am quite certain she didn't want to die."

"It was an accident. Just a lousy accident. But she took the risk of something bad happening when she walked in the front door of a fraternity house dressed like that."

"Is that what your father said?"

Chad nodded, his chin with an arrogant tilt. *My father says so.* Fathers and God can't be wrong.

"So, when a girl walks into a fraternity house wearing tight clothes, she runs the risk of dying?" Karen asked, amazed at her calmness. At her logic. "That's a pretty stiff penalty for being a little horny, don't you think? And tell me, before your father presented you with this explanation—with this justification—what thoughts were you having about what happened?"

He frowned, his chin dropping just a little. "I don't know what you want me to say."

"I want you to tell me what was in your heart while all this was happening and how you felt about it afterward."

"What difference does it make? It happened."

"Yes, *it* happened. Until it happened, I always thought that my love for my children was unconditional. That's how a mother's love is supposed to be. I thought that fathers need more—fathers need children to reflect well on them and make them feel good about themselves and fatherhood. But mothers visit sons on death row. I always thought that mothers loved no matter what. But now I find that this may not be so. Or maybe I'm not such a good mother after all. Because I need to know that *you* know what you did was unjustifiably wrong. That it's tearing you apart—like it's tearing me apart. That you're filled with self-loathing. That you'll never be the same again. That you'll live with the image of that poor dead girl until the day you die. Because if I don't know deep in my heart that you feel that way, I'm not sure I can go on loving you."

"But Dad says that it's my duty to pick up the pieces and go on. That nothing any of us can do will bring that girl back, so there's no point in ruining everyone's life, in putting six families through all that. Or the fraternity. Even the university."

"She has a name, you know. Rosalie Frank. I'd like to hear you say her name."

He looked away. "No. I don't want to do that."

"Why not?"

"Because I just don't!" he said angrily. "It's stupid."

"It's stupid to admit that she was a real person with a name? Let's take it one step further. Rosalie Frank had a mother who loved her. She had a father and a brother. And now she's dead. How do you suppose her family would feel about the boys who did this to their Rosalie 'just picking up the pieces and going on'? What if it was Melissa or Brenda on the bottom of Lake Thunderbird? Would you want the boys who did such a thing to them simply to pick up the pieces and go on?"

His mouth twisted into an ugly grimace. "Brenda and Melissa wouldn't have gone to a fraternity house late at night without a date and dressed like a whore dog."

"So, we're back to that. Rosalie Frank was asking for it. Then what happened to her was okay?"

His hands gestured impatiently. "Not okay. An *accident,* for Christ's sake! Why are you being like this, Mom?" he said, his forehead creased in puzzlement. "Jesus, you're like someone else. I've always counted on you to make me feel better and tell me everything is going to be all right."

"And I've always counted on you to be a decent human being. But you acted like an animal. A depraved animal who contributed to the death of a young girl who had just as much right to life as any of her attackers. Who had all of her rights taken away from her—the right to say no, the right to live on."

"Why are you taking her side?" he demanded, his tone righteous.

"Her *side?* My God, Chad! Rosalie Frank is dead!"

"I didn't start it! I didn't take her upstairs. Dad says that's important if it ever comes to trial."

"But you didn't stop it. You didn't say, 'This is wrong.' And you took your turn. You *violated* her. How could a boy who has a sister and a mother and a girl-friend he says he's in love with not stop what happened to Rosalie Frank? What made you think it was all right to do that? What made you want to?"

"She wasn't even conscious most of the time. She was so full of gin and drugs, she probably wouldn't have remembered most of it. If she hadn't died, who knows? She might have come back for more."

Karen walked across the room and slapped him. Hard. This beautiful young man she had birthed and raised and adored.

"I didn't raise my son to rape," she said, looking down at him, seeing the mark of her hand on his face, unmoved by the tears in his eyes. "What you did was wrong. I don't know what's going to happen to you or this family. If your father has his way, no one will ever know what happened to that poor girl. But whether it remains a secret or whether you go to prison, what you did was wrong. There is no justification. No explaining it away. No blaming it on tight clothes. It was wrong. Hideously wrong."

17

*H*e wasn't a bad person. He'd done stupid things but not bad things.

Last year his sociology professor conducted a survey of several hundred undergraduate males. Chad had been one of only forty-two percent who said no, that they would never rape a girl even if they were absolutely certain they could get away with it. He had been shocked at the results of the survey. Told Brenda how shocked he was. Were young American males really so depraved? He even had felt superior knowing that he wasn't like that.

So how had this happened? How could one of the good guys have done what he thought he'd never do and be up to his eyeballs in hot shit?

Why had he jumped at the chance—and taken poor Johnny up there with him to get laid for the first time?

He'd been borderline drunk—at that stage when he felt like a cross between Superman and a porn star. The stage when sex was best. When jokes were funniest. When he loved his buddies intensely. When putting an Alfa-Romeo from a rival fraternity parking lot on top of a garbage Dumpster and other sorts of mischief seemed like hilarious fun.

It had never occurred to him to say no, that he really didn't want to have gang sex with an anonymous girl. Not until he walked into the room had he realized that he wanted no part of it. And then it was too late.

The room reeked of semen and sweat. Vomit and urine.

The girl had thrown up onto a sofa cushion and someone had tossed it into the corner. The girl had peed all over the cushion under her hips.

A reading lamp on the corner table was turned so that it spotlighted the action on the sofa. The rest of the room was in shadows.

Chad stood with Johnny in the shadows, leaning against the file cabinets that lined one wall. Carter and Jackson were sitting backward on metal folding chairs, their expressions transfixed, as they watched the two bodies on the sofa. Todd was on his hands and knees in the corner, still gasping with exertion, his pants and underwear around his ankles.

Benton was on the girl, the fat of his flabby white buttocks rippling as he pumped up and down.

The blindfolded girl was not quite conscious—the blindfold had been Carter's idea, a precautionary measure. But he claimed the girl wouldn't say a word. Girls like her never did—girls who had perhaps gotten more than they bargained for but sure as hell had been asking for it in the first place. Everyone saw the way she'd been dancing. Every male there knew that her pussy was hot and wet.

The only word that she had spoken was "no"—over and over in a soft litany. Then she was quiet. Her legs limp, flopped open. Her head hanging over the edge of the cushion.

Benton was talking to her as though she were listening. "What do you think of that, bitch? Pretty good stuff, huh?" Then his monologue changed to a series of "fucks" and "shits" as he entered the final frenzy, pumping furiously. Banging the girl. Slamming against her. Holding nothing back.

She began to scream, arms flailing. Carter stepped
forward and placed a hand over her mouth and held
it there until her body once again went limp. Then he
stepped out of his khaki pants and began fondling his
engorged penis, preparing for his turn. As he took his
place on top of her, the girl's swollen lips began to
move, once again mouthing "no" over and over. But
her body was limp.

She was a high-school girl who worked as a waitress
at a Campus Corner hangout. Carter had invited her
and her girlfriend to the party when they got off work.
They came about eleven, the party already loud from
beer and booze and even some coke.

Loose girls, by the look of them. Tight sweaters,
short skirts, lots of makeup, high-heeled boots. The
college girls in their smart blazers, tailored skirts, and
expensive loafers had turned away and rolled their
eyes at the sight of them. *Can you believe those two?*

The girl was still wearing her cheap patent leather
boots. Her skirt was high around her waist, her panty
hose and underpanties ripped open, exposing an
abundant bush of black pubic hair. Her sweater and
bra were ripped open. And there was blood. Down
there. She was on her period apparently. Not a lot of
blood, but it kept oozing out of her, staining the already wet cushion.

The other high-school girl had been wary, refusing
a second beer. This girl went from beer to gin. Probably she'd sniffed some, too. She hadn't protested
when Carter and Benton took her in the downstairs
john and felt her up. That's where she passed out.
They carried her up the back staircase through the
deserted upper reaches of the house to the window-
less fourth-floor storeroom where they had sex with
her unconscious body. She still had been unconscious
later when they'd brought the other four brothers upstairs to share the bounty.

The girl was silent, passed out again. Which was better. She may have been looking for sex, but this was cruel and ugly. Wrong. Most certainly wrong.

The stench in the airless room was overwhelming.

Chad felt sick. And afraid. His turn was next.

And then it would be Johnny's. *Jesus, what had he gotten poor Johnny into?*

But Chad managed.

And Johnny, too. Somehow. He was shaking like a leaf, but his penis was erect as he mounted the girl.

He came almost at once, his body shuddering. "Atta boy!" Chad had said. "Atta boy."

Carter said that he'd take care of the girl. After everyone was in bed, he'd come get her, check her into a motel to sleep it off. And maybe do her again, he said with a wink, when she was awake enough to appreciate it. They all gave him money—for the motel and more than a hundred dollars to stuff into her pocketbook. A night's wages. Paying had made it almost seem all right.

Chad had already showered and fallen across his bed when Carter came creeping into the room, kneeling by Chad's bed.

"I went back up to get the girl," he whispered, panic in his voice. "Jesus, Billingsly, she's *dead*!"

"What the hell are you talking about?" Chad whispered back, rousing himself on one elbow.

"She's fuckin' dead! That's what I'm talkin' about. I swear she is," Carter said hoarsely. "*Dead*. I tried that CPR stuff, but she even feels dead."

Across the room, in his narrow bed, Johnny heard and cried out.

"Shut up," Carter hissed. "You'll wake up the whole house."

Johnny buried his face in his pillow, muffling moans.

"No way," Chad mumbled, half falling out of his bed, heading for the door, stumbling up the stairs to see for himself. *No way.*

Benton was in the room. And Todd. Benton was holding the girl's head by her hair and slapping her. Vomit spurted out of her mouth. Which made Chad think for an instant she was alive. But she wasn't.

"Wake up, bitch," Benton kept saying, hitting her hard, over and over, until finally Todd pulled him away.

Desperately, Chad jabbed at her throat, searching for a pulse. Her skin was cold, rubbery. Like a rubber doll. He couldn't breathe. Couldn't move. Couldn't react.

Dead. The word thudded against the sides of Chad's mind. Like a medicine ball thrown against a gym wall. Over and over. *Dead.*

The girl couldn't be dead. It made no sense. No one had hurt her. Not really. She was passed out drunk, but that didn't kill a person.

Carter, calmer now, was speculating that she could've drowned in her own vomit. Or maybe a blood vessel in her brain had burst. Her head had been hanging over the edge of the sofa.

Chad was sweating. A lot. This couldn't be happening to him. This was worse than anything. Even his powerful lawyer father wouldn't be able to make the reality of that dead girl go away.

And with that realization, disbelief began to turn to fear. Sickening fear. He felt his insides turning to liquid. And raced down the stairs to the third-floor head but still soiled himself. Shit in his underwear. Shit running down his leg. He washed himself and threw away the underwear.

He went to his room for fresh underwear. And a

pair of jeans. Johnny was sitting up on the bed, clutching a pillow to his chest. "Is she really dead?"

"Yeah, she's dead," Chad whispered, zipping his jeans and heading out the door.

His knees were so shaky, he had to crawl back up the stairs to the fourth floor. His T-shirt was soaked with sweat, and he kept tasting the contents of his stomach. Pepperoni pizza and beer. Lots of beer. He stopped midway up the stairs, concentrating on his stomach, trying to quell the nausea.

Would he go to prison? Was his life over? What about his family? And Brenda? Had he lost them? How could this be happening to him?

What were they going to do? What would happen to them? Carter said they had to stay calm. Chad took several deep breaths and concentrated on that. Calmness.

Carter took charge. He sent Benton to drive his car around to the side door. He sent Todd for a blanket to wrap the body in. With the rest of them acting as lookouts, he had carried her down the backstairs. And Carter and Benton had driven off into the night, leaving Chad, Todd, Jackson, and Johnny to clean up the room according to Carter's instructions.

Todd had taken the sofa cushions and stuffed them in garbage bags from the kitchen and put them into the trunk of his car. Jackson brought a wastebasket full of water up to the fourth-floor room, and they scrubbed, not really sure why they were scrubbing. Johnny came upstairs but didn't help. He just sat against the wall, still holding his bed pillow, staring at the cushionless sofa. Finally, Chad led him back to his bed and tucked him in like a baby, then wadded Johnny's clothes up in a bundle with his own. He even went upstairs to the third-floor head and fished his shitty underwear out of the trash. Carter said they'd have to burn the sofa cushions and the clothes they'd been wearing. Just one of that girl's hairs or a drop of her blood could be all the proof the cops would need. They'd burn the sofa, too. Tomorrow. And blame it on a cigarette.

Johnny, lying with his face to the wall, wouldn't talk to him when Chad got back to the room. So screw him, Chad thought, suddenly angry enough to hit him. He couldn't worry about Johnny when he had to take care of himself. Calm himself. He felt like he was running in circles. Little tight circles. And sitting in the center at the same time.

He longed for a joint. Or beer. A six-pack. Something to put him someplace else.

Yes, someplace else. Out of here. He had to get out of here.

He'd go home. Talk to his dad.

His dad thought that being a good father meant attending his children's every sporting event and getting them out of trouble. He had never failed on either count. Well, this time it was trouble. *Big* trouble.

Suddenly the urge to talk to his father was so strong Chad felt as though he could run all the way to Nichols Hills. His father would know what to do. Know if they really could get away with it. Not go to jail. Not become just another campus rapist—like the guys in the athletic dorm back in the eighties. Football players. They'd put a jacket over a girl's head and taken turns. Chad had been in grade school at the time. He remembered the shock. The OU football players were his heroes. The national media had a heyday.

Only that girl hadn't died. She testified at a trial. The football players had gone to prison.

Jackson had wanted them to call the police. After all, they hadn't killed her. She died on her own. The police couldn't blame them.

But Chad knew Carter was right. They would be

held responsible in some way—even though no one forced her to drink herself into a stupor.

And even if her death could be explained away, they would be charged with rape. Six boys and a semi-conscious girl. *Jesus.* It sounded as sick as it was. Why hadn't he just taken Johnny back downstairs? Right away he'd known that's what he should do. That wasn't the way for Johnny to have sex for the first time. And Chad himself didn't need to get his jollies like that.

But even so, as disgusting as it was, his cock had gotten hard. He joined the pack. Six guys humping a nameless girl. Brothers. He was one with them. Johnny, too. Chad had actually felt proud of his room-mate as Johnny found his way into the girl's soggy cunt and got off. A rite of passage. No longer a virgin.

18

$\mathcal{L}$ater, Carter had come into Chad and Johnny's dark room and hunkered down by Chad's bed. "It's taken care of," he whispered. "We weighted her with a backpack filled with bricks and threw her over the dam. The water must be forty feet deep there. No one will ever find her."

Chad went with Carter to burn the sofa cushions and clothes—in a gully out from town, along a dirt road where old refrigerators and mattresses had been dumped. They burned one of the mattresses with the clothes and cushions.

It was close to five when Chad called home. He wanted to hang up when his mother answered the phone. The sound of her tentative hello tore at him. His *mother*. How could he talk to her after what had happened this night?

But he did.

His dad wasn't there. Chad had known that. Known about the fishing trip. With Mr. Parker and an important client. But in his need, he had forgotten. His dad had always been around before when he made early-morning phone calls after car wrecks, fistfights, arrests. His dad had provided cash for an abortion and for bail. And even a gambling debt when two hoods from south Oklahoma City had threatened to break his legs.

But maybe he shouldn't tell his father. Carter said they should swear in blood never to tell.

"Do you really think that's necessary?" Todd had asked dryly. "Like we're gonna to run right out and confess. Like we want to check that place on application forms where it asks if you're a convicted felon."

"Look, the IB house will be the last place that girl was seen alive," Chad insisted. "I think we need my dad to help us get our story straight in case we have to tell the police. Did we or didn't we see the girl leave? What time? Stuff like that? Make sure our stories jibe."

They had agreed. They'd talk to Chad's father, but only tell him part of what happened. No one but the six of them would ever know that she was dead.

That decided, Chad felt a desperate need to get out of there. Get away from Johnny. And the rest of them. This place. Feel normal again.

"I'm going home," he told Johnny. "You going to be okay?"

Johnny didn't answer.

"Look, your folks will be arriving later this morning. Are you going to be able to get it together by then?"

With an arm still thrown across his eyes, Johnny nodded.

"I'm sorry that I got you into this. I guess I'll be sorry about that for the rest of my life."

"You're not my keeper," Johnny said, eyes still covered, voice raspy. "I could have walked out the door."

"You and I both know it's not that simple. It was more than sex you would have been walking away from."

"You think I care?" he demanded, struggling to prop himself up on one elbow. "You've been decent enough, but you think I care about the rest of those shitheads? Hell, I'm here because my old man bought my way in. I'm here because I keep trying not to disappoint him. Ol' Johnny 'Rebel' Fontaine. The sports-

casters still talk about him. And he's got a wimp for a
son. I wanted to be able to tell him I'd had sex. Isn't
that just too stupid? That wasn't having sex. That was
taking sex. Serve us all right if that girl had AIDS. And
now she's dead. We're not only rapists, we're murderers."

"We're not murderers. We didn't kill her."

"Are you sure? I'm not. If I'd walked out the door
and called the police, that girl would be alive and you
guys would be in handcuffs."

Chad hurriedly made his bed and threw dirty
clothes under it. Not the usual game day spit and polish, but it would have to do.

All day Saturday, when his father didn't come
home, Chad had difficulty controlling his panic. He
didn't read one word of his opened text books. He
avoided his mother and slept—the kind of sleep that
made him wake up feeling drugged. He even prayed.
*Please let his father know what to do to make everything all
right.*

He thought in passing that he should be offering
up prayers of forgiveness, prayers for that girl's eternal
soul. Except his own soul was probably in a hell of a
lot more jeopardy. But he'd worry about souls and
forgiveness later. What he needed now was for his father to take charge.

His dad would know how to handle it. His dad always knew what to do. He would be mad as hell. Probably rant and rave. He would lecture him, extract
promises. But right now Chad could sincerely promise
that he'd never again have sex with any girl except
Brenda for the rest of his life. And right at that moment he wasn't all that sure about Brenda.

It hadn't even felt good. Brenda always was tight
and just moist enough for him to slide into. That girl
had been limp and full of slimy cum and blood. And

smelled of vomit. Revoltingly so. He could feel his hard-on fading as he mounted her limp body.

But the others were watching. That was the thrill. *Come on, Chad baby. Give it to her good.* Benton said the word "fuck" over and over. In cadence. Chad's orgasm had been so intense, it was painful.

Should they have known not to leave her on her back? Did he dare hope the girl's body would never be found? Carter insisted that, if everyone kept their mouths shut, there could be no investigation without a body.

Jesus. A body. When there was no reason for her to die.

What if the backpack came off and her body floated to the surface? Chad closed his eyes and imagined fishermen finding her body in the weeds along the shore. And he could see the courtroom scene that would follow.

And so, Mr. Billingsly, even though she was nauseated, incapacitated, and nonconsenting, you not only had sex with her, but you left her there unattended, her head hanging over the edge of the sofa. What did you think would happen to her if she threw up again?

What did he think? He hadn't thought. He had just reacted. And when it was over he had wanted the hell out of there. He couldn't even look at the nameless girl whose body he had just fucked.

He didn't want to go back to Norman and the fraternity house. He didn't want to see any of those guys ever again. Didn't want to face Brenda. He thought about faking an illness. Staying home in his own bed. Indefinitely. But his mother would call a doctor. And Brenda would drive up. He really had no choice but to return to Norman.

Johnny had packed up and left. Gone back to Phoenix with his parents. He'd left a note for Chad. "I'm calling it quits for now. Good luck."

Brenda brought him presents from Tulsa. A new
necktie and pralines that she and her sister had made.
"I'm still not used to Susan being married," Brenda
said. "She says that she's happy, but she sure is careful
around Brad. I don't want things to change like that
when we get married. It won't, will it?"

"I hope not," Chad said, downing the last of the
beer from his mug.

"Don't you like the spaghetti?"

"Sure. I'm just not hungry."

"Is something wrong?" Brenda asked. "You seem
distant."

As always, Brenda looked adorable. Her sweater was
red and furry. Her hair was soft and fluffy on her
shoulders. Her green eyes wide and guileless. A
woman child. Sexy in a sweet, innocent way. They'd
been having sex for almost two years. Before Brenda,
he'd just done straight fucking. He and Brenda had
experimented. Done it all. Loved it all. She trusted
him completely to manage their lives, to plan their
future.

Normally, he would have driven out to the lake to
park in one of the deserted picnic areas. Their spot.
But he couldn't do that. Not the lake. Never again.
Instead he drove south on Twenty-fourth Street—
toward the river. There was a park near the remains of
the old Highway 9 bridge that had once spanned the
South Canadian. Before he was born. The supports
still marched across the sandy bottom of the often wa-
terless riverbed. It used to be a real river, he'd heard,
before it was dammed. Indians could canoe all the way
to the Arkansas.

He couldn't get it up. More correctly, he didn't try.
He knew nothing was there. No semen. No desire.

Brenda offered to pay for a motel room. Or to go
back to his room at the fraternity house and close the

door. After all, with Johnny gone, Chad had the room to himself.

"I don't feel well," he told her. "I drank too much Friday night, and I've felt like shit ever since. I'll make it up to you tomorrow night. I love you, baby. You know that I love you."

Brenda was her usual sweet, understanding self, which made him almost hate her. With relief, he finally was able to kiss her good night at the front door of the Chi Omega house.

He stopped at the 7-Eleven for a six-pack to get him through the night. Already, he dreaded seeing Brenda again tomorrow night. Would twenty-four hours make any difference?

He drank the first beer sitting in the Iota Beta parking lot. Chugalugged it. And immediately opened another. Why him? What had he ever done to deserve a mess like this? Carter, he could understand. Carter bragged about roughing up girls. He claimed that deep down that's the way girls really liked it. That nice guys finished last. But Chad wasn't like that.

Dead. The girl's face flaccid and white. No longer pretty. She had been pretty. Black eyes. Black hair. A wonderful mouth. A small girl—about the same size as Brenda—with big breasts. And now her bloated body was resting in the mud on the bottom of Lake Thunderbird.

His stomach began to heave. Chad opened the car door and leaned out, losing it—the beer, spaghetti, even the ham sandwich he'd had for lunch—a telltale pile of puke by his BMW.

He closed the car door, pressed his head against the steering wheel, and sobbed.

19

*H*er mother used to say that she was sorry Karen didn't have a sister. "With a sister, you have a friend for life," Grace would observe with a knowing nod. And for a number of years Karen had thought that a younger sibling might be forthcoming. Her old baby bed and high chair were waiting in the attic. Whenever her mother was around a baby, she got a soft, silly look on her face, and she would coo as she picked it up and kissed its fuzzy head, caressed its tiny back.

Grace and her own sister, Faith, had been very close. As married women they had lived in equally impressive homes only a few blocks from one another in Tulsa's gracious Southern Hills area and were all but inseparable. They shopped together, belonged to the same ladies' clubs, hosted showers and bridge parties together, chatted over daily cups of coffee, and talked on the phone when they weren't together. Karen found it amazing that her mother and her aunt never ran out of things to say to one another. Their shared world of family, friends, and books seemed to require endless examination. Sometimes Karen couldn't tell if they were discussing real people or characters from the novels they read.

Sometimes she'd hear them talking about John David, her brother who died before she was born—in a fall from his pony. Her mother would be blowing her nose, dabbing at her eyes. Which made Karen sad.

Sometimes she'd stand before the mantel and look up at John David's portrait. Did her parents wish they still had him instead of her?

When Karen was thirteen, Aunt Faith's husband was named to head West Coast exploration for Texhoma Oil and Gas, and they moved to Los Angeles. After that, Faith and Grace saw each other only a couple of times a year. But marathon long-distance phone calls continued up to the time of Grace's last hospital admission, when Faith flew home to sit in the frigid blue hospital room, wrapping herself in a blanket to keep from shivering, holding her sister's hand, never leaving her side except to bathe and change clothes. Karen's father came and went, but Aunt Faith stayed around the clock.

Until Grace slipped into a coma, she would ask Faith to tell stories about when they were young, when their parents were still alive. Faith reminisced about driving the pony cart down the hill to the drugstore for ice cream, getting lost in the Smithsonian, having their picture taken with Mrs. Roosevelt, the summer spent in glorious Florence among art and life.

After a grade-school friend explained to Karen where babies came from, Karen continuously observed her parents, trying to determine if they still "did it." And found herself doubtful. The kisses that they offered to one another at times of arrival and departure were dry and perfunctory. They replaced their double bed with twin beds. The baby bed and high chair in the attic were given to the Negro maid, whose daughter was expecting.

Karen wondered if the intimacy shared by her mother and Aunt Faith had somehow diminished their respective marriages. Certainly, neither sister had the sort of marriage Karen envisioned for herself. They talked more to each other than they did their husbands. And seemed to need each other more.

Karen wanted a lovers-and-best-friends sort of marriage with intimacy and great passion.

She and Roger had been like that in the beginning. Their love had been a spiritual thing. Their very souls merged in the white-hot fusion of truly remarkable lustful, young, trusting sex. Surely no one in the history of humankind had ever experienced what they were experiencing. They had invented love and passion and sex. They alone had the patent. They were the most fortunate people in the world.

But then, as they assumed their separate roles of husband and wife, father and mother, wage earner and homemaker, they retreated from rapture. Taking love to the limits left one with no place to go. Best to leave room for a safety net.

Karen found herself repeating the pattern established by Grace and Faith with her mother becoming a surrogate sister for Karen. And Karen worried that her relationship with her mother contributed to the growing distance in her own marriage. Her mother knew almost every detail of her life. Her mother was her best friend when her husband should have been. But the things she had discussed with her mother Roger would have found boring or trivial.

Then her mother died.

Although Karen didn't have a sister, she'd always had lots of female friends. From grade school on, she'd been popular. Everybody's buddy. An easy person to be around. When her mother died, when the baby was born too soon, Karen's friends clustered around her, offering flowers and food and comfort. They always remembered her birthday. They thought of her first when guest lists were being made. But she couldn't possibly tell any one of her friends that her son had raped a seventeen-year-old girl and was responsible for her death.

And so, on an October night, in the forty-seventh

year of her life, motherless, sisterless, friendless, Karen found herself standing in the upstairs hallway of her home, outside the door to her son's room, unable to move, unable to breathe, the palm of her right hand still stinging from the slap she'd just delivered to his face, her mind reeling from the words she'd just said to him. Behind other closed doors in this house were her husband, father, father-in-law, daughter. Yet Karen was alone. Utterly alone.

Nothing in her life, in her upbringing, no book she had read, no sermon she had heard, had prepared her for this moment. She didn't know what to do. Who to turn to. Where to go. A big tearing part of her wanted to go back into Chad's room and take him in her arms, kiss his perfect face, tell him that everything was going to be all right, that she would love him forever no matter what, that somehow they would make it through—and in doing so make meaningless the death of Rosalie Frank.

The only person she could remotely imagine telling about her son's role in the Rosalie Frank tragedy was George Brown. George was the only close male friend she'd ever had, and she loved him. He was the calmest, kindest, most clear-thinking person she knew. He accepted people as they were and helped them over the rough spots.

Yes, she could tell George. Just knowing there was someone to confide in made her feel better. And gave her the courage to take a step away from her son's bedroom door.

The day she'd learned for certain that in spite of chemotherapy and radiation and leading specialists, her mother was going to die, Karen had cleaned out the attic.

The night she'd finally faced the certainty of her husband's affair with Rhonda Parker, she had sorted though her closet, discarding almost every garment that she owned.

On this night of discovery, she cleaned cupboards. She threw away old spice cans and stale boxes of cereal. She boxed the dishes and cookware that she never used for an upcoming garage sale to benefit Haven House.

When she finished in the kitchen, she tackled the butler's pantry and dining room, working with dispassion. No matter that the copper tray or the crystal vase had been a wedding present. If she'd never used an item, or hadn't brought it out of hiding in years, it went either into the garage-sale pile or, in the case of family heirlooms, to the attic—even her great-grandmother's candelabrum. Karen had always thought it made the sideboard in the dining room look like an altar but felt duty bound to keep it there. Her mother had presented it to her the month before she died—to make sure that her sister, Grace, didn't lay claim to it for her own daughter, who didn't appreciate family, who hadn't returned to Oklahoma even once since her parents moved to California, not even for Karen's wedding.

No matter how Karen tried to concentrate on the task at hand—climbing up and down the step stool, tiptoed up and down the attic stairs, carrying boxes to her station wagon—her mind kept probing the past, looking for clues. Why had this happened?

Had her nightgowns been too revealing?

She tried to remember how old Chad was before she stopped allowing him to see her naked, allowing him to crawl in the bathtub with her, sleep with her. Had she loved cuddling with her children in the night so much that she let it go on too long?

Should she have done something about the cache of *Penthouse* magazines he used to keep under his mattress?

She had been too tolerant of his occasional disrespect.

She should have punished him more severely for tormenting his sister.

She should have demanded that Chad take responsibility for his behavior instead of always allowing Roger to right the wrongs. Chad could have gotten a job after school to pay for speeding tickets. He could have worked summers to pay for car repairs. He could have done without a car.

In the lake. My God, that girl's body was in the mud on the bottom of Lake Thunderbird with sailboats floating tranquilly on the surface.

Roger stayed in his study. After a time the line of light under the door went dark. And Karen knew that he was sleeping on the leather sofa—a first in all their married life. But then, she herself had set the precedent for abandoning the marital bed.

Finally, when every shelf was tidy, and the back end of her station wagon was loaded with items for the next Haven House sale, she wrote a note for Roger and left it in the middle of the kitchen table. *I've gone for a drive. If I'm not back in time to fix breakfast, heat the coffee cake and plug in the coffee pot.*

At this hour of the night, traffic on the turnpike to Tulsa was sparse, and the drive took less than the usual two hours. At ten minutes before four, Karen pulled into the driveway of the home in which she had spent her childhood. The sprawling post–World War II stone-and-brick dwelling was ugly and pretentious, softened only by a spacious, sloping yard with an abundance of mature trees—magnolia, dogwood, pine, redbud.

Using the key that had always hung on her key ring, she let herself inside and roamed about, turning on lights, remembering, but also seeing anew.

The house had changed little since the last interior

decorator redid it in the early 1970s. Oriental was "in" then—lacquer screens, cloisonné vases, vapid watercolors, ornate rosewood chests. In the living room, the only object not a part of the decorator's scheme was the portrait of John David.

She and Aunt Faith had removed her mother's personal possessions from the bedroom the day after the funeral. Even so, Karen opened dresser drawers and bathroom cabinets in search of some evidence that Grace Fullerton had once lived here. Even her wedding picture had been removed from over the bedroom mantel, probably because her father brought women to this room and did not want to make love to them under the watchful eyes of his dead wife.

Only the sunporch retained vestiges of Grace. Her collection of Murano glass birds still lined glass shelves in front of the windows. Her mother had come here in the afternoons to read and do needlepoint—and enjoy the sunlight on the colored glass of her birds. Her chair and ottoman were still in place. Family pictures lined the walls. No Oriental antiques intruded.

And, sitting in her mother's chair, Karen wept. What in the hell was happening? She'd thought that she was doing everything right. She thought she was being a good mother. She'd always prided herself on being as good a mother as her own mother had been.

Her mother. Grace Fullerton. A quiet, gentle unassuming woman with open arms. Always there in the background. Always helpful. Forgiving of all sins. Unquestioning love.

Her mother. A meek, passive woman who retreated into books whenever she had the chance. A bland, almost invisible woman. A nonentity.

Karen sucked in her breath at such irreverent thoughts. *Her saintly mother.*

But then, the woman had been married to Vernon Fullerton, so how else could she have been? He dominated their lives. Her mother maintained order by invoking the omnipotent will of the father—never her own.

But her mother was a dear. Her mother loved her. Karen talked long distance to her mother almost every morning of her adult life. Having someone to whom she could report the small events of her life gave them significance. And Karen needed that. Her mother had cared about what she was cooking for dinner and what the pediatrician said about coughs and rashes. Karen missed those phone calls as much as the woman herself.

Would she have told her mother about Chad? Karen tried to imagine such a thing. Sitting in this very room. Looking at her mother's sweet, concerned face. *Chad, your beloved grandson, raped a girl, caused her death.*

Would Grace have agreed with Roger? *Protect the boy at all cost. Save the family. Too bad about the girl, but she should have been more careful.* Or would she have experienced the same revulsion and disbelief that Karen felt?

But Karen could not imagine her mother doing either.

Grace would have chosen not to deal with it. She would have looked past Karen, waiting for her to finish, then announced that she was sure there had been a misunderstanding and that Roger would get everything straightened out.

Grace fretted about fevers and runny noses but, other than a painful little discussion about Kotex and sanitary belts, never talked to her daughter about anything sexual. Grace insisted on phone calls to know that Karen had arrived home safely but refused to listen when Karen wanted to discuss the growing distance between herself and Roger, her concern over his seeming infatuation with one of the partner's wives, what she should do if her husband strayed.

When Karen was away at college, Grace would send shoe boxes filled with vitamin pills, calcium tablets, Midol, Maalox. And started the stream of newspaper clippings that continued until her death—manila envelopes full of articles about the danger of microwaves, ultraviolet rays, caffeine, sugar, sugar substitutes, allergic reactions, Legionnaires' disease, dust mites, light deprivation. But Grace had never had a mammogram. She didn't go to the doctor until the lump in her right breast was the size of a golf ball. She fussed over small things to avoid what was important. Like happiness. Life. Opinions.

Grace Fullerton would have tuned out any talk of rape and murder and focused instead on the shadows under her daughter's eyes. Had Karen read that article that she'd sent about Vitamin E?

Maybe, after John David's death, Grace had survived by living on the surface. Never soaring. Never plunging.

No, that was too simple. Karen knew that her mother had loved her deeply. Probably more than anything. More than her pretentious house. Her formidable husband. More than the memory of John David. More than Aunt Grace. Her mother had been important, more important than Karen's father. More loving. More caring. More kind. A real person. A mother.

If her mother were still alive, sitting here in this chair, Karen would have made her deal with the reality of what Chad had done. She would have forced her mother to grieve with her about Rosalie Frank and Inez Frank and help figure out if she could have prevented Rosalie's death and what she should do about it now.

On impulse, Karen reached for the telephone,

called information, and dialed the Franks' telephone
number in Norman. All she wanted was to hear Inez
Frank's voice. Maybe she'd even say something back.
Tell her how sorry she was for her trouble. *You don't
know me, but I cry for you.*

Inez answered the phone. Her hello was tense, anxious.

Karen slammed down the receiver. *Dear God.*

She imagined the scene that she had just unthink-
ingly precipitated. The phone ringing in the darkness.
Inez's heart filling with hope as she grabbed the receiver. *Please, dear God, let it be Rosalie. Please.*

That poor woman didn't know that her daughter's
dead body was rotting on the bottom of a lake.
Karen's hands started to shake. *I know, but she doesn't.
And no one is ever going to tell her. That woman is suffering
a thousand deaths while my husband and son are thinking
of ways to make sure she never finds out.*

Karen found her mother's wedding picture in the
attic. She wrapped each glass bird with newspaper and
packed them away in an empty box she found in the
garage.

She left a note for her father explaining that she
had taken the birds. She said nothing about the wedding picture, certain that he would never miss it.

20

Chad and the grandfathers had left. Melissa was still in bed. Karen found Roger in his bathroom, shaving.

"*You went to Tulsa!*" Roger said, shaving soap on his face, his tone incredulous. "In the middle of the night, you went to Tulsa to get your mother's wedding picture?"

"That's not *why* I went," she said, leaning wearily against the door frame. "I needed to think—to try and find the reason why all this has happened."

"Don't make more out of this than it is, Karen. What happened at that fraternity house was a spur-of-the-moment thing. *An accident.* Not something to reexamine your whole life over."

"No," Karen said, slowly shaking her head. "I know they didn't mean for her to die. But rape is not an accident. And that poor girl still would be alive if they hadn't done that. Rosalie Frank still would be alive. They are responsible. Chad is responsible. And us, too. You and me. We raised a son who thought it was all right to violate a girl. Who thought that he could have whatever he wanted."

At dinner, Karen told Melissa about the appointment with Dr. Burk.

"No way," Melissa said, glaring at her mother. "There's nothing the matter with me."

"You don't eat," Karen said from across the kitchen table, glancing in Roger's direction. Surely, he wasn't going to let her do this alone. But he said nothing. "You've taken exactly one bite of rice and one of salad," she pointed out.

"I'm not hungry," Melissa said with a shrug.

"Everyone gets hungry," Karen said, trying to keep her voice reasonable sounding. Not challenging. "You have *chosen* not to eat, and that's not healthy or normal. Your father and I are worried, honey. Can't you understand that? Maybe for no reason. Maybe Dr. Burk will tell us to bug off and leave you alone. That this is just a silly phase and isn't doing you any harm. But we have to check it out."

"Why do you always pick on me? You wouldn't make Chad go to a *pediatrician*."

"If you don't want to see Dr. Burk, we'll find another doctor," Karen said. "But you have to see someone."

"You just don't want me to be thin," Melissa spit back. "You liked me better fat so you could be the concerned, understanding mother, and everyone would wonder how such a perfectly lovely woman could have had such a gross daughter but wasn't it wonderful the way you tried to help me."

"Cool it, Melissa," Roger said. "Your mother and I are worried about you, and you *will* go to the doctor. If you expect to continue driving around in that blue Mustang, I expect to see you at Dr. Burk's office at one-thirty tomorrow afternoon."

"Why are you on *her* side?" Melissa demanded before pushing back her chair and hurrying from the room. Her parents listened in silence as her footsteps thundered up the stairs, as the door to her bedroom slammed.

Karen was stunned. Once again, she had been accused of taking sides against her children.

"She thinks I'm her enemy," she said, staring at her own plate of uneaten food. "Both of my children do."

Roger made no comment. He carried the dishes to the sink then retreated to the family room and began flipping through television channels.

Karen stayed at the table, her hands in her lap. Numb. And tired. So tired. She'd tried to nap this afternoon, to make up for her lost night of sleep. Her body ached with fatigue, but the scene in Chad's bedroom was still too much with her. And she couldn't even begin to guess the future. She had dozed fitfully and finally given up and, promising herself that tonight she would sleep even if she had to take sleeping pills, came downstairs to stew a chicken and make a rhubarb pie. Her mother's recipe.

In Aunt Faith's household, her housekeeper had done the cooking. Faith had never understood why her sister insisted on spending so much time in the kitchen. But the kitchen had been Grace's domain. Exclusively hers. Not professionally decorated. Just a plain kitchen, where she stewed chickens and made pies. Even when she wasn't cooking, Grace often sat at the kitchen table with a book propped in front of her, a pot of tea under the crocheted cozy, the radio on top of the refrigerator playing softly, sometimes tuned to the classical station, other times the voices of Perry Como, Frank Sinatra, Dinah Shore sang softly in the background.

Karen poured a cup of coffee and sat at her own kitchen table, enjoying the aroma of the baking pie, waiting for the chicken to cool enough for her to remove the meat from the bones. She wasn't sure what she'd make with it. Chicken à la king maybe. Or chicken noodle soup with the homemade noodles she had in the freezer.

Melissa always had loved homemade chicken noo-

dle soup and refused to eat the kind that came from
cans. She wanted her mother's kind. She loved to help
make the noodles, standing on the kitchen stool and
cutting the rolled-out dough into strips, sneaking bites
of dough when she thought that Karen wasn't looking.

Melissa had been an easy baby, a sweet little girl—
quiet, undemanding, eager to please. By the hour, she
would quietly play with her toys. And color in coloring
books, laboring with such intensity, taking great care
not to break the crayons or go out of the lines. She
would start with the first picture in the coloring book
and work her way through to the end.

Chad had been a restless baby and a boisterous,
noisy, inquisitive, demanding child. All boy, his father
was fond of saying. He shunned coloring books and
created his own freehand pictures of tanks, airplanes,
and men at war. Chad was constantly looking for new
skills to master, new obstacles to climb over, new tricks
to play on his sister. He'd charm Melissa out of candy
bars and trick her out of her turn to sit in the front
seat of the car. He'd tell her that her doll had died,
that her teddy bear didn't love her anymore, that girls
were stupid and ugly and only boys could be president. But sometimes he would let her sit in his tree
house. And he taught her to play checkers and ride a
bike. He once punched a boy in the nose who called
Melissa fat.

Melissa never got into trouble at school; Chad did
almost weekly.

Melissa proceeded cautiously in all endeavors and
almost never fell off her bike, crashed on roller skates,
or wiped out while skiing.

Chad lived his childhood with skinned knees and
elbows, knots on his head, splinted fingers. Various
falls from trees, ski slopes, and other high places re-
sulted in a broken humerus, collarbone, nose, and numerous ribs.

Melissa was a pretty child. Chad was beautiful.
When they were very young, strangers would gravitate
toward Chad, wanting to know how old he was, re-
marking on his long lashes, his golden curls, his rosy
cheeks. A Raphael cherub. He should be a model, a
child star. Usually, they wouldn't say anything about
the quieter, plainer younger sister. And during Melissa's bout with adolescent plumpness, she became all
but invisible.

Melissa studied diligently and made straight A's.
Chad scored higher than his sister on standardized
achievement tests but never studied and made B's,
C's, and an occasional D. Both youngsters were athleti-
cally talented, but Melissa spent three hours hitting
tennis balls at the backboard for every hour Chad
spent at the driving range.

Karen and Roger bragged about their perfectly behaved daughter to family and friends. They shook
their head indulgently over Chad. He'd settle down.
He was a good kid. Just a little wild.

Until Melissa gained weight, Karen worried far
more about her daredevil son than her cautious
daughter. She worried about Chad's driving, drinking,
flirtation with drugs, study habits, and before Brenda,
she fretted about the girls who called constantly at all
hours of the day and night.

When pudginess set in, Karen enrolled Melissa in a
series of weight-loss programs and sent her to charm
school, where she learned about walking tall and wearing vertical stripes and dark colors. Karen helped her
select clothes that called attention to her pretty face
and dark shining hair and away from her hefty thighs
and thick waist, and Karen quietly reminded her
daughter several times a day to stand up straight.

Karen bought a Weight Watchers cook book and
prepared attractive, low-calorie meals for Melissa, even
packing her lunch to take to school so she could stay

on her diet all day long. But Karen would find candy
wrappers hidden under Melissa's mattress and in her
closet, wadded up in the toes of shoes or the pockets
of clothing. She even found smoothed-out candy
wrappers stashed between the pages of her school-
books. Finally she quit looking.

Tennis had been Roger's idea. He'd coached Melissa until she got too good for him. Then he turned
her over to the tennis pro at the country club. Suddenly her clothes had to be altered and finally given
away. A lean athlete emerged from the adipose. Karen
was enchanted. She couldn't keep her eyes off her
daughter, her *slender* daughter. How lovely she was.
How smart she looked in her new clothes. Boys started
calling. And girls who weren't plump.

For one glorious year, everything seemed practically perfect in her daughter's life. Melissa was overly
concerned about her appearance, but then most teenage girls were. She had been absolutely thrilled when
Trevor Washburn started calling. Trevor was a senior.
Almost as good-looking as Chad. A football player.
Only an inch or so taller than Melissa, but maybe being tall wasn't the end of the world for a girl after all.
Trevor didn't seem to mind.

Karen wanted to blame Trevor for Melissa's emaciated state, but in all fairness, she had begun to worry
before Trevor appeared on the scene. Melissa had already begun avoiding meals. Already dropped another
dress size.

And now she was beyond thin. She was emaciated.

With a sigh, Karen finally rose from the kitchen
table and put away the food. She left the dishes for
Mildred to do in the morning. Right now she wanted
a nice bath and two of Roger's sleeping pills. She wondered what time he'd come upstairs, if she'd wake up
when he came to bed, if he would wake her. If he'd
want to talk. To touch. To make love.

She paused outside the door of the number-two guest room. Did she dare?

Walt had stripped the bed and left the used bed linens carefully folded at the foot of the bed. She stared at the bed. The thought of sleeping alone in that bed was very appealing. Shockingly so.

But she'd always slept better when her husband was at her side. She felt safer when he was there and took comfort in the sounds of his breathing, in being able to touch him in the night.

Except she relished the nights when he was away and she could stay up and read as long as she wanted. Give herself a facial. Pluck her eyebrows without Roger calling out, "What the hell are you doing in there?" With her husband away, she could curl up in bed and watch whatever television show she wanted to. Drink wine in bed. Crunch on crackers with peanut butter. It was like a mini-vacation for her with privacy as its main attraction.

Of course, it would be different if she had to be alone all the time. Then she'd probably hate it.

Tonight she didn't want to drink wine or watch television alone. She just wanted to sleep alone.

Roger was watching a sixties movie—Steve McQueen chasing crooks through the streets of San Francisco. A movie she was certain he'd seen at least half a dozen times. "I'll be in the small guest room," she told him. "I think we'll both sleep better."

Roger muted the sound. "And tomorrow night?" he asked.

"We don't feel the same about what's happened. And that bothers me. A lot. Right now, I couldn't deal with sex. So maybe it's best. . . . " Her voice trailed off. She wasn't sure what was best. But she felt such distance from him. Alienation even. If she returned to their bed, Roger would assume too much. The only sort of sex she could manage right now would be the

dutiful variety. In her mind, she would be thinking of
Rosalie Frank. Feeling violated like Rosalie Frank.

If she could separate herself physically from her
husband for a time, she might be able to work
through things. If she didn't, she was afraid she would
start to hate him.

She went behind the sofa and leaned over him, her
arms around his neck, her cheek against the top of his
head. "Good night," she said.

He clung to her hand for a minute, then with a
pained sigh, let her go.

For a long time Karen couldn't sleep. She wondered if Roger was asleep yet. Imagined him seething
with anger. Hurting to the point of tears. What if he
came here to this bed? What would she do?

She thought about locking the door. She even
thought about giving up and going back to the other
bed. Always before, sex was the salve that cured marital discord. Like homemade pies, it made a marriage
seem normal.

But the sleeping pills were beginning to take hold.
Finally. She felt herself relaxing, drifting away into
beautiful, mindless sleep.

21

*I*va Burk regarded the girl sitting on the end of the examining table, a hostile frown on her young face. Melissa Billingsly's collarbones jutted out so far as to look painful. The girl's hands, clutching the paper gown closed in front, were fleshless, like an old woman's.

"Well, Melissa, two years ago your parents brought you in because they were concerned about your being overweight. Now they've brought you back to me for not weighing enough."

"I didn't want to come."

"That's understandable," Iva said, leaning against the counter, folding her arms. "Most sixteen-year-olds don't want to be taken to a pediatrician. And maybe you do need to see someone else. That's what we need to decide today."

"I don't need to see you or any other doctor. There's nothing wrong with me. This is all *really* stupid."

"You're five foot ten and weigh a hundred and five pounds. That's too thin."

"The *chart* says it's too thin. The *chart* doesn't know how I should look."

"And you think you look all right?"

"No," Melissa said with a defiant tilt to her chin. "I think I need to lose at least five more pounds. I want to weigh an even one hundred. Or maybe ninety-nine. Ninety-five would be perfect."

"Why?"

"Because it would be cool. And I could wear a size two."

"You have a boyfriend, I understand."

Melissa hesitated. "Yeah. Kind of."

"What does this boyfriend think of the way you look? Boys usually aren't attracted to skinny girls."

"Boys don't like tall girls either."

"Oh, I don't know about that. Depends on the boy. Are you trying to make up for being tall by wearing a small dress size?"

"Well, I'd rather be tall and thin than tall and fat. I can't be five-six like my mom, but I can get down to a size two."

"You didn't tell me what your boyfriend thinks. Does he want you to be a size two?"

Melissa lifted her chin again. "No. He says I'm not pretty anymore."

"Yet you still want to lose more weight. If you're trying to get out of a sexual relationship, there're other ways than starving yourself."

"I'm not trying to get out of anything."

"Are you sure, my dear?" Iva asked. "You're awfully young to be having a boy put that sort of pressure on you. Now that you're involved with him, I imagine you feel like you have to have sex with him. Like you have no choice. And that makes you uncomfortable."

"I didn't know you were a psychiatrist, too," Melissa challenged.

"Would you be more comfortable talking to a psychiatrist?"

"No! And don't you go suggesting such a thing to my parents. I don't want to go to some shrink. I don't want to go to any doctor. Besides, I don't have sex with him anymore. He's a jerk. I'm the one who decides how I'm going to look, not some jerky boy."

"Nevertheless, Melissa, you can either put up with

me, or I will find you a specialist, who may very well
put you in the hospital. In fact, if you continue to lose
weight, *I* will put you in the hospital myself and feed
you intravenously—with restraints if you try to pull out
the needles. And we both know how much you like to
be poked with needles."

"I won't go to the hospital," Melissa said, glaring.
"I'd run away first."

Iva took the girl's young face between her aging
hands. "My dear child, we can be enemies and fight
each other. Or you can get a good healthy dose of fear
and help me and your parents to help you. This cannot go on. It may take you a year or two, but you will
kill yourself if you continue your present course—as
surely as if you'd taken a loaded gun to your head and
pulled the trigger."

Iva had striven to make her office look more like a
comfortable living room than a doctor's office, but
the Billingslys seemed decidedly *un*comfortable. They
were seated on opposite ends of the sofa, Roger chewing on his thumbnail, Karen holding an unopened
magazine on her lap. Iva had the feeling she was interrupting an icy silence.

She seated herself in her favorite chair, re-covered
in a dark plaid to look much like it had looked when it
resided in her father's medical office, and took a deep
breath. "As you feared, Karen, Melissa is indeed suffering from anorexia nervosa," she began. "The chief
physical symptom of this disorder is severe and inten-
tional weight loss involving over twenty-five percent of
the individual's body weight. I'm sorry to say that Melissa qualifies. She also exhibits the characteristic side
effects of low blood pressure and slowed heartbeat.
Typically, individuals who suffer from anorexia are intelligent young women from middle- or upper-class

families and have a distorted self-image. By Melissa's own admission, she plans to lose more weight. She'd like to weigh one hundred pounds. Or ninety-five pounds would be better. 'Cool' was how she described it."

"*Ninety-five pounds!*" Karen gasped. "That's ridiculous!"

"Of course it is. But you have to understand that when Melissa looks in a mirror, she doesn't see the same person we see. And no one knows exactly why that is, which makes it very difficult to manage the disorder."

"Why do you think this is happening?" Roger asked.

Iva looked from one concerned face to the other. They were waiting for her to reassure them, to prescribe a pill to make it all go away. "As Melissa pointed out, I'm not a psychiatrist, but I imagine her disorder somehow relates back to the very difficult time she spent as an overweight adolescent. She felt like an ugly duckling in a very attractive family. She told me that all her life people have been telling her how pretty her mother is, what a hunk her brother is, how handsome her father is. She's seems to focus especially on you, Karen. She hates towering over her mother. And she thinks you have no right to try and make her weigh more. It's become a war between you and her, right?"

Karen swallowed before speaking. Iva felt a wave of pity for this woman who had been the most conscientious of mothers. "But we've always told her how pretty she is," Karen insisted, her voice breaking.

"She didn't believe you, apparently. At least, not after she developed the weight problem. She said you spent a fortune on clothes for her, Karen, trying to camouflage the fat because you were embarrassed about the way she looked."

"I just wanted her to feel good about herself," Karen said weakly, her hands tightly clutched in her lap.

"And now she doesn't want you to have any say in selecting her clothes, I imagine," Iva said.

Karen nodded. No say.

"And Roger has sat quietly by while mother and daughter have carried on this battle," Iva observed, focusing her gaze on Roger.

"Yes, I guess I did," Roger admitted. "But food and meals and what the kids wear have always been Karen's domain. And I still don't see this as a major problem. Melissa is very bright. Surely after you point out to her that she's way under on the weight charts and could make herself sick, she'll come to her senses. After all, you're not her mother. She'll listen to you."

"It's not that simple," Iva said. "Melissa is aware of the weight charts. She's stopped having periods and knows very well that this is what happens when the body fat drops below a certain level. But she's in charge here. She has the power to say if she will or will not eat. You can't force-feed a sixteen-year-old."

"But it has to end," Roger said. "She can't keep doing this."

"Some people get over anorexia and some don't," Iva said.

"And what happens to the ones who don't?" Karen asked, fear in her voice.

"They die. Like that singer—Karen Carpenter. It can happen."

"Let's not overreact here," Roger said, puffing up a bit, shaking his head. "Karen Carpenter obviously was a mental case. Children in Africa starve to death because they don't have any food. Melissa has food. She has a life. Everything to live for. She has to start eating. We've been letting her get away with this, but now it's got to stop."

"Fathers usually say something like that," Iva observed dryly. "But if paternal decree solved behavioral problems, we wouldn't have any addicts or alcoholics, would we? Or anorexic girls?"

"What should we do?" Karen asked.

"I'm sorry, dear, but for now I don't want *you* to do anything," Iva told Karen. "I think you should withdraw from the mother-daughter confrontation. Melissa is to have at least one meal a day alone with her father. And she must come in weekly to see me and be weighed. If she doesn't get better, she will have to be admitted to a hospital-based treatment program."

"What about her boyfriend?" Karen asked. "She's lost most of this weight since she started dating him. Should we try to keep her from seeing him."

"Melissa and I discussed him. She's not involved with him anymore."

Karen stared at the top shelf of the hall linen closet. Four boxes of Stayfree Maxi Pads and three of Tampax had accumulated beside a neat pile of beach towels. Shouldn't she have realized that she was the only one using any of it?

Melissa wasn't having periods. Her body had gone into a survival mode. Starving women didn't have periods.

With or without a boyfriend, Melissa wanted to be even thinner. But why?

For years, Karen had sent money every month to save a third-world child from starvation. She had a snapshot of a boy in the slums of Mexico City. Hernando with huge brown eyes, dressed in a ragged shirt. A teenager now. He wrote letters of gratitude. Hernando wasn't starving anymore, but Karen's daughter was. It made no sense. Nothing in her life made sense anymore. And it was her fault. She had

floated through life and motherhood, concentrating
on being nice, on having everyone like her, on being
the perfect wife and mother, on having a showcase
house and showcase children and a showcase marriage. She had lived inside a fairy tale. She had never
presented reality to her children.

Karen went downstairs to warm up the chicken
noodle soup, bake some biscuits, cut up fruit for a
salad.

The three of them played at eating. Karen avoided
looking at her daughter's plate. She was out of it. No
more counting bites. She listened numbly while Roger
invited Melissa to have lunch tomorrow at Ap-
plewood's.

"I only have forty-five minutes for lunch on Tuesdays," Melissa protested.

"Then we'll have breakfast at Denny's before
school," he said.

Roger cleared the table while Karen sat glued to
her chair. She was turning to stone. They could just
carry her outside and give her a place in the garden
by the birdbath that Mr. Song hated. A statue of
Karen.

The table cleared, Roger came and knelt by her
chair. Gently, he stroked her arm. "We'll manage," he
said. "Somehow we'll manage."

Karen tried to nod her head but wasn't sure if she
succeeded.

"I want you to sleep in our bed tonight," Roger
said. "I won't touch you. I just want you there. I promise I'll never try to have sex with you again unless
you're ripping the clothes from my body. Okay?"

"We might lose them," Karen said. "Our children."

"No. This is a bad time, but we'll see it through.
I'm more worried about losing you, Karen. You seem
to be slipping away from me. I didn't realize how up-

set you were by this business with Chad. Of course, it's
been terrible for you. But he's not bad. Surely you can
see that. As for this problem with Melissa, we're on top
of it now. We'll turn it around.''

"What if she dies, and Chad goes to prison?"

"Then I'll need you more than ever. Can I hug you,
Karen? Can I at least hug you?"

He was very close. She could smell his aftershave.
Feel his breath and the warmth of his hand as he continued to caress her arm.

Just a hug. Not so much to ask of a wife. But it
wasn't that simple. A hug would mean she had
stepped back over the invisible line that now separated
them.

She had loved this man. Probably still did. He was a
decent man who, in the only way he knew, loved her
and their children. If she wanted to, she could conjure
up memory after memory of good times. They had
made a family together. And she wanted that family to
continue. But her role in that family would have to
change. She was no longer willing to be simply good
old mom in the kitchen, the dutiful wife in the bedroom. And she wasn't yet strong enough to make sure
that happened. If she crossed back over the line, if she
returned to her husband's bed, she would fall back
into the old patterns. She could close her eyes and
feel herself falling.

The one thing in her life that went beyond her position in this family was her work at Haven House,
which her family ignored. For ten years, she had gone
there twice a week and not one of the three ever had
gone there, ever inquired about what she did there.
Haven House made them uncomfortable. They could
accept her having gone there for one year to fulfill an
obligation. But for her to keep going, year after year,
to a place that had nothing to do with the life they led
made them uncomfortable. It did not fit into the un-

complicated image that they attached to her. And she
had honored their feelings. She never mentioned
Haven House during dinner-table conversation, never
talked about the women and children she met there.
Never talked about George. She never explained how
useful she felt working at the shelter, and how discour-
aged, how frustrated, how much she had come to
question the indifferent society that turned a blind
eye to women who needed sheltering, to the situations
and men who created the need.

Ironically, it was almost out of fear that Karen never
mentioned Haven House, never let her family know
how important it was to her. What if Roger asked her
to stop going there? Then she would have to choose
between defying him and giving up something that
she needed to balance her life. To balance Nichols
Hills and the big house and a maid three mornings a
week. Without Haven House, she would be her
mother.

She touched Roger's face instead of hugging him.
For now it was all she could do. He watched as she dug
her keys from her purse. "I won't be late," she said.

She went to the shelter to price items for the garage
sale. To Haven House. A place of refuge. She sat
among the women—the homeless and battered
women—and discussed how much to charge for used
toasters and incomplete sets of dishes, for a tired sofa,
a yellow dinette set, unused red sandals with five-inch
heels, an orange cowboy hat, an artificial Christmas
tree, a saucepan with no lid.

After everything was sorted and pricęd, she drank a
beer with George in the sitting room of his small
apartment. She told him about Melissa. Mentioned
there were problems with Chad. She didn't tell him
what. She trusted George completely, but she could
hear her husband's voice admonishing her to tell no
one.

"I got a book at the library about anorexia nervosa," Karen said. "Girls really do die of it."

"I don't think that will happen to Melissa," George said. "But if it does, you'll grieve. A lot. The pain will be unbearable, and you'll die a little yourself just to minimize the pain. Then one day you'll see something beautiful, and it will stun you. And you'll realize that you want to feel something besides pain, that you still have yourself, that nothing is worth ruining your life over."

"Was that how it was after your wife left?" Karen asked.

He nodded. Yes, that was how it was.

No one would call George Brown handsome. His skin was not exotically black or café au lait light, but rather a yellowish brown splotched with freckles. His face was big and flat, his cheeks pocked with acne scars, his nose crooked. His huge body was awesome still, not gone to fat like so many middle-aged athletes. His size meant people didn't immediately ignore him because he was black. But what held their attention was the gentleness in that great, ugly face.

"I think that you may be my only real friend," Karen told him.

22

*T*rumps was your basic college hangout. When Karen had been a student at OU, the building was occupied by a bicycle shop, but there had been similar funky establishments on the Campus Corner with mix-matched tables and chairs, graffiti on the walls, painted concrete floors, neon beer signs over the bar, music blasting from overhead speakers.

Karen chose a corner away from the speakers, deliberately sitting at a table covered with dirty dishes. "Are you Sammy?" she asked the boy who came to clear them away.

"Yes, ma'am," he said, pushing his glasses up on his nose and regarding her through smudged lenses. "Do I know you?" he asked.

"No. I used to come in here some. Your sister would wait on me. She told me she had a brother who worked Saturdays."

"You know 'bout Rose?" he asked, busying himself with stacking the dirty dishes on a tray, no longer looking at her.

"Yes, I know she's missing. Your mother—is she okay? I hope you have relatives close by to help out. You and she aren't alone, are you?"

"A friend of ours came for a while from Dallas," he said, wiping away the scattering of crumbs with a dingy rag. "But she's gone now. Some of the nurses from the hospital where my mom works brought over food. My grandmother wanted to come from Mexico, but

my mom doesn't want her to spend the money. She
wants her to wait until we know something for sure."

"I'm glad your mother has a brave son like you who
can help out."

"I'm not brave," he said, picking up the tray and
heading for the kitchen.

Such a frail child. He looked like a little bird with
spindly arms and legs. Not big enough to carry the
heavy tray.

He needed braces. At his age, he should already be
wearing them.

But braces cost thousands of dollars. Poor children
didn't get their teeth straightened. Poor children
bused tables in restaurants and gave half their earn-
ings to their mother to help pay the rent and buy groceries.

Karen had never had a job until she graduated
from college—and then only for three years.

Chad and several of his friends had taken jobs last
summer as wranglers at a Colorado dude ranch—
more as a lark than to earn money. What money he
came home with, Chad had used to buy new components for his stereo system.

Until she was fifteen, Melissa had gone to summer
camp in Missouri. Last summer she had been invited
to return as a paid junior counselor, but by that time
Trevor had entered her life.

Both of her children had always received generous
allowances for which they had few responsibilities.
They were expected to keep their rooms tidy enough
for the maid to vacuum and dust and to put in an
appearance when their parents had guests—to be introduced, offer a handshake, and exchange pleasant-
ries until a nod from their mother excused them.
They were required to write thank-you notes for gifts
and clean out their closets seasonally, culling the
clothing they no longer wore for the next Haven

House garage sale. Their primary responsibility, they
were frequently reminded by both parents, was to do
well in school. Melissa did this all the time, Chad only
occasionally.

Only two weeks had gone by since what Karen had
come to think of as the "tragedy." It seemed longer.
She felt as though she had gone through a mirror or
fallen down a well—and found herself in a place
where time was distorted and nothing made any sense.

Two weeks ago Karen had never heard of Inez
Frank and her two children, her husband, her home,
her life. Now Inez was always in her thoughts. Karen
felt that she personally had wronged Inez. If Karen
had been a better mother, raised her son to be a
stronger, braver person, Inez Frank's daughter might
still be alive.

The "Italian burger" Karen ordered was surpris-
ingly good, made with mozzarella, sautéed onions and
tomato sauce, and served with a side of spaghetti.
When she was finished, she ordered coffee so she
could watch Sammy Frank a bit longer. He worked
hard. And was well liked by waitresses and bartender.
Everyone's pet. Or maybe it was just that they felt
sorry for him.

Monday morning, Karen drove to the VA Hospital,
a sprawling red-brick institution on the University of
Oklahoma Health Sciences Center campus in eastside
Oklahoma City. She left a box of books and magazines
at the first-floor volunteer desk and asked for Joseph
Frank's room number.

She had meant simply to walk by the room and
glance inside. At the man in the "A" bed of the two-
bed room. But the "B" bed was empty, and Joseph
Frank was asleep. Karen stared for a moment at the
ashen, wasted man with tubes in both arms and another coming out of his nose. With each breath, he

made a loud wheezing sound as his chest rose and fell. A man near the end.

A picture of his wife and children was on the table by his bed. Did he know his daughter was missing, Karen wondered. Had he been a good father to her?

She'd seen them all now. Mother, father, brother. Rosalie's family.

The newspapers no longer printed stories about the Norman high-school girl who had vanished without a trace. Karen wondered how many months had to go by before the Norman police marked the Frank case as unsolved and filed it away. Sammy would grow up and get on with his life, but Inez would keep the vigil, think about her daughter every day, observe the anniversary of her disappearance with prayers and tears.

Sharon met Gary at the door, slipping her arms around his neck, kissing him on the mouth.

Behind her, Gary could see the table set with candles, fresh flowers in a silver vase, the good china. Soft music floated out of the stereo speakers.

Instead of her usual faded stretch pants and knit top, Sharon was wearing a dress, her face made up, her hair freshly washed and curled. She smelled of gardenias and shampoo, and she was smiling. Radiant.

Gary recognized the scenario. They'd enacted it three times before. A bottle of champagne would be cooling in the refrigerator. She would have forgone Hamburger Helper for something celebratory. She would have baked a cake or pie.

"You've had a positive pregnancy test," he said.

"Am I that obvious?" she asked, giggling.

"Don't you think we should wait a couple of months before we celebrate—until we're sure this one will take?"

"I've got an appointment with a doctor up at the

university hospital who specializes in difficult pregnancies," she said, grabbing his hand to kiss. Her eyes were sparkling, her voice bubbling with excitement, her cheeks flushed. "Mom met a woman at a craft fair who'd gone to him and finally had a successful pregnancy after *five* miscarriages. Mom said that she had her baby there with her in a stroller. A beautiful little girl with big brown eyes. The doctor put this woman to bed right away and started her on preventative drugs before she had any symptoms. And she couldn't have sex and couldn't take baths—only showers. No riding in the car. A glass of wine every four hours. And she carried to term! Imagine. To *term*. Isn't that wonderful? Mom has already said she'll come up a couple days a week to help out. Mary Ann, too."

She'd already told her mother and sister. He probably should feel jealous, but Gary didn't even care. This pregnancy was more about the three of them than it was about him and Sharon.

But the sight of her flouncing about, chattering about their rosy future, so full of life and plans and hope, young again, beautiful again, made Gary ache deep down inside. Inez Frank had said that where there was sadness, there was still feeling. Well, he was sad, but what he felt was defeated. God help him, he was jealous of the glob of cells inside of his wife that might or might not become a baby. Not even a fetus yet. An embryo. For an embryo, she had climbed out of her bottomless funk, cleaned up the house, and put on a dress. She had gotten out the never-used good china. Ironed a tablecloth. Cooked a fancy meal. Removed the whine from her voice. The prospect of a baby had given her hope, filled her with plans, made her want to go camping again, paint the house, learn how to knit.

He drank a toast with her. To their baby. And si-

lently vowed that it was the last time. If she miscarried
this time, he was going to have a vasectomy. And offer
her three choices. They could adopt, forget about
kids, or she could leave him. He was finished with temperature charts and procreation sex.

During those endless weeks when her mother was in
the hospital dying, Karen had shared the bedside vigil
with Aunt Faith, leaving Chad and Melissa to the care
of baby sitters and friends.

Once a day they would take turns going to Karen's
house to bathe and change. Faith was gone when
Grace patted her daughter's hand and told her not to
worry.

"I've got everything all worked out," Grace said,
her voice stronger than it had been in days.

"What do you have worked out?" Karen asked.

"My dying. I know just how my last minutes will
be."

Karen felt her stomach contract. Until now the
word "dying" had been carefully avoided.

Grace laughed at her. Then coughed. Took a minute to recover. And said, "Don't look so stricken. I've
figured it all out—so I won't be afraid."

Karen fought back tears. She simply couldn't have
this conversation with her mother.

Grace paused to catch her breath, then went on.
"When I was a little girl, Amelia Earhart flew into
Tulsa. Landed at the fairgrounds. We went out there
—Momma and Faith and I. Not my daddy, I don't
think. I don't remember him being there. But he must
have been. Momma didn't drive."

She was silent for a while. Karen thought she'd
drifted back to sleep—or wherever it was she went in
between her moments of wakefulness, which were getting shorter and shorter. They didn't even try to feed

her anymore. Or hook her up for dialysis. She slept most of the time now, her body losing its fight with the cancer that had taken first a breast and had now attacked her kidneys. But suddenly, with her eyes still closed, she was talking again. Slowly. Taking a breath every few words.

"Seemed like the whole town was there. The high-school band. The Shriner band. The roundup club with their horses and flags. A glorious day. Amelia stood on the wing of her airplane—and waved. She was wearing riding breeches and boots. Her hair was shiny in the sunlight. When she flew away, she circled the field—three times. We all waved—and cheered. Just a few months later she disappeared. So sad. But such a life! Goodness, such a life! I'd touched her airplane. Imagine! In my mind, that's where I'll be. In her airplane. Flying away. I've got it all planned. Flying off into the sky."

"But won't you be thinking of us?" Karen asked, indignant. "Won't you think of Daddy and me and John David? Of Melissa and Chad? And Faith? Your parents? The people who loved you?"

"I wanted to name you Amelia," Grace said. "But your father liked Karen."

"I don't want you to be thinking about flying away from us," Karen said, taking her mother's cold parchment hand. "I want you to think about being with us always. Hovering about like an angel, watching over us."

But Grace had already fallen asleep, her mouth open in her skeletal face. Now that she was no longer on chemotherapy, her hair was growing back—completely white. Only in profile did she still look like Grace.

Karen sat there in the chilly, dim room, trying to decide whether to take her mother's words seriously.

She thought not. Her mother's mind was wandering. She wasn't herself. If she was rational at the end, she would be thinking of her family. Not Amelia Earhart.

That was the last semblance of a conversation she'd had with her mother. Over the next week Grace would occasionally open her eyes, say the names of those around her. Ask for water. Then finally, she woke no more. Her lips would sometimes move. Her eyes flutter open. A sound would escape from her lips. But there were no words, no acknowledgment in her eyes. Her final breath had been a formality.

The name Karen meant pure—Amelia meant striving. For Karen, the name Amelia conjured up images of an adventurer, of a woman who dared.

Karen wondered what would have happened if her father had allowed her to be named Amelia. Would it have changed her life? Would she have been a freer, stronger woman?

Chad quit the golf team. Or rather, he stopped showing up for practice. The coach sent him a letter asking for an explanation. Chad didn't bother to answer it.

He still played some, when it wasn't too cold, alone, early in the morning when he and the squirrels and an occasional rabbit had the university course all to themselves. In Oklahoma, golf days popped up throughout the winter. There could be snow on the ground one day and shirtsleeve weather the next.

He still loved the game of golf. He just didn't want to be with anyone, didn't want to make small talk about the guys on the pro tour, the OU football team, demanding professors. Or girls. Most of all, he didn't want to talk about girls.

Eventually, he'd have to tell his dad that he'd quit the team. He'd be disappointed. His dad had thought that he might qualify for an NCAA tournament or have a run at a pro career. But Chad knew better. Good golfers who occasionally have brilliant rounds were a dime a dozen. And Chad no longer had the heart for daydreams.

23

When Johnny answered the phone, Chad offered the usual, "Hey, man, how's it going?"

Chad was sitting on the side of his bed, staring at the room's other bed with its bare mattress where his former roommate used to sleep, watch television, study, read science fiction, live. He never really left that bed much, Chad realized. Just for class, meals, chapter meetings, and church. Johnny went to early mass a couple of mornings a week. Not on Sunday. He said that Sunday mass was for show.

"You really don't have to call me anymore," Johnny said. "Tell your dad that I'm not going to tell anyone what happened. I'd like to, I think, but I can't because of my mother. I don't care about my father anymore, but my mom loves me. Or maybe I'm just a gutless coward."

Chad massaged the center of his forehead. He wanted to protest, to say that he was calling on his own, not because his dad insisted that he keep tabs on Johnny. But Johnny knew better.

"What about your priest?" Chad asked. "Don't you have to confess things to him?"

Johnny laughed. "Things like rape and murder? I suppose some people might. But I haven't been to church since I got back. Everything is different now."

"But if you did go to church and talk to a priest, he couldn't tell anyone what you said, could he?"

"I won't tell a priest, Chad," Johnny said, his voice weary.

Johnny was on a bed, Chad realized. Lying down. His eyes would be closed. He'd probably spent the last two weeks like that. Not going to church. Not doing anything. His parents must wonder. They would have tried to get him to tell them what was wrong.

"I checked with an academic adviser," Chad said. "You need to come back to school by next week or drop all your courses. If you don't come back or officially withdraw, you'll end up with straight F's on your transcript for this semester. The counselor's name is Mary Tuttle. You need to call her. Her extension is one-two-zero-five."

"Thanks. I'll do that."

"Now," Chad said. "Call her as soon as we hang up. Have you thought about what I said yesterday, about us transferring to OSU next semester? We could start all over. No fraternity. No parties. Be ourselves. Study and make good grades. Really learn something instead of just getting by. Hell, man, you've already got a pickup truck. You'd fit right in. Your truck's still parked out back, waiting for you. I keep the bird shit wiped off of it."

"Before that girl died, I might have done that. But before, you wouldn't have asked me, wouldn't even have thought about transferring. Thanks for trying, though. And for putting up with me. I know it was hard for you getting stuck with me as a roommate. I felt sorry for you. What I should have done was stay in the dorms or gone to school someplace else. Join the Peace Corps. Take religious vows, and go live with the good brothers over in Shawnee and make sandals and soap. Anything but what I was doing. But I didn't have the nerve to tell my dad that I hated his fraternity, hated his precious OU Sooners, hated petroleum engineering, hated him actually. I look at him in his gold-nugget jewelry and thousand-dollar cowboy boots, and I want to puke. Strange how it took that poor girl dying for me to realize the last thing I want on this earth is to make my father proud.''

''Look, Johnny, the way I figure it is the only way we can even begin to make up for what happened to that girl is to lead a good life and give lots of money to charity. Turning into a fuckup isn't going to do anybody any good. When our pledge class took those kids from the Cerebral Palsy Institute to the rodeo, you told me that you liked kids more than grown-ups. It was the first time I'd ever seen you have a good time. If you want to stick it to your dad, change your major to education. He'd freak, wouldn't he? Come on back to school, Johnny. Major in education. Be the best teacher you can be. Teach your students to respect people. Come on, man, you can do it. You don't have to live in the IB house. If you don't want to transfer to OSU, we can share an apartment here. We can finish school and get on with it.''

''You're not responsible for me, Chad.''

''Yeah, I am. I took you upstairs.''

''I'm not a retard. I'm responsible for my own fuck-ups.''

''Yeah, I know. You could have left. Could have called the police. But you wouldn't have needed to do anything if you hadn't been up there in the first place. We thought it was such a joke. Getting little Johnny laid. That girl was just someone to stick our dicks into. If I hadn't taken you up there, she might still have died, but you and I wouldn't have had anything to do with it. You could still be sitting over there on your bed reading about the starship *Enterprise* instead of how to drill for oil. I wish like hell I could turn the clock back. But I can't. So, just think about what I've said, will you?''

"I will. I'll write you a letter, okay? You don't need to call anymore."

"Sure. But don't forget to call Mary Tuttle. Extension one-two-zero-five. I hope your letter says that you're enrolling for next semester. I want you back here, Johnny. I want to make things up to you."

The letter from Johnny arrived just two days later. Chad put off opening it until until late afternoon. He wasn't sure what he wanted it to say.

The house was quiet. Most of the guys were over at the intramural field either watching or playing in IB's touch-football game with the Delts. If the IBs won, they'd be in the play-offs.

Chad sat on his bed and looked down at the letter. Did he really want to live with Johnny Fontaine—either here or in Stillwater?

He did and he didn't. He had no problem with moving out of the frat house into an apartment. Lots of guys did that, especially when they had a steady girl. But he and Johnny really had very little in common. Johnny didn't watch sporting events on television. He didn't play pickup basketball or touch football. He didn't hang out at the Campus Corner taverns. Chad had never known him to have a date or get drunk. He drove a restored 1951 Ford truck when he could have driven any vehicle that he wanted to. It was weird to have a roommate like Johnny, but it would be even weirder to live with him in an apartment.

And what about Brenda? They couldn't ask Johnny to leave at night just so they could have privacy. He'd be like their kid. Always around. Brenda wouldn't understand why he'd taken on Johnny Fontaine, and Chad couldn't tell her why.

But like it or not, Johnny was his responsibility. He would move into an apartment with him if that was what Johnny wanted.

Chad tore open the envelope to see what the verdict was and stared at the words carefully printed on lined paper.

Chad,

I can't live with what happened.
Sorry.

Good-bye,
Johnny

"Oh, shit," Chad said out loud and fell backward onto the bed. "Christ Johnny, no! You dumb ass. No."

He rolled to the wall and beat his head against it. Two, three, four times. Then stopped.

Maybe it wasn't so. Maybe Johnny meant something else or had changed his mind. Maybe the letter was just a sick joke, and Johnny didn't send it at all.

Chad rolled back to the edge of the bed and picked the envelope up off the floor. A Phoenix postmark.

He dialed Johnny's private number. No answer. He didn't know his parents' number. He dialed Johnny's number again and let it ring for a long time. He imagined a house so large, a bedroom so remote that the ringing telephone couldn't be heard. Maybe Johnny had disconnected it. Maybe no one was at home.

Chad called Phoenix information for the number of the John Fontaine residence. It was unlisted.

He went across the hall and knocked on the door to Syd Johnson's room. Syd was the chapter secretary. He'd given Johnny's number to Chad and probably had his parents', too.

Syd wasn't there. Chad ran the length of the house to the large corner room reserved for the chapter president. Tom Fitzhugh wasn't in his room either, but the door was unlocked. The cardboard file box where he kept chapter stuff was on the floor next to

his desk. A file with Johnny's name on it was there
behind the "F."

Using Tom's phone, hand shaking, heart racing,
Chad dialed the number in Phoenix.

An older woman with a Spanish accent answered.

Chad explained that he was a friend of Johnny's
and needed to talk to Mr. Fontaine.

He waited, his heart pounding so hard that it hurt.
Please let it not be so.

Suddenly Mr. Fontaine was there, thanking him for
calling. Johnny had thought a lot of him, appreciated
his phone calls. "How did you know?" he asked Chad.
"It just happened yesterday."

"What happened?" Chad asked.

"He was killed. Isn't that why you called?"

Chad broke out in a sweat. *Jesus.* How much did
Johnny's father know? He shouldn't be making this
call. The Fontaines should be calling him. The house.
To inform them that Johnny was dead.

Chad struggled for something to say. A reason for
his call. Mr. Fontaine was waiting for him to say something.

"A friend of one of the guys here in the house just
called," he stammered. "I guess they saw something
in the Phoenix newspaper. I wanted to make sure it
was true. And tell you how sorry I was."

"It happened late yesterday evening and hasn't
been in the newspaper yet."

"Well, maybe he heard it on radio. Or from a
friend. I didn't talk to him." Chad rubbed at his forehead. *Christ,* what had he done?

"Did you talk to Johnny before this happened?"

"I've been trying to get him to come back to
school. We'd talked about sharing an apartment next
semester. How did it happen?"

"He drove his mother's car into an overpass embankment. It caught fire."

Chad groaned. And felt dizzy. Sick.

He had to think of something else to say, something that would allow him to hang up the phone.

"When's the funeral?"

"Tomorrow morning. But don't think you have to come."

"I want to," Chad heard himself saying. But he didn't want to. All he wanted to do was hang up. And cry. Scream. Kick down a door.

"That would be very nice of you," Mr. Fontaine was saying, his voice breaking. "Johnny didn't have many friends. He wrote to you, didn't he? I saw the letter he left for the mailman. Did he tell you he was going to do it?"

"He told me good-bye. I just got his note a little while ago. I'm really sorry, sir, if I've caused you more pain. I shouldn't have called. I wasn't thinking."

"I was pretty sure that was what happened. There weren't any skid marks. The highway patrolman said he must have been going over a hundred. And he'd been depressed. Just sat up in his room all day. I looked for a note among his things. Maybe he had one with him in the car. But I'd hate for his mother to ever think his death was anything but an accident."

"Yes, sir. I'll tell everyone here at the house. An accident. When's the service?"

"Ten o'clock. At St. Stephen's. The burial is the day after tomorrow. Out of town. His mother insists on taking him to the mountains for a private burial. In a country churchyard outside Claypool. We used to have a cabin up there when Johnny was little. He was a cute little guy. Liked to fish. We have nice memories of that time."

Chad staggered down the hall to his room. Without looking at Johnny's bed, he called Southwest Airlines. Packed a suit and some underwear. Then he called

Brenda and started sobbing at the sound of her voice. "Johnny's dead," he kept saying over and over.

Brenda offered to come over. To meet him someplace. Drive him to the airport. As soon as she dried her hair.

Chad drove himself, barely making the six fifty-five flight. He had one beer between Oklahoma City and Dallas. Three more on the flight to Phoenix.

He stayed in a Holiday Inn near the Phoenix airport. The bar was crowded. The Seahawks were playing the Raiders on the big screen and half a dozen smaller sets scattered about the room. He tried to buy a drink, but the bartender carded him. He offered her a twenty for a beer, but she ignored him. "Bitch," he said under his breath.

The woman on the next bar stool heard him and turned her back to him.

He finally dozed off watching a pay-per-view movie in his room. *Terminator II.* But he woke in the night. And watched the Three Stooges, the 700 Club, a surfing competition in Hawaii, anything to keep at bay the image of Johnny burning up in his mother's car. He should have offered the bartender a fifty instead of a twenty. Tomorrow night he'd drink himself into a stupor before he closed his eyes.

He felt like shit in the morning. And realized he'd forgotten his razor.

The adobe church was small and starkly plain. Somehow it seemed more like a real church than the one Chad attended in Nichols Hills. The closed casket in front of the altar was plain, too. Wood. Beautiful, shiny wood with shiny brass handles.

Chad was unfamiliar with the liturgy. And wasn't sure if he should participate in a Catholic service. But he felt like a wooden statue, just sitting there. Conspicuous. Like a godless heathen.

There was no eulogy—just a sermon about death and resurrection. Not about Johnny.

Chad tuned out the priest and stared at the casket. So hard to believe that Johnny was inside of it. Burned up. Wrapped in a sheet probably. Or inside a plastic body bag. Johnny was dead. And the girl. *Rosalie.* She died with his and Johnny's semen inside of her. Poor Johnny. The only sex he'd ever had.

At the last instant had Johnny still wanted to die? Had he tried to get out of the burning car?

The girl most certainly hadn't wanted to die. When Chad closed his eyes, he could see her dead body. Her exposed crotch. Johnny, as white as the bed pillow he was hugging, sitting on the floor. The smells. The horror.

The mourners were directed to file by the casket. Johnny's parents first. Mr. Fontaine stood to one side while his wife put a hand on the casket containing their son's remains. Her shoulders shook.

Chad began to cry. He cried all the way up the aisle, not seeing where he was going, bumping into the woman in front of him.

Like Johnny's mom, he put a hand on the casket. And whispered, "Peace, brother. Peace."

The Fontaines were receiving in the vestibule. Mrs. Fontaine hugged him. And told him thank you over and over. Then hugged him again.

Mr. Fontaine shook his hand. His eyes were rimmed with red. "I'm glad you came. It meant a lot to both of us."

"I wanted to come," Chad said, his voice breaking. "I'll never forget him. I wish I'd been a better friend for him."

They shook hands again, and Chad remembered to ask about Johnny's truck.

"Would you like it?" Mr. Fontaine asked. "If not, I'll have it towed to a salvage yard."

"Yeah. I'd like to have it."

He drank beer on the way home, not allowing himself to doze off. He wanted to be able to sleep tonight. At home, in Nichols Hills. Not in his room at the IB house with Johnny's empty bed across the room.

He wished that he could sleep with Brenda tonight. Not have sex. Just sleep. Maybe he and Brenda could move in together. Get married even.

When he was six or seven and been afraid of monsters in the closet and under the bed, he'd go crawl into bed with his mother.

That's how he felt now. Six or seven years old. Scared of monsters in the night. And his mother didn't love him anymore.

24

From the airport, Chad drove north to Nichols Hills. It was almost five o'clock when he walked in the front door. His mother appeared in the entry hall, carrying a piece of needlepoint, a thimble on her finger. She looked at his face and asked, "What's wrong?"

"Johnny Fontaine's dead," he said. And began to cry.

His mother led him into the family room. His father rose from the easy chair, pointing the remote at the television to switch off a football game.

Chad sank to the sofa, his mother beside him. He heard Melissa's footsteps on the stairs. He wanted to stop crying. He shouldn't cry in front of his sister. But he couldn't stop.

His mother was stroking his arm, asking how it happened. "A car wreck," Chad said, choking back his sobs. "I just got back from his funeral. In Phoenix."

"That was nice of you," his mother said softly. "I'm sure his parents appreciated your being there."

His father sat on the other side of him. "Do you want something to eat?" he asked, which struck Chad as odd. That was his mother's line.

"Yeah," he said, accepting a handful of Kleenex from Melissa. "I haven't had lunch."

His mother was still stroking his arm. It felt nice for her to touch him. Maybe that was why he came home, because he knew she'd have to touch him if his roommate had just died.

"How did it happen?" she asked.

"Get the boy something to eat, Karen," his dad said. "We'll talk about this after he gets something in his stomach."

"I thought you didn't like Johnny," Melissa said from her perch on the arm of the easy chair.

"I didn't want him as a roommate. But he was okay. Just different. I got used to him."

And he began to cry again. He'd thought that he was making such a great sacrifice, agreeing to room with Johnny for a semester. For the fraternity. For the pool table, new deck, and other compensations that Johnny's dad would provide. He'd felt sorry for Johnny. Nobody wanted him. During their pledge year, Chad had lived just a few doors down from Johnny in Walker Tower, and Chad had fallen into the habit of walking with him over to the IB house for the Monday and Wednesday dinners that pledges were required to attend. When Tom Fitzhugh asked Chad at the end of last year if he'd room with Johnny next fall, Chad said no way. But no one else would either. And Johnny would have to have a roommate to live in the house. Only the president got a room to himself. Finally, Chad had agreed. Somehow the fact that he'd walked four blocks with Johnny two evenings a week made him feel responsible.

Mr. Fontaine never should have tried to buy his son's way into his fraternity. The chapter shouldn't have gone along with it. Johnny should have refused to come to OU. Chad should have been a straight enough guy to tell Johnny he didn't belong in a fraternity. He shouldn't have taken Johnny upstairs. Lots of shoulds. A pretty worthless word.

His mom offered to fix an early dinner, but all Chad wanted was a bowl of soup and some crackers.

His dad hovered, refilling his glass of milk. Offering him a second helping, a banana, cookies. His mother sat on a bar stool, not saying much, watching him. Both parents were waiting to hear the details of Johnny's death.

Already, Chad was regretting his decision to come home. He'd have to face his empty room at the IB house eventually. And he had a calculus assignment due in the morning that he hadn't finished. Of course, he had a good excuse. He'd been out of town —at his roommate's funeral. But if he didn't get it done, he'd be behind in starting the next assignment. Mostly, though, he didn't want to face his mother's questions. He hadn't anticipated her reaction. Did she know that Johnny had been involved in what happened to Rosalie Frank? Even if his dad hadn't told her, she was probably suspicious, with Johnny leaving school the day after it happened. Explaining Johnny's suicide to his dad was one thing, but the idea of telling his mother made him uncomfortable. *Johnny couldn't live with what happened to Rosalie Frank. He drove his mother's car into a concrete wall and killed himself.*

He lingered for a while, opening a beer, watching the evening news with them. An apartment fire on the south side. The presidential press conference. A cold front on the way. Even Melissa sat with them. The four of them in the family room. It had been a long time. But it wasn't the same. Melissa looked like a scare-crow. His mother was distant. Only his father was trying to be just the same. The urge to start sobbing again was so strong it made Chad's chest hurt. Not for Johnny this time. For himself. He took a deep breath and another swallow of beer.

When the sports news ended, he explained about the calculus assignment. Probably he'd better get on back. There really wasn't all that much to tell about Johnny. He'd been driving too fast and crashed his mom's car into a wall. Chad hugged his mother. Melissa blew him a kiss from the stairway. His dad said he'd try to drive down to Norman tomorrow—they'd have lunch at Legend's.

As he approached the I–35 exit, for half an instant, Chad considered going north instead of south. Heading for Colorado. Forget about finishing out the semester. Forget about everything.

But he knew there was no such thing as forgetting.

He thought about his mother's hand on his arm. Had that meant anything? Or was it just an automatic gesture on her part?

Karen stepped back to admire the new bedcover—a quilt she'd bought at the Haven House sale. A country quilt—the sort that women made out of random scraps of clothing with fine little stitches put in when they could.

The quilt replaced the starched white Battenburg lace coverlet that was totally impractical for a bed that was being used every night—as this one now was. For a week now, Karen had slept in the smaller of the two guest rooms. One night had followed another, every night a decision anew. Karen didn't plan ahead anymore. She just got up in the morning and wandered through each day.

Putting the quilt on the bed seemed to indicate that now she was a resident of the room.

She needed to sleep alone—here in this house or someplace else. At this point in time, returning to her husband's bed—and she had come to think of it as his bed—would soften the boundaries of her resolve to think for herself no matter where those thoughts took her.

The guest room was just a place to spend the night. She still dressed in the other bedroom. Bathed in her large bathroom. But every day she found herself carrying a few more possessions down the hall. A hairbrush and a toothbrush were now in the guest room's adjoining bathroom. Her clock and a bottle of hand lotion occupied the bedside table. The little black-and-white television from her bathroom was on the dresser.

The homey quilt inspired a trip to the attic to bring down the old rocker that used to sit in the corner of her and Roger's bedroom when the children were babies. Of course, it didn't go with the room's French provincial settee. But neither did the quilt. Maybe she'd move the settee someplace else. Or maybe not.

She'd forgotten how soothing it was to rock, how comfortable the chair was with its contoured seat and bowed back. She'd been pregnant with Chad when she bought the rocker at an estate sale on a farm west of Perkins—a sturdy old chair constructed of native pecan with broad armrests that made it perfect for nursing a baby, one of the few pieces of furniture she'd kept from back then when she was in the nesting period of her life and her decorating tastes ran more to cozy.

Her mother had been with her that day. Grace seldom bought anything during their mother-daughter excursions to such sales. Collectibles wouldn't be appropriate in her home. But she was usually the one who saw the announcement in the newspaper and suggested they meet at some town along the turnpike for an excursion to Beggs, Okfuskee, Oilton, Cushing, wherever. Adventures down country roads. Lunch prepared by the ladies of the local home demonstration club. Browsing through the past. Grace's aunt Lura had had that same ruby-red glassware. The jars of watermelon pickles made her think of her great-aunt Beth. Her father had listened to war news on a radio just like that one. She'd pick up a Log Cabin Syrup tin and recall pouring syrup on her pancakes from one just like it.

The rocker had been a real find. It didn't even need refinishing. They'd wrapped a blanket around it and put it in the trunk of her mother's Lincoln, tying the lid down with a rope.

Karen leaned her head against the chair's high back and closed her eyes, seeing herself as a younger woman holding a baby, rocking in this chair. Good times.

She waited for a few nostalgic tears to dampen her eyes. Wanting them. Needing their warmth to help her remember who she was. Karen, daughter of Grace, mother of the babies she'd rocked in this chair. But tears wouldn't come. The present was intruding on her past.

When she opened her eyes, Roger was standing in the doorway, taking in the quilt on the bed, her in the rocker.

"What about dinner?" he asked.

Karen glanced at her watch. Yes, it was dinnertime. "I'll fix sloppy joes," she said. "It won't take long. Did you see Chad today?"

"Yes. I had breakfast with Melissa and lunch with Chad. A real shame about Johnny Fontaine. I called his dad. Told him how sorry we were. He said that he and his wife really appreciated Chad coming to the funeral and kept telling me what a fine young man that Chad is and that he'd hire him in a flash if he ever wants a job." Roger remained in the doorway, not setting foot on her new turf. Karen wasn't sure if that was a sign of disapproval or respect.

"Was Johnny one of the boys who raped that girl?" she asked.

"I'm not at liberty to say."

"Oh, for Christ's sake, Roger, don't pull that lawyer crap with me! *Was he one of the boys?*"

Roger nodded. He was.

"Was Johnny's death an accident?"

"Chad seemed to think not."

"Dear God. *Two* young people dead now. Doesn't this change something?"

Roger frowned. "How do you mean?"

"I'm not sure. But it's twice the tragedy now."

"No, it's doesn't change things—not for us. Not for our son."

Karen shrugged and rose from the chair.

"Where's Melissa?" Roger asked, glancing down the hall toward Melissa's room.

"I don't know."

"She's supposed to call if she's going to be late for dinner."

Karen nodded. Yes, Melissa was supposed to call. Karen had been pointing that out for months.

"Did she eat anything for breakfast?" Karen asked, folding her arms, then unfolding them, not knowing quite what to do with herself while her husband was standing there. She should have stayed in the rocking chair.

"Not much," he admitted. "I warned her that her weigh-in with Dr. Burk is tomorrow, and she did take a couple bites of toast and drank some orange juice."

"You want me to take her to the doctor's in the morning?"

"No. I will. I'm marked out at the office," he said, unbuttoning the top button of his shirt. "I didn't know you still had that old rocker."

"You remember it?" she asked, touching the back of the chair.

"Jesus, Karen! Of course I remember it."

He headed down the hallway to change out of his work clothes. Karen went downstairs to see about dinner. She took a package of ground beef and one of hamburger buns from the freezer. She put the meat in the skillet to brown and searched for something to make a salad out of.

But the greens were slimy, the bell peppers and tomatoes soft. She hadn't shopped since Chad's birthday. There wasn't even a carrot to slice into sticks. She threw out the rotting vegetables and put mustard and pickles on the table.

The phone rang. That would be Melissa phoning in her excuse. Karen let it ring. Roger could answer it.

She already knew that Melissa would not show a weight loss tomorrow. Melissa wasn't about to let herself gain weight, but she was savvy enough to have eaten just enough during the week so she wouldn't lose weight. And as insurance, she'd probably drink two diet Cokes in the morning instead of her usual one. Maybe the weekly weigh-ins would keep her from losing any more weight, but they were nothing more than a holding pattern. The crisis or cure was yet to come.

"Melissa said to save her half a sloppy joe," Roger announced. "She and Debbie are studying for a chemistry test. I told her that I planned to sit and watch her eat it no matter what time she came in."

He was wearing gray sweats. His hair was freshly combed. "Want me to help?" he asked.

"That would be nice," Karen said, hacking browned beef away from the frozen lump.

He waited a minute for her to tell him what to do. When she refused to state the obvious, he set the table, put ice in the glasses. Then he sat down, a folded *Wall Street Journal* at his elbow. He no longer read his newspapers before dinner, but he continued to bring one to the table with him, as though to remind Karen of his sacrifice.

"How was your tennis game?" he asked.

"I didn't play," she said, opening a box of frozen broccoli.

"I thought Monday was your foursome day."

"It is. I'm sure they found someone to take my place. I worked at Haven House."

"You didn't even call to cancel, did you?" he asked.

"To be perfectly honest, I forgot all about it until you mentioned it," she said, putting the broccoli in the microwave. "Tennis is the farthest thing from my mind right now."

"You blow off your friends for a bunch of losers at a women's shelter? God, Karen, I don't understand you anymore."

"So you've said."

"I think this family would be a lot better off if you didn't spend so much time at that place."

"Oh?" she said, feeling the skin on her face tighten as she turned to face him. "How's that?"

He tapped his fingers on the unread newspaper. "I've worked hard to provide a beautiful home and a good life for you and our children, and I never could understand why you insisted on seeking out the seamy side of life. But at least you were only going down there a couple times a week. Now you're going every day, and your involvement with that place certainly isn't helping you deal with the situation in Norman. Haven House has done nothing but give you a skewed image of relationships and men."

"*Skewed?* Because I don't condone physical abuse against women? Because I'm devastated that our son raped a girl?"

"Damn it, Karen," he said, slamming his fist down on the table, making the plates and silverware jump. "I don't condone abuse either. And just because our son was involved in that one incident doesn't mean that he's some kind of monster. You know damned good and well that he isn't like those men who beat up their wives. What happened to that girl was a tragic accident. And she is as much to blame as they are."

Karen took a step forward and slammed her own
fist on the table. "Like hell she is! One drunk, semi-
conscious girl against six boys doesn't sound like an
equal division of blame to me. Do you really believe
that it's okay for those boys to have done what they
did to that poor girl and walk away unscathed? That
it's okay for them to do whatever they want to a girl
and get away with it?"

Roger got to his feet, and Karen tensed. But he
stayed on his side of the table, his face an angry red
mask. "I'd hardly call Johnny Fontaine *unscathed*. He
drove a car into a concrete wall and burned to death.
And you saw how distraught Chad was last night. Is he
unscathed?"

"And just what did you tell our distraught son at
lunch today?" Karen demanded, spitting out the
words, her anger matching his. "I'll just bet you told
him to put it all behind him. That it's not his fault that
Johnny Fontaine was a weakling. That Chad Billingsly
has to be strong."

Roger picked up a plate and threw it against the
cupboard over Karen's head. She jumped but didn't
scream.

He stared at the shattered plate for a long moment
until his shoulders slumped, and he sank back into his
chair.

"Just what do you want from Chad and me?" he
asked, calmer, but his voice still full of challenge. "Do
you want our son to go to jail. Is that what you want?"

"All I know is that it's not right for them to get off
scot-free—like that girl didn't matter," she said, still
standing, glaring down at him. "I don't know what
should happen to them. I don't know if they should
go to prison. But what else means that what they did
was so wrong that they have to give up something that
means a lot to them—like their freedom for a time?
Nothing can ever wipe the slate clean, but at least a

prison term is a payback of sorts. But you don't want
them to pay back. You don't even want them to feel
bad. And now you're diminishing not only Rosalie
Frank's death, but Johnny Fontaine's as well. I can't
accept that.''

"Don't you know what happens to good-looking
young men in prison? They'd probably get raped
themselves. They'd never be the same again. Is that
what you want?''

"You act like that's a worse fate than what happened to Rosalie Frank.''

He pointed at the telephone on the wall. "So call
the police and tell them your son and five of his
friends raped Rosalie Frank and caused her death.
Turn him in. Then will you be happy?''

"Of course I won't be *happy*. I'm not sure what
should be done. But you and I are worlds apart. You
are killing that girl all over again. Erasing her. She
doesn't even have a tombstone in a cemetery. You
want it to seem like she never lived, like she never
existed.''

"Chad is my son, and I will do everything in my
power to see that he never sets foot inside a prison—
which now means keeping the whole mess a secret. I
will listen if you have some other suggestion. Perhaps
you'd like him to join the Peace Corps and work in a
third-world-country. But nothing's going to bring that
girl back. Or Johnny Fontaine. It's time to prevent further tragedy, not create more.''

Karen sank into the nearest chair. "What if Chad
and those boys help support Rosalie's family. Put her
brother through college. Give her mother a decent
place to live. A new car. An annuity. Something.''

"Right now no one knows that there was a crime,''
Roger said. "The girl could have run away. But if her
mother suddenly gets a lot of money, it would be like

an announcement to her and the police that someone out there is feeling mighty guilty."

Karen could think of nothing else to say. Roger always bested her with his lawyer's logic. And logically, maybe he was right. But it didn't change the emptiness inside her. The desolation. The loneliness. And most of all, the guilt.

She returned to the stove, adding a can of tomato sauce and a tablespoon of chili powder to the beef. Without looking at her husband, she said, "Maybe the parents of boys who rape and kill should be the ones to go to jail. Chad wrecked cars, and you bought him a new one. If he'd lived in south town, he'd probably have done time on drug charges by now. I stood by and allowed you to deny him the lesson of accountability. And I covered for him when he skipped school —lied for him. The attendance clerk must have wondered how a boy with such pretty teeth would have so many dentist appointments."

"We only did what we thought best at the time. That's all any parent can do." She heard Roger's chair being pushed back. Then he was standing behind her. Very close.

"Can't we help each other get through this?" he asked.

She knew that if she just stood there, he would slide him arms around her waist and press himself against her. Intimacy would signify a close to the discussion. An acquiescence on her part. That was the pattern of their marriage.

She reached into the cupboard for two plates. "Hand me that package of buns, will you?"

25

*H*e could hear doors opening and closing, footsteps muffled by the worn carpet as, up and down the hall, other second-floor residents began migrating downstairs for dinner. It was Monday evening, and the freshmen pledges would be arriving from the dorms. After dinner, they'd sing Iota Beta songs, some raunchy but mostly rather beautiful songs of brotherhood. Chad had always felt very close to his IB brothers as they raised their voices in song to pledge loyalty forever to the grand old fraternity. After the singing and whatever announcements Tom Fitzhugh had for the group as a whole, the pledges would go downstairs to the rec room for their weekly meeting, and the members would conduct chapter meeting in the dining room.

If he missed chapter meeting tonight, it would be the third time this semester. Chad wondered if three was the final straw, or if missing number four was when they kicked a guy out of the house. Only active members and upperclass pledges were allowed to live in the house.

He also hadn't shown up for a meeting of the rush committee or the IB touch football game with the Sig Eps for the interfraternity championship, and a midnight pinning serenade in front of the Gamma Phi Beta sorority house.

If he didn't shape up, he would have to emerge from his current listless state long enough to find other lodging. He reminded himself of Johnny—staying in this room most of the day, his back against the headboard, a book propped against his knees, leaving only to go to class and eat. And see Brenda. Johnny hadn't had a Brenda. He hadn't really had anyone. Last year in the dorms he'd at least watch the nightly reruns of *Star Trek* down in the lounge with the other Trekkies. But there weren't any Trekkies in the IB house.

Lunch and breakfast at the house were come-and-go and could be eaten with a textbook or newspaper propped in front of his face. The evening meal, however, was a more formal occasion, served on time and usually followed by announcements, kudos, and periodically the latest warning from the university concerning underage drinking of alcoholic beverages, hazing, fire and parking regulations, whatever. Sometimes one of the university administrators came in person to discuss one the university's concerns with campus fraternities—usually hazing. Fraternities made problems for the university, but OU's strong Greek system was a big recruiting draw for more affluent students. OU was really two schools—a party school and a place where serious students came to learn. Frat guys mostly majored in political science, communication, business administration, all of which could be demanding but were certainly less challenging and left more time for partying and sports than engineering, geology, physics, meteorology, math, chemistry, and the like, which were mostly the province of foreign students and computer nerds. Few frat guys majored in foreign languages or English, both of which were also demanding and a bit squirrelly. And fraternity men never majored in drama, art, music, or dance. Johnny Fontaine had been one of only three engineering majors who were active IBs, and the other two had moved out of the house. Chad was the only fraternity

member in his Japanese class—at least for now. Maybe
next week he'd be the only defrocked fraternity member in his Japanese class.

For whether it was this week or the next, the ax was
going to fall. Fitzhugh had already dropped by to have
a "little talk." The chapter president reminded Chad
of a grown-up Opie Taylor straight from the streets of
Mayberry, but in spite of his wholesome demeanor, ol'
Tom had turned out to be a consummate politician,
working behind scenes to form coalitions, getting
himself elected president of the house his junior year
—an honor normally saved for a senior. But then Tom
planned to be president of the student body his senior
year—and a U.S. senator by the time he was forty.

President Tom had pumped Chad's hand, saying
once again how deeply sorry he was about Johnny,
how his death was a great tragedy. And he knew that
Chad was having a hard time dealing with his roommate's death.

"I hadn't realized that you and Johnny were that
close," Tom said. "I know you agreed to room with
him only because nobody else would. I think it's great
that a real friendship came out of it. Hell, man, that's
what fraternity is all about."

"Cut the crap," Chad said. "*Fraternity* and yours
truly made Johnny feel about as welcome as jock itch.
So deliver your fuckin' ultimatum and get out of my
room."

Fitzhugh stood and, with a hand on the doorknob,
had quickly explained that, because of Johnny's death,
the executive board was willing to overlook Chad's recent absences from chapter meetings and other house
functions but felt that he needed to start pulling his
own weight again, or he would be put on inactive
status and asked to leave the house.

So, Chad reminded himself, unless he got off this
bed and went downstairs for Monday-night roast beef

and the tedious chapter meeting that followed with
minutes, reports, motions, and endless discussions
about a bunch of crap he no longer cared about, he
truly was going to have to find another place to live.

Thanksgiving break was next week. That would be a
good time to move out. He could be gone by the time
everyone came back on Sunday evening.

Since the night that his father referred to as the
"accident," unless he was with Brenda, Chad would
eat a sandwich at the Penny Hill Sub Shop, not because he wanted a steady diet of submarine sandwichs,
but following a set routine was easier than making a
decision. When he was with Brenda, she decided.

He thought a lot about him and Brenda living together. Then she could decide everything. What to
eat. What to wear. What to do. Even when to make
love.

But Brenda loved Chi Omega. And she wouldn't
live with him unless they were married, and she didn't
want to be a married woman until she was finished
being a college girl. She viewed his current funk as
temporary, something he'd get over as soon as he got
through finals and enough time had passed for him to
put Johnny's death behind him. Changing rooms at
the end of the semester would help. And a new roommate. It must be terrible for him looking over at
Johnny's empty bed, sleeping in the room where
Johnny had slept.

Brenda made him feel normal. He needed that.
But she mistook his need for love.

Chad didn't respect Brenda enough to love her.
She never pondered. Never questioned. Her constant
need to please him made him angry at times. He
didn't want her solicitous phone calls or her little gifts
of food. He especially hated her little messages—often
written on sappy greeting cards—that she would leave
in his car or send through the mail. *I'm thinking of you.*

Your grief is my grief. Our love will make us strong. Hell,
she went through practically the same routine with
Deeann Norton-Jones, the pledge who was her sorority little sis, leaving cute little presents and saccharine
messages on Deeann's bed or in her coat pocket. Not
that Chad doubted Brenda's sincerity, but all that
sweetness bored him. And made him worry that she'd
still be that way at forty.

But he wasn't sure if he could manage sex with a
new girl. The strangeness would make him think
about what he was doing. And thinking might make
him impotent. With Brenda, he didn't have to think.
With her, he could fall back into old patterns—patterns developed before Rosalie Frank. There was a
comfortable familiarity about their lovemaking that,
with the help of alcohol, allowed him to find his way
to climax.

But how long would Brenda hang in there with him
if he quit the fraternity? She wouldn't have a midnight
pinning serenade in front of the Chi Omega house.
She would be different. Only a handful of her sorority
sisters dated unaffiliated guys.

Of course, Chad could move out of the IB house
and still remain active by paying his dues and showing
up for chapter meetings and functions. Probably he
should be willing to do that much for Brenda, but it
seemed dishonest to let her think that, philosoph-
ically, he was still a member of the club. A frat guy.
Elite. Cool.

He had liked feeling that way before. A lot. He
liked having Greek letters on his car window. Liked
knowing that he was one of the privileged few. What if
these feelings of alienation that he was experiencing
now were only temporary? Maybe he'd hate being on
the outside looking in.

He could go to chapter meeting tonight and give
himself another week to think about it. He should at

least wait until after the Chi Omega Harvest Ball Saturday night before he upset Brenda's tight little world. She was on the arrangements committee. The sorority had rented the Marriott ballroom in north Oklahoma City, hired one of the hottest bands in the state, chartered buses to transport everyone up and back so there'd be no arrests for drunk driving or automobile accidents on the way back to Norman. Brenda had been talking about the ball for weeks. She'd gone on a quest for just the right dress. She was going to wear her hair up. Have her makeup done professionally. Have another set of party pics for her album.

Yeah, probably he should hang in there for Brenda. Go downstairs and eat a decent meal. Go to chapter meeting. Not do anything permanent until he was sure.

But he knew he wouldn't. Couldn't actually. Couldn't make his body go down the front stairs and take a seat among the brothers and pledges as though he was the same old Chad as before. He could no more do that than he could have bench-pressed five hundred pounds.

He'd wait until the floor was deserted and head out. Then he'd come back here after he'd had his sandwich and study until Brenda called. She'd expect to go out for their usual after-chapter-meeting Coke or beer. Or maybe they'd pass on the beverage and have backseat sex before he came back here and gave his Japanese one last perusal in preparation for tomorrow morning's vocabulary test.

Strange how quickly he'd gone from studying as little as possible to studying all the time. He found refuge in memorizing the conjugation of Japanese verbs, struggling over calculus problems, reading and re-reading assignments in political science, sociology, and American history. He was getting weird. Even Brenda thought so. Not that she said so. But she would look at him with such puzzlement, like he was wearing a different nose.

Penny Hill was just south of Main on Hal Muldrow Drive, in an area where several older apartment complexes were located—a pretty street with lots of trees and not more than ten minutes or so from the campus. Without really planning to do so, he found himself pulling into Old Albany apartments and caught the manager just leaving the poolside office. She had a one-bedroom town house available. But it was unfurnished. No, she didn't know if any of the other complexes had furnished apartments.

While he ate he read the for-rent ads in the *Norman Transcript*. The few furnished apartments listed were mostly on the east side. Only two were close to the university—both on DeBarr, a block-long street immediately north of the campus. When he was little, and they came to OU football games, he liked for his dad to park on DeBarr. Back then, the street still had been paved with bricks. He'd always remembered that. The only brick street he'd ever seen. The bricks were covered with asphalt now, and the large boardinghouses that lined the street had been divided up into apartments.

The street was named for one of the university's first four professors. The chemistry building on the North Oval used to be DeBarr Hall. But the notorious Professor DeBarr had ridden with the Ku Klux Klan, and in the 1980s, the black student organization had successfully lobbied to get his name removed from the chemistry building. Chad wondered why the black students hadn't protested the street name as well.

He rented a one-room efficiency on the third floor of an old house with a porch across the front. The large room had a sloping ceiling and two dormer windows. The furnishings consisted of a double bed, sofa, bookcase, table and three chairs. His closet at home

was larger than the kitchen. The ancient stained bathtub had feet. The linoleum floor was worn through in
several places.

He stared at the bed. He and Brenda could make
love there, on their own private bed. Maybe sometimes she would spend the night. Be there in the night
when he woke up sweating. In the morning when he
had to face another day.

He knew Brenda wouldn't be in her room, so he
called the house number, but the pledge answering
the phone informed him that the members were still
in chapter meeting. "Tell her that Chad is moving to
the third floor of 712 DeBarr and could use some
help."

"Just a sec," the pledge said in a perky little voice.
"I don't have a pencil."

Chad waited an indeterminate amount of time and
finally decided that he'd been forgotten.

With any luck, he could get out of the IB house by
the time chapter meeting was over. The last meeting
he went to lasted several hours while members argued
whether or not the house should again cosponsor with
one of the black fraternities a benefit fun-run for the
Cerebral Palsy Center. Some of the members claimed
the pairing was good for their image. The others insisted it conveyed the wrong image. Carter Fugate had
been the most vocal of those not wanting to renew the
sponsorship. "If I'd wanted to hang out with niggers,
I'd've gone to school at Langston," he said, referring
to the state's historically black college.

Without boxes to accomplish the move, it took
Chad a dozen or more trips up and down the backstairs to take all his stuff to Johnny's pickup, which he
had to jumpstart. And it took a dozen more trips to
carry everything up the three flights of stairs at 712
DeBarr.

Then there he was, standing in the middle of the

now very cluttered room with low-wattage lightbulbs and worn linoleum, shocked that he'd actually done this thing, already feeling like he'd made a mistake. Chinks, Arabs, and geeks lived on DeBarr Street. Not regular students.

He wandered downstairs to see if there was a pay phone so he could call Brenda. There was, but he had no change.

He went back upstairs, pushed some books to the floor, and sprawled across the bed's bare mattress.

He slept for a few hours then woke feeling, if not better, at least a little less panicky. Nothing was forever. He probably could move back into the house tomorrow if he wanted to. His dad would know how to make things okay. Pay a few fines. Buy a new stereo system for the rec room.

But he began putting things away. Even made up the bed. Plugged in his desk lamp and turned it on—which helped. Brenda would help him make the room seem less dismal. Maybe go with him to pick out a rug and another lamp.

He studied for a while, then took a bath in his footed bathtub, which he liked. Sitting high up like that made bathing feel important. He imagined being in the tub with Brenda. A nice thought. They'd never taken a bath together.

He drove to Denny's and woke Brenda with a call from the restaurant pay phone. "Buy you breakfast," he said.

"You know I don't eat breakfast," she said. "Where were you last night? I called and called. Deeann was named pledge of the month. I was so excited. I wanted you to go with us to celebrate."

"I moved. I need you to help me fix up my new place."

His announcement was greeted by a few seconds of silence, then a sigh. "You really moved out of the house?" she said. "I thought you were just kidding about all that."

"I slept there last night. I really wanted you there with me. Just think, a place with privacy."

"Yeah," she said, her voice going soft. "That'll be nice. But you'll stay active at the house, won't you?"

"I'm not sure. Maybe. I just couldn't stay there in that room anymore looking at Johnny's empty bed. And I'm tired of making love in the backseat of a car. Let's have a party tonight. Candlelight. A six-pack. Take off all our clothes. Hey, I'm hard just thinkin' about it."

At Target, they bought a rug, lamp, two potted plants, candles and holders, and a package of one-hundred-watt lightbulbs. At Homeland, they spent almost an hour wandering up and down aisles, filling the grocery cart.

After arranging their little love nest, they ordered a Pizza from Godfather's and Brenda fixed a salad in the tiny kitchen. Chad set the table and lit the candles. "This is really nice," he said. "Really nice." He had tears in his eyes.

But after they'd had dinner and made love, Brenda left to go back to the sorority house. And he was alone once again.

Maybe he should move back home to Nichols Hills and make the forty-five- or fifty-minute commute to campus. Except that he wasn't sure his mother would want him to live at home.

His mom had been upset with him before. "Disappointed" was her word for it—after the wrecks, DUIs, drugs, bad grades. She never knew about the abortion he had to pay for during his junior year in high-school. Or last year's gambling debt. But even if she'd found out about those, he didn't doubt that she would have shared her disappointment with him and extracted promises of more responsible behavior. He

and his mom would kind of "break up" for a while
but they both knew that it was temporary, that they
would get back together again.

But now there was a big empty space between them.
If she answered the phone when he called, she would
ask how he was, ask about Brenda, then pass the
phone off to his dad. If his dad wasn't there, she'd say
that she'd have him call. She didn't ask when Chad
was coming home or say that she loved him.

He'd never really thought very much about his relationship with his mother. It was just there. She loved
him and cared for him. But he'd always considered
her the secondary parent. His father was more important. His father had power and answers. When the university asked for a parent's name on enrollment and
other forms, he always put his dad's name.

But having things not right between him and his
mom made him uncomfortable. And angry. What
kind of mother would turn her back on her son when
he needed her?

He'd mailed an application for admission to Oklahoma State University—just to allow himself that op-
tion come second semester. The idea of being an
Aggie still appealed to him. He'd drive Johnny's
pickup. Wear cowboy boots to class. A new image. New
school. New life. Maybe even a new major. But he
hadn't even hinted at the possibility of a transfer to his
dad.

He'd even considered dropping out of school for a
semester or two. Head for the Rockies. With Brenda.
They could run off and get married and get jobs at a
Colorado resort. Or drift for a while. When he was
twenty-one, he'd start drawing some income from the
money his grandmothers left to him. Maybe he'd
never go back to school.

But Brenda informed him that he was mistaken if
he thought she was going to trek off to Colorado and

become a latter-day hippie with Birkenstock sandals
and chapped lips. A girl dreamed all her life about a
big wedding with all her friends and relatives in attendance. She wasn't running off to the mountains. And
she wasn't going to transfer to OSU. She'd decided
that Chad was selfish even to suggest such a thing.
Brenda had been elected sorority rush chairman. She
had a good chance of being president her senior year.
Just because he'd turned his back on his friends and
the lifestyle that he'd been raised to didn't mean such
things weren't important to her.

Chad didn't mention OSU or Colorado again. If he
left OU, most likely it would be without Brenda, which
probably meant he wouldn't go.

Chad knew that if Brenda ever found out about
Rosalie Frank, he'd lose her. Brenda needed respect-
ability. A safe life. No surprises. Maybe everyone did.

Thanksgiving break, he avoided being alone in the
same room with his mother and hung out mostly with
his dad and the grandfathers in front of the television
set. Grandpa Walt barely knew one team from the
other, but he feigned interest for the sake of polite-
ness and quietly read the morning newspapers. Finally, he produced a jigsaw puzzle that he'd brought
along. The box, with a fading picture of Notre Dame
Cathedral on the lid, was held together by yellowing
cellophane tape. Chad helped him put out the pieces
on the round game table and get the lower edge
pieced together.

His mom went all out for Thanksgiving dinner, like
always, but Chad wasn't very hungry. All he wanted
was the wine.

After dinner, Melissa cornered him at the foot of
the stairs and asked what was going on with him and
Mom. "I can't believe that she's upset with Bonnie

Prince Chad, the anointed one. You must have really had a major screwup for her to be like that. What'd you do, kill someone?"

"At least I eat," he said, grabbing her arms and pushing her aside. "You look like shit, you know. I'm surprised you have the energy to walk around."

"They told you, didn't they?" Melissa demanded.

"Told me what?"

"About them trying to make me eat. Making me go to the doctor every week. They want you to give me a hard time, too."

"Naw. They didn't say anything. I don't need anyone to tell me that you look like shit—like someone they let out of a concentration camp at the end of World War II. Why don't you eat?"

"You didn't eat so much yourself. I saw you pushing food around your plate, not eating the sacramental holiday dinner that our saintly mother spent days preparing."

"And you're accusing *me* of having a problem with Mom. Sounds like you're the one being the offspring from hell," he said, putting a foot on the bottom step, edging toward a retreat. Then he changed his mind and turned to face her. "You still haven't answered my question. Why don't you eat?"

"Because I don't want to. Why did you move out of the IB house?"

"Who told you about that?"

"Carter Fugate's sister. Why did you?"

"Because I wanted to," he said. "At least moving out of a fraternity house doesn't make me a nutcase like you. No wonder Mom and Dad make you go to a doctor. I hope it's a shrink."

"And who are you going to these days? A drug counselor? A parole officer?"

Chad took the stairs two at a time. Christ, Melissa

was screwed up. *He* was screwed up. Their parents
didn't deserve to have such screwed-up kids.

Chad had heard the disappointment in his father's
voice, seen it in his face when he'd talked to him earlier about moving out of the IB house. That jerk Tom
Fitzhugh had called his dad to say how sorry they were
to lose Chad and hoped he would be able to work
through his problems.

Chad wasn't holding up his end of the bargain, his
dad pointed out. Everyone involved in the "accident"
was supposed to be keeping a low profile, going on
like nothing had happened. Then Johnny commited
suicide. Now Chad had moved out.

Chad had promised his dad that he'd try to smooth
things over at the house so he at least could remain on
the active list, but he knew he wouldn't. Not right
now. Maybe next semester—if he stayed at OU.

He stretched out on his bed for a nap but couldn't
fall asleep. His stomach was rumbling, protesting emptiness. His head hurt from overload. Finally, he went
downstairs to work on the puzzle with the grandfathers and watch another football game. Texas and
Texas A&M. Tomorrow was OU-Nebraska. In Lincoln.
Chad supposed that he'd watch. But he really didn't
care. Last year, in Norman, he'd screamed himself
hoarse at the battle of the two Big Reds.

Jigsaw puzzles were pointless. What did you have
when you finished except a picture to take apart and
put back in the box? An exercise in futility. But it
passed the time. And was better than thinking. Melissa
even came down for a while and put together a few
pieces. His mom would pass by and stop for a while,
search a bit. And his dad would lean over and work for
a time. For a few poignant minutes, the whole family
was there around the table just like three generations
of your basic sitcom family.

But they weren't.

Chad kept looking at his sister, at her wrists, her neck. He hadn't realized until he grabbed her in the hall just how disgustingly thin she really was. Like a skeleton. Did she want to die? Hell, she didn't have nearly the shit in her life that he had in his. And he didn't want to die. He just wanted things to be normal again. He wanted to feel good about life. He wanted to push Rosalie Frank to the deepest, darkest recess of his mind and bury her there in the darkness. Make her really dead.

After the house had quieted for the night, he knocked on Melissa's bedroom door. She was watching an old movie on television. *Singing in the Rain.* Debbie Reynolds and Gene Kelly being innocent and happy.

"Sorry I made fun of you today—about being skinny," he said awkwardly. "Guess it's not a joke, is it?"

"Not with me. I like being thin. No one's ever going to make me fat again, especially not Mom and Dad."

"Hey, Missy. *They* never made you fat."

"That's your opinion. Now bug off, will you. I happen to be watching a movie."

The next morning Chad woke up remembering the huge messy breakfasts he and Melissa used to make sometimes on Saturday mornings. Pigs in a blanket. A big batch of scrambled eggs. Blueberry frosties. He went downstairs and began cooking. Then he took a pitcher of ice water up to Melissa's room. Holding the pitcher over her head, he announced that breakfast was ready.

Melissa shrieked and ran into the bathroom and locked the door. "So, starve to death," Chad said to the closed door. "Mom and Dad's friends can make contributions to the charity for stupid girls with eating disorders in lieu of flowers."

His mom was surprised and pleased about breakfast. She actually kissed Chad's cheek. But Melissa's empty place stole away his pleasure.

After breakfast, Grandfather Vern announced that he and Roger were going to take advantage of the glorious weather and get in a round of golf. Chad refused to join them, bringing a look of irritation to his father's face.

He drove Grandpa Walt back to Tulsa instead. Walt needed help cleaning up his yard and pruning his overgrown trees and shrubs. "I've let things get out of hand," he admitted as they surveyed the overgrown beds choked with winter-dead flowers, weeds, vegetables. "It's hard to make myself get things done now that your grandmother is gone. She never let things go undone, you know. She believed in living life to a schedule."

They worked side by side, with Chad doing all the heavy work. "I planted all these vegetables last spring out of habit," Walt said as he pulled up another dead tomato plant. "I never bothered to pick most of it. Told the neighbors to help themselves. Think I'll put the place up for sale now that we're getting the jungle cleared away."

"Where will you live?" Chad asked.

"Sallisaw, probably. With an old friend. An ornithologist who retired from the university about the same time I did. Sounds kind of nice. Two old naturalists living out their dotage together." Something about the way his grandfather said the word "friend" made Chad wonder if the ornithologist was a man or a woman.

They got an early start the next morning. Walt was sore and limited his efforts to supervising and instructing as Chad pruned the shrubs and trees. Redbud and dogwood are tolerant of shade, he explained. That's why they could be planted in among other

larger trees. The dogwood "flower" is really a group
of modified whitish leaves, or *bracts,* around a cluster
of small true flowers. The Oriental arvorvitae is native
to northern China.

"Remember when we had a tire swing in the elm?"
Walt asked. "And we nailed some boards up in the Y
of that big oak. You and Missy liked to take a picnic
lunch up there. She called it her magic carpet. You
children used to like being here, helping me in the
garden. Those were nice years. Your grandmother
liked having you here, too. It gave her someone to
organize besides me. Nice years."

"Do you miss Grandma?" Chad asked as they ate
melted-cheese sandwiches in the very cluttered
kitchen.

"Oh my, yes. The house is so quiet. So empty. But
sometimes it's nice to just sit and read and think without interruption. She was never one for sitting and
thinking. Such an incredible woman. Once she set her
mind to something, you might as well go along with it.
Probably she should have married somebody else,
someone more like her. I never even made chairman
of the department. That was a big disappointment for
her. But then without her, just look at me. And this
house. We're both going to seed."

Chad watched as his grandfather fussed around,
opening and closing cupboard doors, trying to find a
can of applesauce or pears to round out their lunch.

"Does your friend in Sallisaw like to read?"

"Yes. And take long walks. Listen to old records."
Walt's faded blue eyes looked past Chad, a small smile
teasing his lips.

The ornithologist was definitely a woman, Chad decided. He wondered if his mother knew. She'd been
pissed because Grandfather Vern started going on
dates so soon after Granny Grace died. But surely

she'd approve of Walt's friendship with an old colleague.

"If you had your life to live over, what would you change?" Chad asked.

"Ah, Chad boy, is that why you came with me to Tulsa, to ask an old man to tell you how to avoid pitfalls?" Walt asked, stopping in his search to come sit across from Chad. "You want to know if you should marry that nice young woman who expects to marry you or wait and see if one comes along who warms your heart. Should you take the safe road and be assured that you can meet your responsibilities in life, or should you go for the gold? I can't tell you things like that. I don't know how my own life would have turned out if I had taken another road, but what I've had hasn't been so bad."

"When you were my age, did you want to be a botany professor?"

Walt laughed the dry, raspy laugh of an old man. "No, son. I wanted to be a fighter pilot and fly combat missions against the Huns, but I couldn't see worth a damn, and they wouldn't have me. But just think, if I'd gone off to bomb Berlin or Tokyo, I might never have come back. I never would have married your grandmother. Your father never would have been born. Or you and your sister. Old people like me can't tell you anything, Chad. It would dishonor those we'd spent our lives with to say we wished our lives had been otherwise. And if I told you to follow your heart, would you even have the faintest idea what that was? Life's a crapshoot, son. All I can tell you is that my main comfort has come from learning. If it wasn't botany, it would have been chemistry or math or some other orderly discipline. But your father, he takes comfort in being in charge—like your grandmother did. And your mother, she takes comfort in your pretty house and raising you children. Maybe comfort is what you should be looking for. What makes you comfortable, Chad?''

Chad closed his eyes. He was adrift and the waterfall was just ahead. He could hear its roar. Comfort? How could there ever be any of that for him?

26

*C*hristine Worthington was a bright young woman. And a striking one now that her bruises had healed, with her blond hair, blue eyes, classic Nordic features, and long, slim body. She had fit in well at the shelter, taking her turn with chores, taking a teenager with a week-old baby under her wing, teaching her how to care for her tiny daughter. Christine had the ability to turn her life around and raise her children well.

But Karen was no longer hopeful.

Christine had been been in touch with her husband—not that she'd told Karen. Or anyone else. But Karen could tell. A woman stopped talking with the other residents when she'd been talking to her man. She stopped being one of the girls and retreated into isolation. It was only a matter of time until she left. Usually without saying good-bye.

Karen had stepped up her arrangements to get Christine and her children relocated. She made telephone calls, searching for employment opportunities. She accumulated a few basic household items and some toys. She located a used television at a TV repair shop and found extra clothes for the family at the Junior League Thrift Shop. She helped Christine obtain copies of her and her children's birth certificates so they could apply for food stamps.

In early December Karen drove Christine and her two children in the Haven House van to Edmond, a

city immediately north of Oklahoma City, and helped
them get settled in a tiny apartment across the street
from a grade school. Karen had made arrangements
for Christine to work in a day-care center at a nearby
Methodist church. She would be able to get by without
a car for the time being and make enough money to
cover the rent and buy groceries. Karen helped Christine make up the beds, put the groceries away in the
kitchen's only cupboard, put away their few possessions.

Afterward, Christine walked her out to the van.
"You can do this," Karen said, hugging the younger
woman. "You don't ever have to see him again."

Christine looked away.

"He won't stop hurting you," Karen said. "No matter what he says, he'll do it again and again. You'll end
up disfigured or dead. Your daughter will marry a
man like her father, and your son will beat his wife.
Don't call him, Christine. Don't tell him where you
are. You're safe here. You have a place of your own.
You are in control of your own life."

"Is that how it is for you?" Christine asked. "In
control? George said you don't get paid for working at
Haven House. Why would you come spend all that
time down there for free unless you're running away
from something, too?"

As Karen drove away she wondered. For years she'd
thought of Haven House only as the place where she
did good works. But there was more to it than that.
She always felt such freedom as she walked up the
sagging front steps. At the shelter, she didn't have a
last name. She was just Karen. She could get paint
under her fingernails and laugh at bawdy jokes and
have opinions and be a person.

But she couldn't build the rest of life around
Haven House. Eventually, she would have to move on.

For now, however, there was comfort in structure.
Most days she went there.

The day after getting Christine settled, however,
she drove to Tulsa to have lunch with her father. It was
time for her to tell him what was going on with her
family. Before Christmas. For Melissa's sake, she'd
have to stage some sort of family Christmas, pretend
that nothing had happened. And for Walt's sake, too,
she supposed, unless Roger wanted his father to know.
But she needed her own father to know that things
had changed. That she was not the same sweet Karen.
The good mother. The good wife. Passively going
through life like her mother before her.

Vernon served quiche and fruit salad from the
French deli. They were in the dining room with its
Chinese Chippendale furniture and thick Chinese rug
underfoot. Usually they went to the country club for
lunch. She tried to remember whether she and her
father had ever had a meal in this room together, just
the two of them.

Vernon, it turned out, already knew about Melissa's
eating disorder. And about Chad. Roger had told him.

Karen fought down a wave of irritation. Roger
might have checked with her before he talked to
Vernon. After all, he was *her* father. "Well, as you can
see, Roger and I aren't communicating too well these
days. I guess there was no need for me to drive up
here today."

She shook her head when her father picked up the
carafe to offer her a second glass of wine. One glass of
wine had become her limit.

"It sounds as though Roger is handling things
well," Vernon said, filling his own glass, then sitting
back in his chair. Her meticulous father. Every hair on
his handsome gray head in place.

"But what about Chad?" Karen demanded. "How
do you feel about what he did?"

"I'm very disappointed in him," Vernon admitted. "I understand about the psychology of the pack, but just as I'd expect him to turn down an injection of heroin, I'd expect him to decline to participate in what legally could be called a gang rape."

"Does that mean other sorts of rape are okay?"

Vernon lifted his eyebrows. "Karen, don't get on your high horse about this. Sometimes one doesn't have the luxury of righteousness. You have to be strong like your mother would have been. She buried a son and survived. Nothing is as bad as that."

"Maybe," Karen said, toying with her empty wineglass. The Waterford. Her mother had used the Waterford only for company. "At least all of her illusions were left intact," she added.

"So, would you rather have a sainted dead son or an imperfect living one?" her father demanded.

Karen allowed herself a sigh. "It's not that simple, Dad, and you know it. I'm devastated by what my son has done, by what happened to that poor girl. But when I look for reasons why it happened, I find lots of them. Chad's upbringing and my marriage don't hold up well under scrutiny."

"And *your* upbringing, too, I suppose?" he challenged.

Karen took her napkin and wiped her lipstick from the edge of the wineglass. So beautiful and delicate. A crystal status symbol. "It's not that I blame you or Mom. Right now I'm having a hard time accepting that the affluent Roger Billingslys of Nichols Hills have more rights in this world than the family of an Hispanic LPN who lives in a duplex in east Norman. The Billingslys and their son are relatively untouched by this tragedy. The LPN's family has lost a daughter and doesn't even know for sure that she's dead. They don't even have the right to bury her body."

"And you want to sacrifice your son to these high-minded principles that you have so lately acquired?"

"No, damn it! " Karen said, throwing her napkin down on the table, pushing her chair back. "I want what is best for my son. And I'm not sure that means avoiding all responsibility for what happened to that girl."

"Some people do have more—if not 'rights' then opportunities," Vernon said, leaning back in his chair, assessing his daughter. "Some parents work harder to provide opportunities for their children, to give them good schooling and family traditions, family pride."

"That LPN works damned hard. I've seen her. She's an honest, hardworking woman who loves her children every bit as much as I love mine."

"All right, then. You've made your point. Life is not fair. So, what do you plan to do about it?"

"I don't know," Karen admitted. "Maybe nothing. But nothing will ever be the same again either. I feel different about everything. *Everything.* Even you. And this house. And Mom."

When Vernon walked Karen out to her car, he hugged her for a long moment. "You and your children are all I have," he said. "Don't change so much that I don't even recognize you."

"Has anything ever changed you?" Karen asked. "What about when John David died? Didn't that change the way you felt about everything?"

"Yes, for a time," he said with a sigh. "Nothing seemed to matter anymore. But that wasn't so. You and your mother mattered. My parents. Her parents. The firm. Politics. Patriotism. The church. And life itself. Accomplishing. Doing what needs to be done. Being strong and healthy. Swimming forty laps in the pool. Sipping good wine. Smoking a good cigar. Enjoying the company of like-minded people. *Life* mattered."

* * *

Karen dropped an opened envelope with a Dallas postmark in front of Roger. "This came today. I thought it peculiar that a letter from a girl's boarding school came addressed to you."

They'd just finished dinner—with the evening news taking the place of conversation.

It wasn't much of a dinner. Spaghetti with Prego sauce. A tossed salad. Spiced peaches from a can. Rolls from the freezer. She'd set a place for Melissa more out of habit than any expectation that her daughter would actually join them.

Karen watched while Roger took the single sheet of paper from the envelope. "Melissa was accepted for the second semester—as you requested," Karen said before he had a chance to read it. "She does have two parents, you know. How could you have arranged to send her away to school without discussing it with me first?"

"I was waiting to see if she was accepted."

"Do I have no say in the matter? What about Melissa? And Dr. Burk?"

"Dr. Burk suggested it. With all of her meals taken in the school cafeteria, her eating habits will be under scrutiny from the other students. Dr. Burk thought a little peer pressure might be good. The school nurse can monitor her weight. If she keeps going down, the next step is a hospital. Dr. Burk has been looking into hospital-based programs for eating disorders."

Karen felt her anger dissolving into anguish. She used to think that she was a good mother. She used to feel superior to mothers in the supermarket who lost their tempers and spanked their children. Karen never spanked. Never raised her voice. Never lost her temper. She always was understanding. Always the perfect mother. No wonder her daughter hated her. All that perfection must have been nauseating. No won-

der Chad assumed that his mother would be calm and
forgiving, no matter what.

"I should be the one who moves out," Karen said.
"At least you have a meal with Melissa every day. The
only time I ever see her is when she comes in the back
door and heads upstairs to her room. If I do insist that
she join us for dinner, she doesn't eat. You tell me
that she at least eats a salad and a couple of bites of
bread when you take her to lunch. She insists that she
eats when she's with her friends. It's only my food that
she seems incapable of chewing up and swallowing."

"All the more reason why we should at least try a
boarding school. I thought you'd be pleased. The
school has a wonderful reputation. You've said so
yourself."

"I'm sure it's a wonderful school. But we'd be send-
ing her away. Washing our hands of her. When maybe
what we should do is forget about the whole mother-
in-the-kitchen bit since it obviously isn't accomplishing anything. And these meals that you and I have
with CNN don't accomplish much either. Maybe Melissa should stay, and I should move out."

"Don't say that!" Roger said. "Without you here,
there wouldn't be a home for any of us to come to."

Karen felt like he'd hit her in the stomach. Tears
stung her eyes. "Oh, Roger, that's not true. Not anymore."

"It's always been that way for me."

"Not always," she said, remembering that awful
time when he made up reasons not to come home,
when she knew he was with another woman, making
love to another woman. "Not when you were having
an affair with Rhonda Parker," she said, not knowing
she was going to say the words until they were out of
her mouth.

Roger sat there for a long silent moment, looking
down at his empty plate. "You knew all along?"

"Yes."

"I'm sorry. Truly sorry."

"Sorry that I know or sorry that it happened?"

"Both. It was a long time ago."

"Not so long. I still think about it when you come home late, and I wonder if it's happening again."

"Why didn't you ever say anything?"

"Suffering in silence was more my style."

Roger shook his head in disbelief. "And why are you breaking that silence now?"

"I hadn't planned to, but maybe it's best. If there's to be any hope for us, we have to understand each other. I didn't make a single wave during one of the most hurtful periods of my life. But I can't be that way anymore. I have to speak up and let you know how I feel. And if nothing else, I insist that you acknowledge my right to feel the way I do."

"Our marriage will never be the same, will it?"

"Oh, Roger, you aren't hearing me at all!" Karen said, raising her voice in frustration, clenching her fists. "It can't stay the same. *I'm* not the same."

"No, you're not. And look what's happened to this family."

"Damn you!" she said. And left him sitting there with the unwashed dishes.

She retreated to her room and sat in the rocking chair, rocking furiously, charged with righteous anger. *Damn him.*

Karen was finishing the paperwork on two new arrivals when she looked up and realized Chad was standing in the doorway. It was shocking to see him there. No member of her family had ever set foot in Haven House. The two parts of her life had been totally separate until this moment.

He was wearing jeans with the green crewneck

sweater she'd given him last year for Christmas. A handsome young man. A *very* handsome young man.

She hadn't yet bought any Christmas presents this year. And Christmas was only two weeks away. Normally, she would already have the tree up, the presents wrapped, the cooking under way.

"Have a seat," she said, indicating the worn plaid sofa that used to sit in the waiting room at Roger's office. "Or would you like me to show you around?"

He shook his head no and sat down. "Dad says that you think I need to be punished. Do you want me to go to prison?"

"Not prison necessarily, but I do feel that you should assume some sort of responsibility for what you've done," she said from behind the small desk, her hands folded in front of her. But it didn't feel right—looking at her son from the other side of a desk. She pushed back the chair and went to sit beside him on the sofa.

"I'm sorry about what happened, Mom. And all those things you said were right about how I should feel haunted and remorseful for the rest of my life. But I still want my life. I don't want it to be ruined because of one mistake. Is that so awful to feel that way? I'm not a bad person. And now I want to be a better person. I want to make damned sure I never hurt anyone again. Can't that be enough?"

"That's for you to decide. Your father told you to come see me, didn't he?"

"Yeah. He thought it would be a good idea. He's worried about you. He says you spend more time here at the shelter than he does at his office. Melissa says you guys don't even sleep together anymore. And it's almost Christmas. There's no tree. No presents. The house looks like no one lives there. Please, Mom. I can live with what happened to Rosalie Frank. But I don't want to lose my family."

Karen allowed herself the motherly gesture of smoothing a lock of hair back from his forehead. And ached for more. She wanted to take his hand. To kiss his forehead. Stroke his arm. Rub his back.

"I know what you want me to say," Chad went on. "You want me to dedicate my life to helping people or in some way do penance for what's happened. Instead of prison, a life of good works."

"Just tell me what you want, not what you think I want for you."

"Always before, I wanted to be successful. Like Dad. To make a good living for my family. To have a good marriage. Be a good father. A nice house. Drive great cars. Vacations in the south of France. Celebrate holidays with you and Dad in the home I grew up in. But now I'm not sure."

He paused, but Karen could tell he wasn't finished. She waited while he looked past her, out the window, searching for words.

"Sometimes I think about living on the side of a mountain. Or out in the country someplace. Seeing how many plant names I remember from all those treks with Grandpa Walt. Sometimes I almost wish that we'd all turned ourselves in and were serving time. At least, that way, Johnny would still be alive, and there would be an end to it. But then, if we'd done that, people would know. Brenda would know. Melissa. It's bad enough that you know. I don't want anyone else to know. They wouldn't understand."

"What wouldn't they understand?"

"That I'm not a bad person. That I wish like hell none of it had ever happened. But it did. I'll pick my friends more carefully in the future. Drink less. Stick close to Brenda. But I can't change what's already done."

"So you feel changed by what happened but not responsible?" Karen asked.

"God, you're hung up on that word," Chad said, not hiding his irritation. "I wasn't the only one involved."

"You're the only one who is my son."

He sighed. Nothing had been accomplished by his coming here.

Karen felt uncomfortable with his disappointment. He'd come to prove his sincerity, to woo her. And she wanted to respond. To soothe. To tell him that she knew how sorry he was. That he had learned by his mistake. That he'd feel better in the morning. That's how she had raised him. Good ol' Mom with her Band-Aids and soothing.

27

Melissa found the folder of clippings in the back of the file drawer in her mother's kitchen desk. She hadn't been looking for anything in particular. Just snooping. Trying to figure out if either of her parents was having an affair. Her friend Debbie insisted that when parents stopped sleeping together, one of them was screwing around. That was the first step. Then comes separation and divorce.

Melissa wasn't sure how she'd feel if she discovered that one of her parents was committing adultery. Such an awful word—adultery. In the Bible they stoned adulteresses. She wasn't sure what happened to male adulterers.

She'd probably hate the offending parent. Maybe never forgive him or her.

In a way, it seemed more likely that her mom was having the affair. After all, she'd been the one who'd been acting weird. But somehow it was hard for Melissa to imagine her perfect-at-all-times Mom doing something sordid and sneaky. Dad kind of flirted sometimes. But then he did it in front of Mom, so it couldn't mean anything.

Except that men had secretaries. Men had opportunities. And he probably got tired sometimes of being married to a woman who always was calm and reasonable, who never yelled or lost her temper. Melissa got tired of having a mother like that. She hated her mother's reasonable voice, her classic clothing, her smart-but-sensible haircut, her tidiness. All that cooking. Her mother was irritating. And boring. Of course, having an affair definitely was not something a boring person would do. Affairs were for the passionate, reckless kind of people—the exact opposite of her mother.

Weirdest of all was that her competent, calm, responsible mom had suddenly seemed to abdicate from the family. Dad was now the enforcer of curfews and eating habits. He even checked to see if Melissa made her bed in the morning. Her mom wasn't home much anymore. Sometimes Melissa came home from school to an empty kitchen, which bothered her even though she never had anything to do with her mother when she was there.

When her mother wasn't there, Melissa didn't rush right through the kitchen. She lingered, rummaging through the refrigerator and pantry, pinching off a morsel of cake or cookie, peeling a carrot, taking one cracker from the box, eating an apple if she thought there were enough so that one wouldn't be missed. It was a lot harder not to eat when her mother wasn't around. Which scared Melissa. Without her mother around, maybe she would get fat like before. She'd rather die than be fat again. All of which made her nervous about going away to the school.

In some ways, the idea of changing schools appealed to her. She wouldn't have to pass Trevor in the hall. No one in Dallas would know that her boyfriend had dumped her. It wouldn't matter so much that she didn't have a date to her class Christmas party. Or the prom. But other times the thought of going away to a school where she didn't know a soul scared her.

For some reason her mom didn't want her to go. She'd thought her mom had put Dr. Burk up to suggesting the school.

Dad said that Melissa could come home if she

didn't like it there. He also said he'd give her a hundred dollars for every pound that she gained. He'd buy her a Rolex if she gained ten pounds. A diamond tennis bracelet if she gained twenty.

But she had no intention of gaining any weight at all. No one—not even her friends—understood how much that meant to her. Since first grade, she'd been the tallest girl in her room. All her life she'd felt like an Amazon. Then she'd decided to be thin. *Really* thin. Mind over matter. It was the greatest accomplishment of her life. Being thin was more important than making good grades or being a good tennis player. She really got off on pulling her belts past the last hole and having to poke a new one with an ice pick. She loved wearing a smaller size than her mother, than any of her friends, than any of the Casady cheerleaders.

She looked better than she ever had and felt fine. More than fine. She felt great. Euphoric. High. All she had to do was put her hands on her waist, and she felt positively giddy. And her parents wanted to take that away from her. Dr. Burk, too. Melissa was sick and tired of all that weigh-in crap. Peeing in a cup. Blood tests. Lectures and warnings. Warnings and lectures. She wanted to put her hands over her ears. To tell Dr. Burk to get a life. And her parents. She'd be just fine if everyone would leave her alone.

Sometimes she did feel a little dizzy, but the feeling never lasted for more than a few seconds. And it was strange not to have periods. And for her breasts to have all but vanished. Like she was turning into a boy. Or not turning into a woman. But anytime she had doubts, all she had to do was look at the picture hanging in the upstairs hallway—of herself a couple of years ago in a tennis outfit that showed off her fat thighs, fat arms, no waist, gross breasts. Even her face looked fat. The hands holding the tennis racquet were fat. Melissa hated the picture and would have liked to burn it. But she didn't because it was a reminder of what she'd look like if she ate what her mother put in front of her.

She didn't really hate her mother. But she didn't love her like she used to. Maybe if Melissa went to school in Dallas, her mother would miss her. Melissa kind of liked that idea. But maybe having her gone would be a relief. An end to tension.

If she was away in Dallas, would her parents start sleeping together again? Would Mom and Chad get along better?

Try as she might, Melissa couldn't figure out why her mother had stopped sleeping with her father. And it was her mother who had done the leaving. Melissa could tell by the way her dad's eyes followed his wife when she went up the stairs at night. He looked pissed —and hurt. Melissa couldn't remember her mom ever going against her father before—not over anything serious. Maybe she'd make him go to a dinner party when he didn't want to. Stuff like that. They argued about her last new car. She insisted that she had to have another station wagon. Her dad wanted her to have a Mercedes or a Lexus.

Melissa supposed that lots of parents didn't sleep together. And maybe lots of parents slept together but didn't have sex. Her parents had still had sex until whatever happened to make her mother start sleeping in one of the guest rooms. All her life Melissa had been catching peeks of them feeling each other up, usually when they'd been drinking. She knew what it meant when she heard their bedroom door close, the lock click.

Chad didn't want to talk about it. He said that where Mom slept was her business. Maybe Dad snored. Maybe Mom had insomnia.

Melissa had gone through her parents' dresser

drawers. Her father's desk. She looked in the top of
their closets. Searched through pockets. Her mother's
purses. Gone through the dirty clothes hamper.

She didn't find any love letters. No packet of in-
criminating photographs. No telltale lipstick smears
on collars or scraps of paper with mystery phone numbers. Her mother hadn't purchased any sex-kitten lingerie and hidden it away under the folded sweaters in
her bottom drawer. Her dad still used the same old
aftershave.

The only thing of interest that had come out of her
search was the manila folder of newspaper clippings—
about a missing high-school girl in Norman named
Rosalie Victoria Frank. The last place the girl had
been seen was at a party at the Iota Beta house. The
middle of October.

Melissa checked her mother's desk calendar. That
had been the weekend that her dad went on a fishing
trip to Padre Island. He'd a hard time getting home
because of the hurricane. Chad came home early that
Saturday morning. He'd been there when she'd gotten up. And hadn't come out of his room until dinnertime. When Melissa made a remark about the OU–
KSU football game, he hadn't even known who'd won.

Melissa picked up the clippings one by one, read
them, tried to figure out why her mother would have
them. The girl's mother was a nurse, her father a patient at Veterans—not people Melissa's parents would
have known. Rosalie Frank had worked at Frumps on
the Campus Corner. Vanished without a trace, her car
left in the parking lot behind the restaurant. The paycheck she had received that evening had never been
cashed.

Vanished without a trace after going to a party at
the IB house. Did that mean anything?

Probably not, Melissa decided, returning the folder
to the file drawer, in the very back where she'd found

it. All that folder meant was that her mother was weird. She had all sorts of dumb stuff filed away. A report on the bacteria count in the various brands of bottled water. An article about psychic phenomena. Directions for making candles.

But what if that missing girl had something to do with her mother's weirdness? With Chad freaking out over Johnny Fontaine's death? With him moving out of the fraternity house? With her parents' not sleeping together? Melissa had wondered if their separate bedrooms were somehow her fault. But this new possibility was even more worrisome.

Suddenly Melissa felt dizzy. She closed her eyes and waited for the feeling to pass. It took longer than usual. Not a few seconds.

She drank a glass of water then opened the refrigerator door and stared inside for a long time. The refrigerator motor started to run. And still she stared. At the butter. Mayonnaise. Cheese. Cool Whip. Fruit. Salad greens. She opened the freezer door and regarded the ice-cream carton. A frozen coffee cake. A loaf of sourdough bread. She held both doors open and stared and stared.

Finally, she took a diet Coke and went upstairs to sprawl across her bed. She hadn't even eaten a single grape. She was in complete control.

"Hey, Billingsly, wait up!"

Chad turned to see who was calling to him and was immediately sorry. Carter Fugate, wearing his all-state football jacket and an OU baseball cap, came loping across the library plaza.

"Hey, man, long time no see."

"Hello, Carter."

"Buy you a beer, man."

"Naw. I need to study. I just got out of one final, and I've got another this afternoon."

"Me, too. But what you don't know now, you're not gonna learn between now and then." Carter grabbed Chad's arm and steered him across the deserted plaza in the direction of the union.

During the semester, the large plaza would be full of students hurrying back and forth to class, and on a sunny day students would be sitting on the low walls in front of the fountains, either studying or visiting with friends. But today Chad and Carter were the only people occupying the large expanse of masonry that surrounded the clock tower in front of the library's futuristic west wing, which in no way related to the traditional collegiate Gothic architecture of the original structure to which it was attached. Many students had already taken their last final and had cleared out for the holidays. The rest were either hunched over their books and notes or over examination papers. And the day was gray, cold, and windy, the fountains frozen. Not a day to be out.

"Your dad tells me you're thinking about transferring to OSU," Carter said. "Surely you jest."

They cut behind the administration building, walking past a solitary smoker. Chad recognized the university provost, huddled in the back doorway of the building, getting his hourly dose of nicotine.

"When did you talk to my dad?" Chad asked.

"Not too long ago. He stays in touch, checking to see that no one else is going off the deep end like Johnny Fontaine. I guess we're lucky that ol' Johnny didn't leave a written confession. Or maybe he did, and it burned up in the fire. Wouldn't that be a hoot! The grand gesture of retribution going up in smoke, his suicide becoming just another traffic fatality."

"You don't know that he committed suicide," Chad said, slowing his step.

"Hey, man, it doesn't take a rocket scientist to figure that out. Johnny was a wimp of the first magnitude."

Chad stopped walking. "Hey, Carter, I just remembered that I can't stand you. I think I'll pass on that beer."

Carter glanced over at the provost, who was staring at the ground, apparently lost in thought. "How come you moved out, Billingsly?" he asked, his voice low and challenging. "You're not freaking out, are you?"

"Look, Carter, I know the rules. I know that none of us can ever say a word to anyone. But that doesn't mean I have to hang out with you guys."

"Hey, man, you fucked her just like the rest of us," Carter said, his breath vaporizing in the cold air.

"Doesn't it bother you—what happened to that girl?" Chad asked.

"No. What would be the point? Like your dad said, we didn't kill her. It was just a lousy accident. I'm sorry it happened, but I'm sure as hell not going to become a monk over it. And I'm sure as hell not going to drive a car into a fuckin' wall."

"Do you have a girlfriend?"

"Sure. The kind I can take home to mother. But I still have sex with drunk girls on the side. And not-so-drunk girls. I take it where I can find it."

28

Melissa looked around at the place where her brother lived. He called it an apartment, but it was really just a big room with a cubicle for a kitchen.

The place was neat—not the sort of neat like he'd just kicked clothes under the bed and stuffed things into drawers—but sincerely neat, with dusted surfaces, a stack of plastic organizers on the wooden table that served as a desk, a Peg-Board in the tiny kitchen hung with pans and utensils, coats hung on an old-fashioned hall tree. Chad himself even looked neat, shirt tucked in, his jeans belted. Freshly shaven. Hair combed—longer hair that curled around his ears. Not fraternity hair.

The room's neatness didn't conceal the worn linoleum, scarred furniture, dingy walls, thick cracked paint on the woodwork.

"Why here?" Melissa asked.

"It had furniture," Chad said. He looked awkward, standing in the middle of the room, not quite knowing what to do with a visiting sister.

"If you can call it that," Melissa said, regarding the worn sofa and brown metal bed. "What does Brenda think about it?"

"She's afraid someone will see her coming in the front door."

"Yeah, I noticed some of your neighbors. Pretty ethnic."

Chad shrugged. "Beats the IB house. I was even invited to the International Student Association banquet last week. It was awesome. Want something to drink?"

"You have a diet Coke?" Melissa asked, seating herself on the sofa, dropping her backpack at her feet.

"A *diet* Coke? Christ, Missy, if you had sores on your arms, you'd look like you were in the last stages of AIDS. And you want a *diet* Coke?"

"Forget it. A glass of water would be fine."

He got himself a Coke, her a glass of water. "Don't you ever eat?" he asked, handing her the glass.

"Sure. When I feel like it."

"Why in the hell are you doing this to yourself?"

"Why in the hell does everyone want me to be fat again?"

He sat next to her and grabbed her wrist, the water in her glass spilling on her jeans. She tried to pull away, but his grip was firm. With his other hand, he felt her arm, her shoulder, ran his hand down her back before relinquishing his hold. "What does the doctor say?"

"That I'm going to die if I don't eat more." Melissa put the glass on the footlocker that served as a coffee table and rubbed at her wrist.

"Doesn't that scare you—having a doctor say that you might die?"

"Why should it? It's not true. I'm not sick."

"What do Mom and Dad say?"

"That I'm going to die if I don't eat more. Gives them a wonderful excuse to get rid of me. To send me off to a school in Dallas. They think that I'll be shamed into eating."

"Maybe that's not such a bad idea."

"Don't any of you understand?" she said. "I don't want to get fat again!"

"Do you like being like *that*?" Chad asked, nodding toward her torso.

"No. I'd like to lose more. Dad put you up to this, didn't he? 'Ask your sister down to the basketball game and see if you can talk some sense to her.'"

Chad shook his head slowly back and forth. "Don't you know how awful you look? No wonder Trevor broke up with you. No guy wants to put his arms around a bag of bones. The way you're acting is not normal."

"And this is *normal*?" Melissa said, indicating the room around them. "Your moving out of the IB house to live in a dump with a bunch of Arabs, Africans, and Asians is normal? Is it normal that Mom and Dad aren't sleeping together? Nothing is *normal. Nothing.*"

She reached for her book bag and pulled a manila folder out. "And I'll show you something else that's not *normal.* I found this in Mom's file drawer, right next to the warranty on the freezer."

Chad opened the folder and silently looked through the dozen or so clippings. Then, very carefully, he closed the folder and placed it on the footlocker, then walked over to one of the room's two windows. Melissa watched as he stood there, his hands in his pockets, staring out at the winter-bare treetops.

"What do you know?" he asked, not turning around.

"About that girl? Nothing except what I read in those newspaper clippings. What's going on? Why has Mom saved them?"

Chad didn't answer. Melissa realized his shoulders were shaking. Her brother was sobbing. Like after Johnny Fontaine's funeral. He'd shed tears at their grandmothers' funerals, but he hadn't sobbed.

She stared at the folder. And felt as though the blood in her veins had turned to ice water.

She hugged her shivering body. The bones in her

upper arms were right there under her skin. Cold
bones. Cold skin. And the dizziness was starting again.
It had almost caused her to run off the road on the
way down here.

The whole world was falling apart. The whole
fuckin' world.

She wanted to go to her brother and offer what
comfort she could, but was afraid she didn't have the
strength to cross the room. "Tell me what happened."
she demanded. Even her voice sounded weak. She
wondered if he'd heard her.

But he shook his head no. Then, without looking at
her, made his way to the bathroom. Melissa could
hear him blowing his nose, the water running. She
drank what was left of her glass of water and carefully
made her way to the tiny kitchen. She took a Coke
from the refrigerator. Not a diet Coke. She took sip
after sip, almost feeling the sugar surge through her
body, easing away the dizziness.

She put the folder of clippings in her backpack
then waited for a long time, sipping on the Coke, to
see if Chad was going to come out of the bathroom.
Finally, she went to the door. "Do you want me to
leave?"

"Yeah."

"Will you ever tell me?"

"I don't know."

"You're my brother. I'll love you no matter what."

She picked up her backpack, got another Coke
from the refrigerator, and left.

In years past, the Christmas tree stood in the middle
of a mountain of presents, mostly purchased by Karen.
Extravagant presents. Thoughtful presents. Practical
ones. Frivolous. All beautifully wrapped.

By comparison, the pile of packages under this

year's tree was sparse. Karen had bought everyone a hand-knit sweater. And for each grandfather, a case of fine wine. A reproduction of a Remington bronze for Roger. A gold charm bracelet for Melissa. Ostrich-skin cowboy boots for Chad. Ten presents total.

She received a ski sweater from Melissa, and a handsome western belt of tooled leather with a sterling buckle from Chad. Her father gave her an exquisite cameo pin. From Walt, there was a coffee-table book of North American birds, the writing and exquisite photography done by a former faculty colleague of his at Tulsa University. And Roger gave her a cashmere robe and a note from George Brown acknowledging that a five-thousand-dollar contribution had been made in her name to Haven House. Karen was so touched that her hand started to shake as she folded the note and put it back in the envelope. "That's really lovely, Roger," she said, and blew a kiss to her husband. He blew a kiss back, pleased.

With fewer presents, the gift opening went quickly and there was an uncomfortable pause when it was over. Walt suggested that they take advantage of the beautiful weather and go for a walk. Karen looked around at less-than-enthusiastic faces, but no one offered an alternative suggestion. "That's a good idea," she said. "Just give me a minute to put the ham in the oven."

Karen insisted everyone bundle up. But the temperature was more crisp than cold. Invigorating. No wind. The sky so blue it looked painted.

As the six of them hiked across the deserted golf course, Walt identified the leafless trees—by their shape and bark, he explained. Chad was at his side, asking questions as if he was really interested.

Karen linked arms with Roger for a time. "Thanks for the contribution to Haven House. That means a lot to me."

"I'm trying, Karen."

"I know you are." She gave his arm a squeeze.

At the second-hole tee box, Roger demonstrated, sans golf club, the perfect swing that had garnered him a hole in one on the par-three hole. Melissa gathered up some pine cones. Karen started singing "Jingle Bells," and they all joined in. Then Walt sang "Luther's Cradle Hymn" in the original German, which he'd learned at his grandmother's knee and had remembered all these years. When he was finished, they sang it in English. Badly. Karen imagined how they all must look, singing as they traipsed along. Three generations of a family taking a Christmas walk. A Norman Rockwell painting. Which, at that moment, maybe they where. Maybe Norman Rockwell wholesome wasn't a continuous state.

The dinner was less elaborate than previous years but still bountiful. A glazed ham, homemade rolls, scalloped potatoes, fresh broccoli, a jelled cranberry salad. For dessert, Karen had made the traditional steamed pudding with brandy sauce—her mother's recipe, of course. Melissa kept looking sideways at her brother, and actually ate a bite or two of everything—even the steamed pudding.

The grandfathers left after dinner. Vernon had a social engagement, which Karen translated as "date." And Walt was expecting an old friend from Sallisaw for a cup of Christmas cheer.

Karen and Melissa watched a video of *Sleepless in Seattle* in the family room while Roger and Chad watched a football game in Roger's study.

Then they ate again. Leftovers. Melissa was leaving on a skiing trip in the morning with a church youth group and had to finish packing. Chad had a date with Brenda. And Karen was left alone with Roger. She began gathering up her gifts to take upstairs. "I'm going to Haven House," she said. "I have gifts for the children. And I've helped them put together a skit for their mothers.''

''Would you like me to come with you?''

Karen paused. ''How strange after ten years to hear you say that.''

''Well, what about it?''

''Tonight you might make everyone uncomfortable. But during the day, you could drop by sometime. I've always been kind of afraid that you wouldn't want me to go back if you ever saw it. It's not a pretty place. Some of the women are tough customers. Others are pitiful.''

''If it's that bad, why do you go there?'' he asked.

''For the same reason you go to your law office. It's got something to do with who I am, but I haven't got that all worked out yet.''

''You used to know who you were,'' he said.

''I thought I did.''

''Should I wait up?''

''I'd like that.''

They made eggnog when she got home—the way her mother used to make it. A thick, frothy concoction of cream, eggs with the whites beaten separately from the yolks, laced with brandy and sprinkled with freshly ground nutmeg.

They carried their glasses into the family room. Roger put another log on the fire.

The eggnog was obscenely rich—and so strong that Karen felt it after the first sip. ''I don't think my mother put that much brandy in it.''

''If your mother were still alive,'' he asked, ''would you have told her what was going on between us, that we no longer sleep in the same bedroom?''

''I'm not sure. She was wonderful for recipes. And it was nice to have someone who wanted to hear about every new tooth the children sprouted, every new word they said, who I had lunch with. But if I told her that I'd moved out of our bedroom, I'd have had to tell her why."

"I wish you'd tell me why." His skin was warm and golden in the firelight. He looked younger.

"Because of all that's happened," she said, putting her glass on the coffee table. "Because it's changed me and hasn't changed you—at least not as much. And that's made me feel separate from you. And confused about sex. When you'd close the bedroom door and lock it, I'd know that you expected sex. Sometimes that was okay. Sometimes it wasn't. But I never thought I had the right to say no, and now we've raised a son who raped a girl."

"Do you really think that one thing has something to do with the other?"

Karen nodded.

Roger stared at her, even squinting his eyes a bit as though he was trying to decide if he'd ever seen her before. "What did you think would happen if you said no?" he asked.

"That you'd be pissed. That I'd have to make it up to you somehow."

He didn't say anything for a time. He just sat there, unmoving, watching the fire. When he spoke again, he didn't look at her. "I thought we were happy."

"I thought we were, too."

He reached for her hand. His eyes glistened in the firelight. "Let's get drunk, Karen. Get a little maudlin. I want to make love with you. Hold you in the night. Know you'll be there in the morning."

Karen refused to get drunk. But they did make love. In Roger's bed. Sweet love that made them both cry.

He didn't want her to go back to the other room. And she did stay for a while, curled in his arms. But when she felt him dozing off, she kissed his neck and left.

Were separate bedrooms the answer, she wondered when she was back in her own bed. What if she continued to sleep here and, when she was in the mood for lovemaking, went down the hall?

But then she'd be the one closing the door and turning the lock. She'd be the one in charge. And she didn't want either one of them to be in charge.

And after twenty-five years of one kind of marriage, were they even capable of new ground rules?

The weekend after New Year's, Melissa began packing for her new school, putting carefully folded bed linens, towels, underwear, nightclothes, in the new footlocker Karen had bought for her.

Karen sat on the bed, watching her daughter making trips back and forth between the footlocker and her bureau.

"You excited?" Karen asked.

"More like nervous," Melissa said. She was wearing workmen's overalls over a sweatshirt. In the oversized clothing she almost looked normal. Only her wrists and collarbones indicated that an exceedingly thin person resided under the bulky clothing. And she seemed pale, but maybe it was just that her summer tan had faded.

"Maybe you should transfer to Bishop McInnis or Northwest Classen. It seems a little extreme for you to go all the way to Dallas in search of a new school," Karen said.

Melissa knelt in front of the bottom drawer and began sorting through the folded sweaters that were stored there—mostly ski sweaters. "Why don't you want me to go away to school?"

"It just doesn't feel right," Karen tried to explain. "You're sixteen years old. Sixteen-year-olds live at home with their parents. For you to go away seems too

risky. A sink-or-swim approach—either you start eating
or you get worse.''

Melissa closed the bottom drawer and opened the
one above it, then sat back on her haunches. ''And
maybe I need to go away to get you and Dad and Dr.
Burk off my back. You just don't get it, do you? I don't
need to get *well*. I just need to be left alone. If you're
planning to deliver one last lecture before I leave,
don't bother. I'm forced to hear them every week
from Dr. Burk—about what happens when you don't
get nutrients, how diet pop doesn't have nutrients.''

''Do you think she's lying to you?''

''I think she went to medical school a hundred
years ago and doesn't know what she's talking about. I
think you want her to say those things. I think she has
big hips and needs to lose weight herself.''

Karen patted the bed beside her. ''Come sit down
by me a minute, baby. I want to talk to you.''

''*Baby*? You haven't called me that in forever.''

''I guess I haven't. Please, come sit by me.''

Reluctantly, Melissa obliged and sat on the bed
beside her mother, not too close, feet firmly on the
floor, ready to take flight.

''You are my baby,'' Karen said, longing to stroke
her daughter's hair, but not daring. ''And I love you
and wish I had done a better job being your mother
these last six or eight months. I didn't even know what
we were fighting about. I thought it was about food. I
didn't realize that being thin is a way for you to be in
charge of what happens to your own body. I can understand that. Women need that. Of course, I'd rather
you'd taken up bodybuilding or even tanning yourself
until you're shoe-leather brown. But maybe you chose
eating because I tried so hard to help you lose weight
back in your pudgy days.''

''I don't know what you're getting at,'' Melissa said

warily, brushing away imaginary lint from the bed-spread.

"I understand that you wanted to change the way you look. What I can't understand is that you are jeopardizing your health."

Melissa bolted from the bed, but Karen grabbed her wrist and jerked her back. Firmly. A power move from a parent who was stronger than a frail daughter. Melissa actually cowered against the headboard, which angered Karen. She'd scarcely taken a hand to the girl in her entire life—nothing more than a few swats on her plump rear when she was a toddler to get her attention when she was too near the fireplace, the edge of the pool. Karen actually wanted to squeeze Melissa's wrist harder and make her feel her mother's anger and strength. But she held just firmly enough to exert control. Such a tiny wrist. It felt as though the bones could snap under Karen's grip.

"Hear me out, Melissa. You owe me that much. Then you can go off to Dallas or not. Eat or not. Love me or not. All right?"

Melissa nodded, her eyes wide, and Karen tentatively released her wrist. Melissa stayed put, plastered against the headboard, her arms wrapped around her middle.

Karen took a deep breath. "You're not having periods because your body has gone into a survival mode. Women who are starving to death never have periods. They don't have the blood to waste. They're not healthy enough to maintain a pregnancy, so nature renders them sterile. Up to a point, starvation is a reversible process. But some people never regain their health. Their bodies are prematurely aged. Their bones are fragile and break easily. Their digestive tract is permanently impaired. And some women are never able to have babies." Karen paused, wanting her words to sink in. *Never able to have babies.*

"So, that's supposed to be a great tragedy," Melissa said, her chin lifted to an arrogant tilt.

"For me, not having children would have been a tragedy. A very great tragedy."

Melissa frowned. Her chin came down a bit. "You can say that in spite of everything that's happened?"

"I can say that in spite of everything that's happened. Even though I wake up in the night paralyzed with fear that my daughter will die because she's starving herself."

"And even though you have a son like Chad?"

Something in the knowing way that Melissa said her brother's name made needles of apprehension pierce Karen's flesh. "Are you referring to something specifically?" she asked.

"Yeah, as a matter of fact. I was referring to Rosalie Victoria Frank."

Karen felt her body sag. And the breath rush from her lungs. Her daughter's lips had spoken that name. The name of the secret. The name of the other young girl Karen had taken into her heart—the other young girl she thought about and would think about until the day she died.

Karen found herself gasping for air. *She knows. Melissa knows.*

Karen closed her eyes and put her hands over her nose and mouth, concentrating, taking deep breaths instead of panting like a winded dog.

She had wanted so to believe that Melissa would never have to know—which didn't make sense given all Karen's idealistic notions about prison and punishment. Prison and punishment were not accomplished in private. Prison meant that her fragile daughter who was fighting her own demons would know and suffer because of her brother's crime, be dragged down, publicly humiliated. Roger was right. *Protect the family.* Melissa was a member of this family, too.

"Are you okay?" she heard Melissa asking.

Karen willed her breathing to slow. *Inhale and exhale. Inhale and exhale.* "How did you find out?" she managed to ask, opening her eyes.

Melissa's eyes were wide, frightened. "All I know is what was in those newspaper clippings you had in the back of your file drawer," she said. "I showed them to Chad."

"What did he say?"

"He didn't say anything. He just fell apart. Like you just did. What happened to her, Mom? Why did she disappear? Why do you have all those clippings?"

The last thing in the world Karen wanted was to tell her daughter what happened to Rosalie Frank, to tell Melissa what her brother had done to Rosalie Frank. But she had no choice, it seemed.

Even so, she had not lied about having children. For her, it would have been a great tragedy not to have had Chad and Melissa, whom she loved more than anything and for whom she had thought she was being a superior mother. Her poor babies. Inez's poor babies. They had not been able to protect their children.

Late that night Karen was in bed, attempting to read in hopes of putting herself to sleep, when Melissa came to the second guest room and sat in the rocking chair. Surprised, Karen put down her book and sat there, hardly daring to breathe, not knowing what to say.

"Do you really think that I'm going to die?" Melissa asked.

Karen put her hand to her breast, quelling a gasp. "If you lose more weight, I think that you might," she said carefully.

"I don't want to go to school in Dallas. Do you think Daddy will be mad?"

"No. He won't be mad."

Melissa leaned back in the chair and took a few experimental rocks. "I remember this old rocking chair," she said, rubbing her hands on the wooden arms. "It used to be up in the attic."

"I rocked you and Chad in it when you were babies. I saved it in case I ever had grandbabies to rock."

"Why did you bring it down now?"

"I guess I needed to rock myself."

"Do you still love Chad?"

"Oh yes. And I love you. I'm your mother."

Melissa rocked back and forth a few more times, then stopped abruptly and left as suddenly as she had come.

Karen got up and sat in the rocker, putting her hands on the arms where her daughter's had been. And wondered if she would ever be allowed to touch her daughter again.

29

*I*nez Frank was a widow.

Gary put the newspaper down. *A widow.*

He actually felt light-headed. He took a couple of breaths and went out in the hall for a drink of water.

Back at his desk, he picked up the newspaper again and read through the entire obituary. Joseph Matthew Frank had died following a lengthy illness. A funeral mass was scheduled in the morning at St. Joseph's Catholic Church, with the interment at Norman's IOOF Cemetery immediately following.

Frank had been born in St. Cloud, Minnesota, fifty-eight years ago. His parents and older sister were deceased. He had served with the army in Vietnam, earning a Bronze Star during the Tet offensive. Then been a carpenter in El Paso until moving to the Oklahoma City area six years ago. The family requested memorial contributions to the American Lung Association in lieu of flowers.

Gary was surprised to see Rose's name mentioned along with her mother and brother as "survivors." He knew that Inez had all but given up hope of ever seeing her daughter again but apparently not so completely that she could bring herself to have Rose listed with the dead.

A widow. Not that it was unexpected. Her husband had been dying for some time apparently. But the knowledge that Inez was no longer a married woman was disquieting. He almost wished he hadn't seen the obituary.

He stared out the window at Andrews Park. He and Sharon used to have picnics there as newlyweds. And attend summer concerts at the WPA-era amphitheater. Sweet Sharon. He still loved her—the girl of his memories.

The next day he waited until midafternoon to stop at the Frank home. Cars were still parked out front, several bearing parking decals from the Norman hospital. A U-Haul trailer was hooked to Inez's battered station wagon. A pickup truck with Texas plates had pulled into the yard.

The scene inside was familiar. The small living room and kitchen were crowded with people still in their funeral clothes. Casseroles, pies, cakes covered every surface in the kitchen. Gary was relieved. He had worried that Inez would have no one with whom to share her grief. Even her mother was there from Mexico, holding young Sammy's hand while they talked to a young priest. Something about a mass in the morning. Gary ruffled Sammy's hair as he walked by.

Inez was sitting at the kitchen table with Beverly and Grady Martin, her friends from Dallas, a plate of uneaten food in front of her. Inez insisted on taking Gary around to introduce him to her visitors. People she had worked with at University Hospital and her current colleagues from the Norman hospital. A couple of neighbors. The priest. Her mother. Sammy's homeroom teacher from Irving Middle School. When they returned to the kitchen table, Beverly presented him with a plate heaped with food.

"I noticed the trailer. Are you leaving?" he asked Inez.

"Yes. Sammy and I are moving to Dallas. I was going to call you tomorrow and give you my new address and telephone number. I have a job with the Dallas Visiting Nurse Association.''

Gary dutifully ate a few bites of ham, tossed salad, and pie, then went to visit with Sammy and his grandmother, a remarkably handsome woman who wore her white hair in a braid on top of her head. She was going to help Inez and Sammy get settled in Dallas and stay for a few weeks she said in heavily accented English.

Sammy was excited about moving. His two best friends lived in Dallas—Beverly and Grady's sons. He and his mom were going to live close to them, and he was going to work after school in Grady's grocery store. "And Mom says I can take guitar lessons. She'll buy me a guitar with her first paycheck.''

Gary lingered until Inez was free to walk him out to his car. The harsh sunlight was not kind to her. She looked tired. Older. Thinner. A few gray hairs were visible against the shining black ones. He could hear sirens on Alameda. Heading for the lake. A drowning probably. A sunny day brought out the boaters no matter what the time of year.

"I'll keep the case open and do what I can," he promised.

"I know. Maybe someday we will know. Thank you for everything. You're a good man.''

"I guess you know that I admire you.''

She touched his cheek. "Yes, and I you.''

He grabbed her hand and pressed his lips into the palm. "For a long time I woke up every morning planning how I would manage to see you that day—what excuse I could use. I'd think about you a lot—silly things like driving in the car someplace with you or going for a walk. I thought about taking you and Sammy camping. And I still think about finding Rose. Every day I think of that—bringing Rose home to you. God, Inez I'm so sorry I couldn't do that.''

She touched the tears on his cheeks, then took him in her arms. "Yes, such a beautiful dream. It's been my dream, too."

And they held each other as they let go of the dream—the beautiful dream. The feel of Inez's hair was smooth against his cheek.

Finally, she began to ease away from him, and reluctantly he let her go. "If my life ever changes . . ." he said, his voice trailing off. His life would change only if he changed it, and he wasn't sure that he could do that.

"Then you'll know where I am," she said. "But be sure that's what you really want."

"She's going to have a baby."

Inez smiled. "You'll be a wonderful father."

Gary drove to the end of the block before he stopped the car and put his head against the steering wheel, an ache swelling painfully in his chest. He could have been friends with Inez as well as love her. And Sammy. Sammy was real. The baby in Sharon's belly didn't seem real.

That night, he reached for his wife in the darkness and felt her stiffen.

"Christ, Sharon, I just want to hold you!" he said angrily. "I know what the doctor says. Or at least I know what you say the doctor says. But does that mean I can't even touch you?"

He rolled onto his back, his heart pounding. He thought about rolling on out of bed. Leaving. Getting in the car and driving far away. To Dallas. But instead, words came pouring up. He loved her so much. Always loved her—since they were kids. Always wanted to marry her. Always thought that she loved him, too. But ever since that first miscarriage, she'd loved the idea of a baby more than she loved him. And now that it looked like this pregnancy was going to take, and there really would be a baby, he felt like he might as

well leave her to her mother and sister, that she would
have the baby she'd always wanted more than anything and he would just be in the way. All she'd need
him for was monthly support checks.

Sharon struggled to a sitting position and turned
on the bedside lamp. He sat up, too, and leaned
against the headboard. He was sweating, his heart
pounding. But he was glad to have it said. Finally.

"But I want the baby for you," she said, her hands
cradling her belly, her eyes filling with tears.

"I don't think so, Sharon. Pregnancy has become
an obsession with you. I feel real sorry for the kid.
There's no way any real, live baby can ever measure up
to your expectations of the joys and bliss of motherhood. I want a wife more than I want a kid. And you
haven't been a wife for a long time."

Sharon was silent for a while, staring at him, her
swollen breasts rising and falling under her flowered
nightgown. He half expected her to reach for the telephone and call her mother. Tell on him. Maybe pack
up and drive to her mother's house. He hoped that
she would. Tomorrow she could call a lawyer. Demand
that he give her the house. The car. Everything. He
didn't really care. Maybe he could work in Grady's
grocery store, too. Lead a simpler life. No paperwork.
No Sharon.

"You're seeing someone else, aren't you?" she
blurted out. "I can't believe it. Here I am pregnant
with your baby, and you're out screwing another
woman."

"No, I'm not, damn it! But would you really blame
me if I was? When was the last time you had sex with
me without praying the whole time that a baby was
being conceived? When was the last time you felt passion and had an orgasm? You've just kept me around
for stud."

"How dare you," she screamed. "Having a baby is a

holy thing. It's what marriage is all about." She tried to slap him, but her body was at the wrong angle to deliver much of a blow. Awkwardly she got to her knees and began to beat on him with her fists, telling him that she hated him, that he didn't deserve to be a father.

He rolled out of the bed and headed for the kitchen. Without turning on the light, he drank a beer sitting at the kitchen table. Then retrieved his guitar from the crawl space over the garage. A guitar for Sammy. He didn't even bother with shoes, driving barefoot the mile or two to Inez's house. He left the guitar in the back of the U-Haul trailer.

Sharon met him at the back door. On the edge of hysteria. "I thought you'd left for good," she said, slipping her arms around him, frantically kissing his neck, his face.

And back in their bed, she kept kissing him—his face, his shoulders, his hands, his arms. "Don't leave me, Gary. Please don't leave me. I need you. I can't raise this baby by myself. I'm not the sort of woman who can manage without a man. I want us to be a family. I want us to be happy. In my mind, I see all these photographs in an album of you and me and our baby at its first Christmas, at its baptism, its first birthday, its first day of school. So many good things are waiting for us—maybe even another baby now that my stupid body has figured out how its done. And we'll make love a lot. I promise. I'll get my figure back, and we'll make mad, passionate love. Mom can keep the baby sometimes, and we can get as kinky as you want."

"You haven't felt kinky since we made love in the back of my truck, have you?"

"Not like before," she admitted. "Back when we were kids, I loved getting hot with you. For the last four or five years I know I haven't worked at it like I should. Getting pregnant was more important. I know that wasn't fair to you. But now it will be different. I do like sex. You know that. I've always liked sex."

Gary started to cry. The second time in one day. He cried and cried in his wife's arms, her pregnant belly between them.

"You won't leave me, will you, Gary?"

"I can't promise, Sharon. I'll see you through this pregnancy. Then I just don't know."

But even as he said the words he could see his whole life spread out in front him. Him and Sharon and the kids. A family, just like she'd always wanted. Him, too, but with the darling Sharon of his youth at his side. And that Sharon was gone forever.

She reached for his hand and put it on her belly. He could feel a fluttering inside—like a tiny bird. He stroked her belly for a time, caressing the child within. Their child.

30

*C*had put two bulging garbage bags in the bin in the front of the Salvation Army store. The clerk handed him a blank receipt for his donation.

"For your taxes," she explained. "You put down what you think it's worth."

Chad thanked her and stuffed the receipt in his pocket, wondering how one assigned value to a bunch of purged fraternity paraphernalia. He wasn't even sure that the poor of Cleveland County would even be interested in goods that bore the letters "IB." He imagined a shopper's puzzlement. *IB?* Indian Brotherhood? Iowa Barrister? Impulse Buyer?

Last night, in the middle of writing a paper for his marketing class, he suddenly found himself bagging T-shirts, sweatshirts and pants, golf shirts, athletic shorts, a billed cap, stocking cap, beer mug, jigger, ice bucket—all bearing the Greek letters and/or crest of the grand old fraternity—and tossed the garbage bags in the back of Johnny's truck, which he now drove unless he was going out with Brenda. The Iota Beta key ring, money clip, and signet ring—all gifts from Brenda—he left in his jewelry box along with his dad's Iota Beta pin, but he couldn't imagine ever wanting to use any of it again.

He'd considered getting rid of his collection of Chi Omega sweatshirts and T-shirts, which indicated the wearer had attended the sorority's tricycle race, bingo party, African safari, sock hop, hoedown. Also, he had a Chi Omega piggy bank, shaving mirror, stocking cap, muffler, Nerf ball, and Frisbee. But those, too, had been gifts from Brenda. And he didn't mind that stuff so much. He even wore the T-shirts sometimes. It was just IB items he needed to clear out.

Before leaving the store, Chad took a minute to look around at the amazing assortment of donated items for sale. Several shoppers were pushing shopping carts up and down the aisles. Normal-looking people. A young mother with a baby. An elderly Native American couple, both wearing braids and beaded headbands. A bearded man in a tweed overcoat who could have passed for a professor—or maybe he was. A woman about the age of Chad's mother—neatly dressed. She looked at Chad and smiled. She wasn't even embarrassed to be seen shopping there, in effect admitting that she was poor and in need. But then, she probably thought that he was here for the same reason.

Chad turned his truck into the drive-through lane of the eastside McDonald's and waited impatiently in the long line for his Egg McMuffin, feeling the need to get back to the unfinished paper that was waiting for him on the table of his now less-cluttered apartment. Less clutter seemed appropriate for his pared-down life that now consisted mostly of classes, studying, and Brenda—a Chi Omega party when he couldn't avoid it. And when the weather allowed, he'd play an early-morning round of golf at the university course. Last Saturday, he played with his dad at the old Lincoln Park course by the Oklahoma City zoo. He and his dad seldom spoke about "the accident." After almost four months there wasn't anything else to say. Every day that went by meant less likelihood of anything happening, that there would be no arrests, no trial, no punishment. Chad didn't think about it so much now. Sometimes a whole day would go by, and he'd realize he hadn't thought about it.

He stopped at a convenience store for milk, bread, and a small package of single-edged razor blades—to scrape the IB decal off the back window of his BMW.

As soon as he and Brenda had gone through rush and knew for sure what their Greek affiliations would be, they'd gone to Balfour's and bought two sets Iota Beta and Chi Omega decals for their cars. They couldn't wait to affix them, side by side, on their cars' back windows to announce to all who saw them that the occupants of the smart black BMW and the snappy red Firebird were both affiliated and committed.

So important, it had been, that everyone know they were not independents. Not ordinary.

He was an outsider now, and as such found himself an observer and critic of the campus Greek community. Sometimes, frat guys seemed like real dickheads as he watched them saunter about campus and its environs, almost always in the company of other members of their house, seemingly unaware of the other occupants of the sidewalk, beer hall, sandwich shop, weight room, classroom.

And Chad was bored by Brenda's running commentary on life at the Chi Omega house. He'd come to think of her and her sorority sisters as childish. They even looked childish. Chi Omegas usually didn't pledge tall girls. And like the Kappas, Chi Omegas were "bow heads," which was campusese for sorority girls who wore large hair bows clipped or tied to the back of their heads. Brenda had a bow to match every outfit. And Chi Omegas even spoke in breathless little-girl voices. Nonthreatening, he supposed. Telling the world they were really sweet girls. Which they were. But it still irritated him that they talked like that.

The most annoying aspect of Brenda's sorority prattle concerned the institution of big sis/little sis. In the nomenclature of sorority, a "little sis" was a pledge assigned to a member, who then became her "big sis." These relationships were often extended to "great big sis" and "great little sis" as big sisses advanced a year and pledges became members with little sisses of their own. Fraternities had big and little brothers, but it wasn't nearly the big deal that it was with sororities.

Big sisses helped indoctrinate their charges in the unwritten rules of dress and behavior. Sorority girls smoked only while seated. They didn't wear their sorority or pledge pin with jeans, shorts, or sweats. They avoided public drunkenness, were under great pressure to keep their grades up, and to dress in classic collegiate attire—purchased at Harold's, if possible.

Brenda had both a big sis and a great big sis. She herself was big sis to Deeann Norton-Jones, whose parents lived in Brussels, where her career-diplomat father was assigned to the American embassy. Chad found it amazing that Brenda knew by heart the extended big sis/little sis relationships of the more than one hundred Chi Omega members and pledges.

Brenda exchanged gifts with those up and down her big-sis/little-sis family tree on every usual gift-giving occasion and some created ones, such as anniversaries of pinnings or an improved grade-point average. She sat with Deeann during designated big-sis/little-sis meals. Deeann often spent the weekend with Brenda and her family in Oklahoma City. Brenda tutored Deeann through her math and science classes, which she was obligated to take under the university's general education requirements.

Deeann was not a typical OU sorority girl. She had grown up abroad and attended private girls' schools in France and Luxembourg. Her parents had decided to send her to OU because her mother was an alumna of the school and her mother's parents lived in Norman.

Deeann was Dresden-doll beautiful, spoke three languages, was sweetly shy, and incredibly grateful to Chi Omega for the instant friendships and support they had extended to her in what had at first seemed a completely alien world. Brenda said that Deeann was a blond Audrey Hepburn. Chad had to agree. She was delicate like Hepburn. Not sexy. She would have been cast as the young nun in a white habit.

Most of first semester Deeann had written nightly letters to a boy in Brussels named Claude. According to Brenda, his picture smiled from a frame on Deeann's desk—a beautiful boy with thick eyelashes, smooth skin, and thick, curly black hair.

Since she had a boyfriend, Deeann refused to go through the traditional first-semester series of organized blind dates with members of fraternity pledge classes. But apparently her long-distance relationship ended while she was in Europe during the Christmas break, because for the last month Deeann had gone out with a very blond international exchange student from Switzerland. Chad would see them together in the student-union food court, the two blondest people in the room, eating American junk food, conversing in French.

But last week Chad saw Deeann walking across campus with Carter Fugate. Which made his blood run cold. But then walking across campus didn't mean anything. They weren't holding hands. But Deeann was smiling up at Carter. Her cheeks were rosy with the cold. Her blond hair bouncing as she walked along. Her coat a brilliant red. Little Red Riding Hood in the presence of the Big Bad Wolf.

Chad asked Brenda about it. "Deeann isn't seeing Carter Fugate, is she?"

"Not that I know of. Why?"

"I saw them together."

"Well, I doubt if that means anything. He's hardly her type."

"Check on it, will you? It wouldn't be a good idea for Deeann to go out with him. He's mean."

Brenda checked. Carter was in Deeann's American history class. He had asked her out, but she'd been busy.

"Besides, I think that she really likes Louis," Brenda said. They were sitting on his sofa, drinking beer and watching *Law and Order*. "Louis is as shy as she is. All they do is kiss good night."

Chad mentally marked the Carter-Deeann problem off his list and began unbuttoning Brenda's blouse, reaching around her to unfasten her bra—a feat he could accomplish with one hand. He really got off on Brenda's breasts, which were wonderfully full, with large rosy-brown nipples. Sometimes during the day, he'd just think about them and get turned on.

He knelt in front her and buried his face between them, inhaling the smell of her, wanting to live his life here between her breasts. Brenda took his face between her hands and guided his mouth to her right breast. And moaned as he clasped his mouth over her nipple.

They made love almost every night now. Chad wondered if he could have managed these last four months without Brenda. He'd given up on transferring to OSU when she wouldn't go with him. She knew how much he needed her, but she didn't know why. She thought it was true love. But then, Chad hardly understood it himself. He just went with it, never thinking about any girl except Brenda, ignoring the fact that she was a spoiled sorority girl. As long as she would allow him the comfort of her body, he was hers.

* * *

The Sunday before midterm examinations were to begin, Deeann's roommate called Brenda. Melanie was
spending the weekend studying at her aunt's house in
Oklahoma City. "Deeann was supposed to drive up
here yesterday afternoon to study for our psych test.
But she didn't show. When I called, she said she was
sick. Just an upset stomach, she said, but she sounded
funny—like she'd been crying. I called again this
morning but got no answer. Her grandparents are out
of town, and I thought maybe you should check on
her."

"Sure. But she's probably just freaked out over her
tests. If she doesn't make better grades this semester,
she won't get initiated."

Brenda went back to her books, thinking that she
probably should have gone home, too. The Chi
Omega house was almost too quiet. Like a tomb. Ste-
reos and televisions were silent. The residents were
either at the library or holed up in their rooms, cram-
ming, wishing they'd taken better notes, read more of
the assigned chapters. Before lunch, Brenda dialed
Deeann's dorm room but got no answer. She waited
for the answering machine to kick in. But the phone
just kept ringing.

Probably, Deeann was feeling better and had gone
out to get something to eat. Brenda went downstairs
for lunch then allowed herself a short nap before she
tackled her sociology notes. She didn't always keep up
with outside readings, but she took wonderful notes.

About two, she tried Deeann again. Still no answer.
Maybe she'd gone to the library. Or her grandparents
were back in town. Brenda reached for the Norman
telephone directory but didn't know the grandparents' last name. Wanda and Burt something. Norton,
maybe. But no Burt Norton was listed.

She and Chad had carryout Chinese for dinner.

Then she tried Deeann again. "I'm worried," she finally admitted.

The first floor of Walker Tower was quiet, with only
a few guys playing pinball in the lounge. The seventh-
floor television room and hallway were deserted. But
there were sounds of life behind many of the doors.
Music. CNN. Water running. A door being slammed.
Muted voices.

When Deeann did not answer their knock, Brenda
whispered at the door, "Dee, it's Brenda and Chad.
We're worried about you. If you're in there, I want you
to unlock the door right this minute, or we're going to
get the RA."

They heard a sound. And after a lengthy wait, the
lock turned.

Chad opened the door. They stepped into the dark
room, the shaft of light from the hall showing Deeann's form already back in bed, buried under blan-
kets, her back to them.

Brenda turned on the desk lamp and sat on the
side of the bed. "Hey, sugar, what's going on?" she
asked, rubbing a hand up and down Deeann's back.

"Nothing. Please, turn off the light. My eyes hurt."

Brenda obliged. Chad had closed the hall door, but
a thin light came through the room's one window,
drifting up from the streetlights below. "Don't you
have a psych test tomorrow?" she asked.

"I'm not going to take it."

"Have you made arrangements with the professor?"

"No."

"What about your other midterms?"

"I'm not taking any of them."

"Why?"

"I can't."

"Why?"

"I just can't."

"Are you hungry?" Chad asked from across the room. "We brought you a sandwich and a Coke."

"I don't want any food. Leave the Coke. I'll drink it later."

"Come on, Dee, talk to us," Brenda said. "Do you want me to call your grandparents?"

"They're gone."

"Where? I really think I should call them."

Deeann's shoulders began to shake. Brenda turned the light back on. Deeann struggled as Brenda pulled away the covers. Then gave up. Her head fell back on the pillow, her face a mass of bruises, her eyes swollen shut, her upper lip hideously swollen. Brenda gasped. Chad swore.

"My God, Deeann, who did this to you?" Brenda asked.

"He said that he'd cut my face if I ever told. But I won't tell. I don't want anyone to know. Please, Brenda, don't ever tell. It would kill my grandparents. My parents would be so ashamed. I'd never have a normal life. I can't be one of those women who go on talk shows and march in rallies and carry signs about taking back the night."

"A boy raped you?" Brenda whispered, horrified, panic taking hold of her. She needed to do something, but she didn't know what. Something to help Deeann. She should call someone. Notify the resident adviser. Call the campus police. Pass the problem off to someone else. Do anything except just sit here by this brutalized girl that she could hardly even recognize as her friend. Her little sis.

"Did you know him?" Brenda asked, still whispering.

"A little. I thought he was nice. He's in a fraternity. He said he wanted to borrow my notes." And Deeann covered her mouth with both hands, sobbing.

Brenda knew, even as she was asking her next ques-

tion, that she shouldn't. She'd attended the lectures.
Taken a women's studies class. She knew that victims
weren't to be blamed. But she couldn't help herself.
Maybe Deeann could have prevented this. Maybe
she'd acted imprudently—like walking alone down a
dark alley at night. Not having a canister of Mace
ready. "Why, Deeann?" she demanded, suddenly angry. "Why did he do this to you? Were you drunk?"

Chad was instantly beside her, pushing her aside.
"Christ, Brenda! Cool it."

He knelt beside the bed. Touched Deeann's poor,
damaged face. "We'll help you, Dee. Tell us what to
do."

Chad helped her struggle to a sitting position. Her
nightshirt had a pink teddy bear on the front.

"My grandparents are away for a few days," she
said, speaking only to Chad. "Help me get out of
here. Get me over to their house where I won't have
to see anyone. I'm meeting my parents in Paris spring
break. I'll tell them I was in an automobile accident.
I'll tell them that I'm not coming back here. That I
want to stay in Europe next year. I'll think of some
reason why."

Chad pointed to the Coke on the desk, and Brenda
dutifully handed it to him. He popped the lid and
handed it to Deeann. She just looked at it for a second, then took a swallow. And another. Then handed
it back. "Just last week I wrote to my parents and told
them how much I loved it here. How much fun it was
being a Chi Omega. How good the professors were.
How there already are pansies and jonquils blooming
all over campus." She was crying again. Her nose running. Chad pulled some tissues from a box and wiped
the snot away, then pulled her into his arms, putting
her head against his shoulder, stroking her hair. Such
a little person, he thought. Smaller than Brenda. Frail.

No match for any guy. But then, she shouldn't have to
be.

He felt sick and twisted inside, filled with hate for
the male who had done this to her. And for himself,
because he, too, was a male.

He wanted to avenge her. To hurt the man who had
hurt her. To put his hands around that man's throat
and choke him. Stomp on his face. Mutilate him. Stab
him. Beat his brains in.

He didn't want it to be Carter Fugate. Probably
there were lots of guys around capable of doing this to
a girl. Just because he'd seen Deeann with Carter that
one time didn't mean that he had done this to her.
Just because he and Dee had a class together. Not
Carter. *Please not Carter.*

He had to ask her. As soon as he said Carter's
name, Deeann began to scream. Chad had to put his
hand over her mouth to quiet her. Just as Carter had
done to stop the screaming of Rosalie Frank.

Brenda knelt beside him, and together they tried to
calm the hysterical girl, holding her, rubbing her back
and arms. Brenda began to whisper soothing words
that none of them believed. It would not be all right.
It would never be all right.

Chad added up the devastation. Rosalie Frank was
dead, and her family didn't know what had happened
to her, hadn't buried her body, was probably still praying for her safe return. His own family was in bad
shape. Johnny Fontaine had deliberately run his truck
into an embankment and burned to death. His relationship with Brenda was based on deceit. And Carter
Fugate continued to rape girls.

31

"*Y*ou hold the ball like this," Karen said, pushing up the sleeves of her windbreaker and putting the small rubber ball in her right palm.

She watched while her three young companions imitated her. They were kneeling on a corner of the cracked concrete slab they referred to as the "patio," warmed by the afternoon sunshine, protected from a chilly wind by a metal storage building and from the outside world by the six-foot chain-link fence that surrounded the backyard.

"Other hand, Tammy. The one you use to hold a pencil. That's right. Now, toss the ball straight up, and while it's in the air grab a jack and put it in your spare hand. If you do it fast enough, you're ready to catch the ball when it comes down. Like this."

Karen demonstrated the maneuver several times, then watched the girls try. Jasmine was very coordinated, the other two girls less so. Karen enjoyed watching the concentration on their smooth faces, loved the innocent curve of their young cheeks.

"When you get good enough at onezees," Karen explained, "we'll try picking up the jacks two at a time. That's good, Jenny. Almost, Tammy. You don't need to throw the ball quite so high."

But Tammy was looking toward the back door, alarm on her thin little face. The back door was open,

and a man was watching them through the screen
door. Not George. A white man.

Karen scrambled to her feet, ready to face an in-
vader, wondering where George was that this man had
entered the house. Karen put a hand on Tammy's
shoulder, ready to send her to find George.

But the screen door opened, and Chad stepped out
on the stoop.

Karen's heart stopped for an instant, making the
changeover from fear to joy. *Chad.* She hadn't seen
him since Melissa's birthday last month.

His hair was longer, curling around his ears, darker
than it was when he was a little boy, but still blond.
Her golden boy.

George was working in the office, and the living
room was occupied by three women watching television. Karen led Chad out to the broad front porch,
which had once been gracious but was now unsightly
with rotting boards and peeling paint. And the view
was of a parking lot that occupied the space under the
elevated expressway. But they were out of the wind,
and the afternoon sun cast warming rays across the
sagging floor.

Karen sat on a wooden bench that George had
nailed to the wall to discourage thieves in the night,
Chad on an old-fashioned metal glider that was apparently too heavy to be carried away.

He had finished his midterms. Yes, he thought he'd
done okay. Brenda was fine. Yes, he still liked living on
DeBarr Street.

"Are *you* okay?" he asked.

"Yes and no. Your dad and I are in a holding pattern. Melissa and I muddle along. She announced that
to get everyone off her back, she would gain two
pounds and get her weight up to one hundred. And
she did just that—not an ounce more. I've applied for
admission to the OU graduate school, but I have to

take the Graduate Record Exam before I can be accepted—and I'm not sure that I'm up to that."

"Sure you are. What would you study?"

"Social work."

Chad nodded. "Yeah. You'd be good at that. I liked
watching you with those little girls. You pay attention
to people. I used to be embarrassed by that—the way
you'd talk to just anyone. Salespeople. Waitresses. The
guy who came to fix the furnace. Old ladies in the
park."

"That wouldn't embarrass you anymore?"

"No. I've been trying it myself. Talking to people.
After I moved out of the IB house, I suddenly found
myself without any friends. Except Brenda. And she's
not interested in talking about some things. I actually
have an invitation to Nicaragua—from a guy I've been
hanging out with. He's from a little town called Rivas.
He said there are more rocking chairs per capita in
Rivas than any other town in the world."

"Yes. Go. Don't miss anything."

"That's what Grandpa Walt said. Maybe I will—
someday."

"I talked to Walt the other day. That was nice of
you to help him move to Sallisaw. He seems happy,
doesn't he?"

"Yeah. He's a great old guy. He calls Professor
Winslow 'Birdie.' They really seem to like each other a
lot. I think he loved Grandma, but I don't think they
liked each other much."

Chad slid the glider back and forth and looked
around the spacious porch. "I wonder why they
stopped putting porches on houses. This old house
must have been something in its day. Mr. Brown
showed me through. Told me about what goes on
here. And how there's never enough space, never
enough beds, how the plumbing is rusting away, how

the city needs other shelters. It makes me feel sick to my stomach."

"Why's that?"

"Because women need shelters." His voice wavered. Karen realized that he was fighting for control. She went to sit beside him. And took his hand.

"Will you come with me to Norman?" he asked.

"Why? What's going on?"

"I want you to go with me to the police station."

Karen looked at her son's face. At the pain there. No longer the face of a boy. She hurt so for him. His pain was her pain. Like a wound.

Yet, this was the the moment she'd longed for—the moment when she would know with absolute certainty that her son felt pain and sorrow and remorse in his heart and brain—feelings that he would carry with him throughout his life and take with him to the grave —as she herself would.

Was knowing that he felt that way not enough? Was another form of retribution still necessary? The law would say that it was. But she wasn't the law. She was his mother.

"Are you sure that's what you really want?" she asked.

"It has to be done. This thing is like a monster that keeps getting bigger."

"But your father. Think of what it will do to your father. What if they send you to prison?"

"I'll face that if it happens. All I know now is that I have to do this."

"Maybe so. But you've got to talk to him before you do anything irrevocable."

Chad shook his head. "He'll try to talk me out of it. He'll tell me that I owe it to the family and to the grandfathers and to the fraternity to hang in there and be brave. But I have to put an end to it, Mom. That girl is dead. Johnny is dead. And now, I've found

out that Carter Fugate has raped another girl. If I
don't put an end to it, I'm no better than he is."

Karen's stomach contracted. *Another horror to face.
Another girl raped.* A young life irrevocably altered. So
many lives irrevocably altered. Two snuffed out completely. But Chad was right. *Hang in there*—that was
exactly what Roger would say. The male credo. Being
brave. Never shedding a tear. Never reconsidering or
admitting error. But for all the wrong reasons, maybe
in this case Roger was right. Hanging in there would
take its own sort of bravery. Without confession, there
was no absolution, no closure, no peace.

"You owe your father the chance to try and talk you
out of this," she said. "And he owes it to you to listen
to what you have to say. In the end, whatever is done,
we all share the consequences. The whole family."

"Remember when you said that you weren't sure
you could go on loving me if I didn't know what I'd
done was unjustifiably wrong. Did you mean that?"

"Yes. Probably so. But I've discovered since then
that there's a lot of blame to go around. Your father
and I raised you to think that you got to play by a
special set of rules."

Chad shook his head. "You and Dad were the greatest. I knew what I was doing was wrong."

"Of course you did. But you also knew it was wrong
when you did lots of other things that led up to Rosalie Frank's death, and somehow all those things got
taken care of, erased, forgiven, whatever. Maybe it
wasn't so much that I couldn't love you as I couldn't
love myself for having raised a son capable of violating
a girl."

"I want you to know that it's okay for you to love
me," he said, wiping tears from his eyes. "I have
nightmares about that girl's body in the lake. I see
stuff like in a horror movie. Only sometimes it's not
her. It's you or Melissa or Brenda. I'd give anything to

go back and make her still be alive. To make *Rosalie
Frank* still be alive. Anything. I am so sorry, but it
sounds stupid to even say the word. I can't even tell
her mother that I'm sorry. The only person I can tell
is you.''

Karen put her arms around him. And cried with
him. Mother and son. And through all the pain and
sadness, she felt such love for him. Boundless love.
Mother love.

George vacated the office so that Chad could use
the phone. While Chad called his father Karen
watched the three jack players out the kitchen window. Their mothers had joined them, sitting on a
blanket with Tammy's baby sister, their backs against
the metal shed, sheltered for a time from the abuse
and fear that had brought them here.

Would the police be able to find Rosalie's body in
the lake if they had some idea where to look, Karen
wondered. If they found it, Inez could have a funeral.
A grave in the cemetery on which to put flowers. Next
to Rosalie's father. Inez wouldn't have to keep hoping
against hope. Karen wanted that for her. And someday
she herself would go to the cemetery and visit Rosalie's grave. Just the thought of doing that brought
more tears to her eyes. Rosalie had become her
daughter, too.

George had come to stand beside her, to watch the
mothers and children in the yard.

"I like your son."

"Would you still like him if you knew he'd done
something terrible—if he'd committed the very sort
of horror that you've dedicated your life to overcom-
ing?"

"He said that he was in trouble. Big trouble."

"Yes. We're on our way to the police station so he
can turn himself in."

"Is he sorry?" George asked softly, still looking out
the window at the sweet scene in the yard.

"Yes. Very sorry. And I love him. God, how I love
him."

"That's what he said about you."

The door to the office opened, and George called
out, "Your mother's in here, son." He squeezed
Karen's hand and left her to her boy.

Chad's face wore a defeated look. "Dad thinks that
you talked me into this."

"Did you ask him to go with us?"

"He said that he wouldn't take part in ruining my
life."

Chad admitted that he hadn't had lunch, and
Karen insisted on making him a sandwich before they
left. He sat at one end of the long kitchen table and
watched as she bustled about. "Melissa and I were always embarrassed that you came here," he admitted.
"We never told any of our friends."

Before they left, Karen brushed her hair, put on a
bit of makeup, tucked her shirt in her jeans. She regarded her image in the bathroom mirror. Hardly the
Nichols Hills matron that she used to be.

George was waiting by the front door to tell them
good-bye. He shook Chad's hand and helped Karen
into her jacket before giving her a hug. "Good luck,"
he told them, "and be thankful that you have each
other."

They made the drive to Norman in Johnny Fontaine's old truck, a symbolic gesture that Karen found
quite touching.

"I can't remember ever riding in a truck before,"
she said. "It makes you feel different, doesn't it? Like
you should be wearing dusty boots and have calluses
on your hands?"

"Yeah. Old guys in overalls come up to me and tell
how they used to have a truck just like this one.

Johnny put it back just like it used to be, even down to
the AM radio and hubcaps. I think he drove it to say
that he was different and not just another spoiled rich
kid. But he hadn't screwed up the courage yet to tell
his dad that he didn't want to be in his old fraternity.
Or to tell me and the other brothers that defiling that
poor girl was wrong. If all that hadn't happened,
though, if he'd lived, Johnny would have gotten his act
together eventually. He already understood a hell of a
lot more than I did."

The Norman police station was next door to the library and across the street from a park with huge old
trees and picnic tables constructed of native stone. A
pair of young mothers huddled out of the wind on the
south side of a small stone building while their children raced about.

Roger and Melissa were waiting outside the police
station.

At first, Karen thought that they'd come to stop
Chad. The four of them met there on the sidewalk in
front of the building, mother and son facing father
and daughter.

"You're sure, son?" Roger asked.

"Yes, sir."

"Well, then, that's the way it has to be. I've called a
Norman attorney," Roger said, putting his arm
around Chad's shoulders. "He's on his way over. Billy
Russo. He's top-drawer. I figured that since this is a
Cleveland County case, we'd be better off with some-
one who knows the lay of the land."

Karen realized that she'd been holding her breath
and let it go. "You are entitled to ask Chad not to do
this," she told Melissa. "Your life will never be the
same."

Melissa looked over at Chad. "No. Dad explained why. It's Chad's decision."

With Roger's arm still around his son, he and Chad began walking toward the door. Melissa and Karen fell in step behind them. And Melissa reached for her mother's hand.

ABOUT THE AUTHOR

While growing up in a military family, JUDITH HENRY WALL developed a lifelong passion for travel to distant places but continues to find much inspiration for her writing closer to home. She lives in Norman, Oklahoma, where she raised her three children and works at the University of Oklahoma as a research writer and editor of the alumni quarterly. She is the author of *Love and Duty, Handsome Women,* and *Blood Sisters,* and is presently at work on a new novel.

DON'T MISS THESE FABULOUS
BANTAM WOMEN'S FICTION TITLES

On sale in June

From the blockbuster author of nine consecutive *New York Times* best-sellers comes a tantalizing tale of a quest for a dazzling crystal.

MYSTIQUE by Amanda Quick

"One of the hottest and most prolific writers in romance today."—USA Today
Available in hardcover   ___ 09698-2 $21.95/$24.95 in Canada

VIOLET by Jane Feather

"An author to treasure."—Romantic Times
From the extraordinary pen of Jane Feather, nationally bestselling author of *Valentine*, comes a bewitching tale of a beautiful bandit who's waging a dangerous game of vengeance—and betting everything on love.   ___ 56471-4 $5.50/$6.99

MOTHER LOVE by Judith Henry Wall

"Wall keeps you turning the pages."—San Francisco Chronicle
There is no love as strong or enduring as the love of a mother for her child. But what if that child commits an act that goes against a woman's deepest beliefs? Is there a limit to a mother's love? Judith Henry Wall, whose moving stories and finely drawn characters have earned her critical praise and a devoted readership, has written her most compelling novel yet.   ___ 56789-6 $5.99/$7.50

THE WARLORD by Elizabeth Elliott

*"Elizabeth Elliott is an exciting find for romance readers
everywhere . . . . Spirited, sensual, tempestuous romance at its best."*
—New York Times *bestselling author Amanda Quick*
In the bestselling tradition of Teresa Medeiros and Elizabeth Lowell, *The Warlord* is a magical and captivating tale of a woman who must dare to love the man she fears the most.   ___ 56910-4 $5.50/$6.99

- -

Ask for these books at your local bookstore or use this page to order.

Please send me the books I have checked above. I am enclosing $___ (add $2.50 to cover postage and handling). Send check or money order, no cash or C.O.D.'s, please.

Name _____

Address _____

City/State/Zip _____

Send order to: Bantam Books, Dept. FN158, 2451 S. Wolf Rd., Des Plaines, IL 60018
Allow four to six weeks for delivery.
Prices and availability subject to change without notice.   FN 158 7/95

DON'T MISS THESE FABULOUS
BANTAM WOMEN'S FICTION TITLES

On sale in July

DEFIANT
by PATRICIA POTTER
Winner of the 1992 *Romantic Times*
Career Achievement Award for Storyteller of the Year

Only the desire for vengeance had spurred Wade Foster on, until the last of the men who had destroyed his family lay sprawled in the dirt. Now, badly wounded, the rugged outlaw closed his eyes against the pain . . . and awoke to the tender touch of the one woman who could show him how to live—and love—again. _____ 56601-6 $5.50/$6.99

STAR-CROSSED
by nationally bestselling author SUSAN KRINARD

"Susan Krinard was born to write romance."
—New York Times *bestselling author Amanda Quick*

A captivating futuristic romance in the tradition of Johanna Lindsey, Janelle Taylor, and Kathleen Morgan. A beautiful aristocrat risks a forbidden love . . . with a dangerously seductive man born of an alien race. _____ 56917-1 $4.99/$5.99

BEFORE I WAKE
by TERRY LAWRENCE

"Terry Lawrence is a magnificent writer." —Romantic Times
Award-winning author Terry Lawrence is an extraordinary storyteller whose novels sizzle with irresistible wit and high-voltage passion. Now, she weaves the beloved fairy tale *Sleeping Beauty* into a story so enthralling it will keep you up long into the night. _____ 56914-7 $5.50/$6.99

THE VERY BEST IN CONTEMPORARY
❧❧ WOMEN'S FICTION

SANDRA BROWN

____28951-9 Texas! Lucky $5.99/$6.99 in Canada   ____56768-3 Adam's Fall $4.99/$5.99

____28990-X Texas! Chase $5.99/$6.99   ____56045-X Temperatures Rising $5.99/$6.99

____29500-4 Texas! Sage $5.99/$6.99   ____56274-6 Fanta C $4.99/$5.99

____29085-1 22 Indigo Place $5.99/$6.99   ____56278-9 Long Time Coming $4.99/$5.99

____29783-X A Whole New Light $5.99/$6.99   ____09672-9 Heaven's Price $16.95/$22.95

TAMI HOAG

____29534-9 Lucky's Lady $5.99/$7.50   ____29272-2 Still Waters $5.99/$7.50

____29053-3 Magic $5.99/$7.50   ____56160-X Cry Wolf $5.50/$6.50

____56050-6 Sarah's Sin $4.99/$5.99   ____56161-8 Dark Paradise $5.99/$7.50

____09961-2 Night Sins $19.95/$23.95

NORA ROBERTS

____29078-9 Genuine Lies $5.99/$6.99   ____27859-2 Sweet Revenge $5.99/$6.99

____28578-5 Public Secrets $5.99/$6.99   ____27283-7 Brazen Virtue $5.99/$6.99

____26461-3 Hot Ice $5.99/$6.99   ____29597-7 Carnal Innocence $5.99/$6.99

____26574-1 Sacred Sins $5.99/$6.99   ____29490-3 Divine Evil $5.99/$6.99

DEBORAH SMITH

____29107-6 Miracle $5.50/$6.50   ____29690-6 Blue Willow $5.50/$6.50

____29092-4 Follow the Sun $4.99/$5.99   ____29689-2 Silk and Stone $5.99/$6.99

____28759-1 The Beloved Woman $4.50/$5.50

- -

Ask for these books at your local bookstore or use this page to order.

Please send me the books I have checked above. I am enclosing $_____ (add $2.50 to cover postage and handling). Send check or money order, no cash or C.O.D.'s, please.

Name _____

Address _____

City/State/Zip _____

Send order to: Bantam Books, Dept. FN 24, 2451 S. Wolf Rd., Des Plaines, IL 60018
Allow four to six weeks for delivery.
Prices and availability subject to change without notice.   FN 24 7/95